# BETWEEN BLOODE AND CRAFT
BETWEEN THE SHADOWS

**MARIE HARTE**

This book is a work of fiction. The names, characters, places, and plot points stem from the writer's imagination. They are fictitious and not to be interpreted as real. Any resemblance to persons, living or dead, actual events, locations or organizations is entirely coincidental.

BETWEEN BLOODE AND CRAFT
ISBN-13: 978-1642920666
Copyright © February 2022 by Marie Harte
No Box Books
Cover by Moonpress Design | moonpress.co

All Rights Are Reserved. None of this book may be reproduced or used in any manner without express written permission from the author, except in the case of brief quotations used for reviews or promotion. http://marieharte.com

For exclusive excerpts, news, and contests, sign up for **Marie's newsletter**. https://www.subscribepage.com/betweentheshadows

# BETWEEN THE SHADOWS

Between Bloode and Stone
Between Bloode and Craft
Between Bloode and Water
Between Bloode and Wolf
Between Bloode and Death
Between Bloode and Gods

# BETWEEN BLOODE AND CRAFT

# CHAPTER ONE

*SW Queen Anne Greenbelt*
*Seattle, Washington*

"I'm afraid you're going to have to come with me." Macy Bishop-Dunwich had no authority to apprehend a class seven threat. But she needed information. Like yesterday. "Hello? I need you to step away from the men you're assaulting."

The long-haired upir standing over a burly, unconscious man and his musclebound friend currently crying and clutching a broken wrist didn't answer her.

Typical.

But then, she hadn't expected compliance. As a whole, the magir—those creatures other than human, no matter what they looked like on the outside—didn't like being told what to do. But vampires took obstinacy and danger to another level entirely.

The moonlight overhead was spotty at best, but the crunch of dead and dying leaves, in addition to all the sobbing, sounded overly loud in the October night. Fortunately, all the civilians had cleared out, no doubt affected by the spell of oppressive dread

Macy had dropped earlier. Something she wasn't exactly cleared to be using.

With time of the essence, she needed to wrap up this mess before a Special Forces patrol from the Magir Enforcement Command arrived. MEC didn't mess around.

A small part of her wondered if she'd need to scramble the minds of the injured humans. That might be fun, to convince them they'd been on a date together after hearing the way they'd talked about a woman they'd seen. Not nice, by half. Or she could convince them that they'd beaten each other up. She grinned. Maybe that they'd been chasing Big Foot and had finally caught him? An article in *Searching the Needle Weekly* about a Yeti sighting had been super amusing, and she wanted to use it somehow.

Then again, if she waited long enough, the vampire would probably solve her problem by killing them both. But what a waste of blood.

*Wait. What?*

She shook her head, reminding herself to stop watching horror movie marathons where she sided with the monsters over the people. Blood—bad. Helping—good.

*Gah. Focus, you idiot.*

In a deep, menacing voice, the upir growled at the crying man on the ground. "I'm waiting for my apology, human. Make it a good one or I'll drain you dry before feeding the marrow in your bones to my kin."

Macy rolled her eyes. Why did vampires always have to be so damn dramatic?

She cleared her throat. Loudly. *Keep it contained.* "Hey, Mister Bone Marrow, I'm talking to you."

The vampire kicked the still-conscious man so hard he flew off the ground like a soccer ball. The poor guy hit a tree then fell to the grass facedown, unmoving.

Bone Marrow slowly turned to face her.

If she hadn't already dealt with the best-looking guy she'd ever seen in her life, she might have been impressed. But a month after flirting with God's gift to vampires, she felt oddly indifferent to this one.

Bone Marrow was upir, as that tribe controlled the west coast of the United States. And with that the case, he had to be one of the local clan, the Seattle Bloode. Like all vampires, he had dark hair and dark eyes, his particular skin color a pale cream. Contrary to myth, vampires, those Of the Bloode, came in all shades, but they had a few things in common. Every vampire was male, and they were all a *huge* pain the ass, too powerful to be ruled by other magir, demons, or even gods.

Even gods.

*What the hell am I doing here?* Her heart raced as the full import of what she'd been up to for the past month and a half hit her.

Bone Marrow cocked his head and stared at her, as if unsure how to deal with such a foolish human who didn't know better than to be afraid.

Macy hadn't bolted in fear. She hadn't screamed for help. And she hadn't immediately flocked to his side, enthralled by his looks or seductive power. A conundrum for the most feared predators of the magir community. Every paranormal non-human did their best to avoid vampires.

*I really need to rethink my life choices.*

"Who are you?" The upir licked his lips and smiled, hiding his fangs behind a full, handsome mouth. "And why haven't we met before?" He looked her up and down, his grin broadening. "I bet you taste as sweet as you look. Come to me."

A very guy thing to do, vampire or not. His kind seemed to be very slow to the idea of gender equality. Well, in all honesty, they were slow to the idea of *human* equality, so she shouldn't knock him too hard for being true to form.

"Look, I understand the city is your hunting ground, but you can't just break people or kill them on a whim." She paused, because his gaze had fastened to her breasts.

"Of course I can," he said with a winsome smile. "You can't control me, woman." He opened his mouth wider to show sharp, white fangs that elongated. "I'm upir, of the Seattle Bloode. Now come to me that I may feed. Perhaps on more than just your neck, if you're lucky."

She blinked, and he was on her. *So* fucking fast.

But as she exhaled a breath into his face, he froze in place.

Relieved the spell worked, Macy pretended she'd known all along she'd have control and smiled as she stepped back. "No, my friend. You aren't in charge here. *I* am." She freaking *loved* the power coursing through her. With the aid of her secret grimoire, she was working magic that should have been impossible.

Like managing vampires.

Considering that just a few dozen Of the Bloode could wipe out hundreds of human and magir with little effort, she should know better than to involve herself in vampire politics. But Macy refused to be stuck in the Spells & Incantations branch of MEC forever. She had plans.

"Tell me what I want to know about the new clan in town. Why hasn't your patriarch killed them yet?"

She ignored the pang inside her at the thought of one particular vampire dying and knew herself to be a fool because of it. Duncan had intended to play her from the beginning. But oh, had turning the tables on him been fun for a short time.

Just thinking about sexy Duncan with his bedroom eyes and sexy British accent made her heart race, and she had to force herself to focus on the task at hand. Her spell wrapped around the upir, threading into his mind and taking hold.

"C-clan? N-no." He couldn't even blink, able only to speak. "Patriarch... not... can't kill."

"Tell me, upir, tell this pretty witch the truth and she might give you what you most desire," she teased and shifted her hair to expose her neck. "Who are they? What do they want here?"

He swallowed. "They are... the Night Bloode."

She kept hearing rumors of vampire politics heating up, but no mention of Duncan's clan, which had intrigued her from the get-go. A new group of upir in Seattle was big news. "Is Duncan new?" MEC knew all the faces of the Seattle Bloode, something they mandated every one of their people commit to memory.

Because typically, crossing those Of the Bloode meant death.

His eyes widened. "I don't know any Duncan. Not... kin. Not upir."

*Not upir?* "Are the Night Bloode aiming to take over Seattle?"

He shook his head. "Don't know. But th-they're too strong. They're... more."

She didn't know what that meant, but then, her knowledge of vampires was limited to what she'd been able to find out without letting anyone know she'd been researching. Even working a spell on Duncan, she'd only been able to push him so far. And a lot of that night over month ago remained hazy, no doubt from driving herself too hard.

So if the Night Bloode weren't trying to take over the Seattle Bloode's territory, what were they up to? How could they be here, in the vicinity of another clan, and not be fighting until the death? Just how powerful was Duncan, really?

*Why the hell do I care?*

A good question she'd brush aside right now, because a subtle chime on her phone sounded. MEC would be here in five minutes, tops. She leaned closer to the upir, blew her breath over his lips, and whispered, "I was never here. We never had this conversation. You will remember nothing more than a denied need to feed, recalling that your boss won't allow it. Go home."

She felt the press of MEC enforcers nearing, all that power interfering with her spell of dread. Time to go.

The upir nodded. "Have to get back before Eric finds out and loses his shit. Can't be here. Don't want attention."

Macy darted away, erasing her power signature with another spell, this one easy enough to manage without the help of anything but her innate knowledge of witchcraft.

She hustled down the road and eventually into her car then sped away.

But she wasn't ready to go home yet. She fought against a familiar block, wanting her best friend despite her recent need for privacy. *I need to study the grimoire some more, to learn all its secrets. To practice and commit the magic to memory.* Yet... Cho. She hadn't seen her best friend in forever, and that wasn't like her.

Without letting herself think about it, she turned around and headed for Fremont. Like Macy, Cho had something to prove and a host of people who loved him but didn't understand what it was like to be different.

If anyone could help her understand vampires, it was her half-demon friend with an agenda of his own.

"*Are you on crack?*"

"Um, no?" Macy hadn't been expecting all the negativity.

"Macy, you're a witch, a beautiful *human* in the prime of her life who can tap into magic. That's like catnip to fangers." Cho ran a hand through his thick dark hair, which now reached his shoulders.

"You need a haircut."

"I'm growing it to enhance my strength," he snarled. The name Cho, short for the Russian word *chort* (which meant demon), had been lovingly bestowed on him by his badass demon father, a former prince of Hell. Uncle Anton used to scare the bejesus out of her before she'd realized he wasn't like most hellrazers, his kind nature a trait he'd passed down to his stubborn son, another anomaly with a lot of attitude.

Thomas "Cho" Novak stood several inches taller than Macy. Tall, dark, and handsome, he looked a lot like his mom, a lovely Chilean woman tougher than any enforcer Macy had ever met. But Cho's father had given her friend the dark eyes that could turn orange when he grew angry or impassioned about a subject. And of course, the occasional wings, horns, and limited power over fire.

Too close to be anything but family, she and Cho told each other everything.

Normally.

But she hadn't mentioned Duncan. And she sure as heck hadn't told Cho about how she'd found a book that absorbed blood. Or the way she'd been drawn to that particular store to find that particular grimoire, which had expanded her magic beyond anything she might have imagined.

"What is going on with you? Macy, you don't cross the street unless you're at a crosswalk or the light is green."

"Because that's safe."

"You've never stayed out past curfew."

"I've never had a curfew."

He pointed at her. "Ah-ha. Exactly. You never needed one because you got straight A's, never dated, and never partied. You don't even color outside the lines."

"I like order. What's wrong with that?" Besides it being no fun.

"Nothing. But that's why this behavior is so unlike you." He shook his head. "You're acting more like me. And that scares me." He grinned to take the sting out, but she felt judged all the same. "Now don't look like that. I love you no matter what, but I'm worried. Tell me again why you want to know about vampires. And while you're at it, tell me what you've been hiding from me for the past few weeks."

"Hiding? Heh." She faked a laugh he wasn't buying.

"Sad. So pathetic, you and all your lying. That you're criminally bad at."

"Cho, that's mean."

He smiled, but the expression didn't reach his eyes, which sparked with flame. "Don't make me pull it out of you." By tickling, which she absolutely hated.

"Fine. I'll tell you... But *after* you fill me in on vampires."

"Swear?" He looked as if he didn't believe her.

"Cho, that hurts."

He continued to stare at her.

"Fine. I promise I'll tell." They hooked pinkies, then he filled her in on what she was up against. And it wasn't pretty.

# CHAPTER TWO

Cho took a deep breath and let it out as he settled next to Macy on the couch. The small cottage he called home sat between two larger remodeled houses on a quiet street in Fremont. A few blocks away, his parents lived equally quiet lives. On the surface.

Since both worked for MEC, they had lively-enough jobs. A lot like her own parents. All of them working to protect humanity and their fellow magir.

Which made growing her knowledge about how to handle new vampires in town crucial. She'd meant to learn all she could after meeting Duncan. But for one reason or another, she hadn't had the time to look into blood-drinkers. Odd.

"You know those Of the Bloode look down on us non-vamps," Cho said. "They refer to us as 'lesser beings.'"

"Assholes."

"They really are." Cho agreed. "Okay, the basics—there are ten tribes of vampires. Each tribe is anywhere from a thousand to fifty thousand strong. They're all male and all powerful, and each tribe has different gifts. Strigoi seduce mortals, change into ravens, and are pretty fierce among their kind. Vrykos can hypnotize prey, tend to be bigger than other vamps, and are drawn to water. Revenants tend to be super fast, super smart, and can also assume the shape of a raven. Upir are—"

"I know about the ten tribes." Impatient to get to what she *didn't* know, she motioned him to move along.

He frowned. "I will not be rushed. Facts are important."

She rolled her eyes.

"Each tribe is made up of individual clans. Clans have, like, anywhere from ten to sixty members. Within a clan, they refer to themselves as kin. Family."

"An odd concept for vampires."

"Yeah. But outside the clan, none of them get along. You know tribes hate other tribes. Well, clans hate other clans, even in the same tribe. The only thing stopping them all from wiping each other out is the strength of their leaders. For clans it's a patriarch. For tribes, a master. The master controls the patriarchs of his clans."

"So a master could have control over what? Like, up to fifty patriarchs spaced over thousands of miles?" Now that was some kind of powerful.

"Think bigger. Rumor has it a few masters have the strength to control *all* their members. Not just through the patriarchs."

She blinked. "Like, one guy controlling *thousands* of vampires?"

Cho nodded. "Ever heard of Master Vampire Atanase? He's a strigoi and supposedly controls all of his kind mind-to-mind. I don't know if that's fact, but people talk about him in whispers. What I do know is that MEC has reports of him killing and drinking down his own people when not butchering nearby lycan packs and witch covens. That guy is seriously messed up and starting a new magir war in Europe."

She nodded, feeling ill. Was Duncan strigoi? Did they intend to start a war here? "The masters are why vampires haven't all killed each other yet."

"Exactly. If you consider that a small clan, like the Seattle Blood, who are what? Thirty-five members? They're powerful enough to kill their way through all of Green Lake *and* Fremont, ending humans and magir alike. And then you have rumors of a fight between the Seattle upir clan and some other vamps new to town, but we don't have any bodies. MEC Intel is looking into it."

Using the same program MEC had been promoting to increase their intelligence network across the city.

She nodded. "I know. I volunteered to take a job downtown and listen for anything that sounded strange." And had been denied her request, but he didn't need to know that.

"I signed up too. I've been working at a gas station a few nights a week. But so far, I haven't heard much." He shrugged. "The city's a big place, and there are only so many of us. But I'm sure Spells & Incantations is working on scrying for the new big bad in the city."

Crap. Would S&I have seen her searching for Duncan and his friends? Hopefully, her magic protection had been strong enough to repel the same people she worked for.

Cho's eyes narrowed in thought. "That we haven't seen a bloodbath between the new guys and the local vamps is unnerving MEC. Right now, a vamp war is our biggest concern."

She nodded. "Dad said they've been strategizing about how to contain this new threat."

"Yeah, my dad told me the same."

They looked at each other, knowing to be worried. Their parents rarely shared the details of the job with them.

Studying Cho, she felt an urge to share. Macy badly needed to let someone know what she'd been dealing with on her own. "Well, it's funny you should mention these new vamps." She cleared her throat, nervous about admitting what an idiot she'd been. "I met one of them."

Cho froze. "Say that again?"

"His name is Duncan. Last month, when I was working at that dive bar to listen up for any weird rumors, I ended up meeting the actual threat."

"Holy crap! Wait. You didn't report it. I'd have heard." He glared at her. "What are you thinking?"

"Don't worry. I cast a spell on him when he tried getting into my pants. He thought he could seduce me for information." She shot Cho a dazzling grin, trying to ignore the growing horror on his face. "Instead, I soaked *him* for info and let him believe we had a lot of amazing sex. But no, just his own imagination making him happy."

"Are you kidding? *Please* tell me you're kidding."

*I wish I was. I don't know what the heck I've been thinking.* "I know it doesn't make a lot of sense, but I've gotten a huge power boost from a spell book I found at an old antique shop."

Cho scowled and studied her, his eyes glowing orange before fading back to brown. "Something's off with your magic."

"I know. That's what I'm telling you. The grimoire—"

"Wait. Now it's *a grimoire?*" His lips thinned. "That's a lot more iffy than a spell book. Grimoires are dark magic." He looked her over. "Not going warlock on me, are you?"

He sounded teasing. And worried.

She groaned. "No, I'm not." A warlock, like a witch, was a human who could manipulate magic. But witches focused on terrestrial magic, using their connection with the earth for good. Warlocks, on the other hand, tapped into negative energy, dark magic. A lot of attraction to pain and sacrifice. Bad stuff.

"You sure?"

"I am." She paused at his look of shock and amended, "*Not* a warlock. I'm sure I'm not, I mean. And that grimoire... I used it once and it crumbled to dust. I can't even use it anymore." She hated to lie, but she didn't want Cho even more worried about her. Right. A lie for his benefit. Because she was a good friend.

"Well, good. Grimoires are nothing but trouble."

"Right." She let out a breath. "It was cool, but it scared me too. I'm honestly glad it's gone." And if he heard mostly truth in that, so be it. "But the magic boost it gave me was amazing. Cho, I can not only create spells now, I can cast them too. I worked a vampire!"

"That's fantastic. I mean, mind-blowing." Cho nodded, but the concern remained. After a pause, he added, "You're sure you're good?"

She recalled thinking about the injured men earlier, about what a waste of blood it might have been if the upir had gotten to them first. "I'm good. Just adjusting to a lot of power I'm not used to."

*And it's not nearly enough.*

# CHAPTER THREE

*Mercer Island, 2AM, Monday night*

Duncan, now a full-fledged member of the Night Bloode clan/tribe/whatever they were calling themselves, stared at the white-haired bastard who continued to have way too much power over his kin.

Trying to hold onto his legendary patience, Duncan—the calm, intelligent, smartly-dressed one of the bunch—leaned back against the kitchen counter and tried not to think murderous thoughts. But really, one of these nights he had a feeling he'd attempt to slice his ex-patriarch's head off. Duncan had been practicing, strengthening his claws and working to speed up his attacks.

As if Mormo knew what he'd been thinking about, he just smiled.

Mormo, a powerful creature, neither young nor old, with eyes that had a tendency to see what others couldn't, ate a banana and twirled a strand of his long, white hair around his finger. He wore a white robe that dragged on the floor and had been insisting everyone call him "Mormo the White" since the group had binged *Lord of the Rings* last night.

They didn't know what exactly Mormo was save that he was in no way human. Despite Duncan's attempts, he'd learned nothing that Mormo didn't want him to know. Personally, Duncan thought him part demon or demi-god, but his kin had all settled on referring to Mormo as a magician. It described him well enough and sounded a lot nicer than half the names Varu—their new patriarch—called him.

After a few seconds, Duncan forced his voice to remain even and said, "So let me get this straight. The witch *you* had me question about the goings on in town put a spell on me using a grimoire from Hell that has the potential to destroy all vampires in existence. Is that right?"

"Technically, Varu had you talk to her. I merely steered you all in the right direction."

Mormo tossed the banana peel toward the kitchen sink and propped his chin in his hand, his elbow on the counter. Come to think of it, he *did* look a lot like a young Gandalf minus the staff, hat, and beard. Then he smiled, flashing a fang, and laughed, his eyes blazing red. "You've been bamboozled, my young friend."

"I'm two hundred and two. Not exactly a schoolboy."

"Yet young enough not to notice an enchantment." Mormo tapped his fingers on the counter, and his nails lengthened into sharp, slender black claws as he studied Duncan.

Like everything else in the goddess-touched house, the granite counter sparkled. The kitchen was of high quality and classy. With white cabinets, fancy dishware, high-end appliances, and no end to the food that could be found all over the place despite the fact no one really ever went grocery shopping, the house's interior in no way reflected what it looked like from the outside.

A two-story, nearly seven thousand foot square home in Mercer

Island, the house had a current worth valued at more than ten million U.S. dollars. Hecate, goddess of magic, witches, and the dead—to name a few of her interests—had claimed it as hers. So while it looked expensive if pedestrian on the outside, inside the place, doors appeared and vanished with little rhyme or reason. A basement that connected to other magical planes occasionally took the place of the gymnasium, weight room, and lounge space. And sometimes, odd animals walked and flew through the place like they owned it.

Mormo's upper level of the home remained mostly off limits, though Varu and his mate had been spending a lot of time up there looking for Bloode Stones. Another nightmare Duncan could have done without.

Yet, as much as he mentally complained about being in this house with a bunch of vampires that now felt like kin, Duncan did his best in the thick of things. A genius in matters of intelligence-gathering and strategizing, Duncan had been having a surprising amount of fun learning all he could about Hecate, Mormo, and the others. Because information was power.

Mormo continued to tap the counter as he studied Duncan. "A witch cast a spell over you, though I see no lingering effects."

Duncan forced himself not to look bothered by the realization he'd been bespelled. He typically handled obstacles with ease. Laidback and agreeable, almost nymph-like in his ability to adapt and overcome.

It took a moment for the truth of the matter to sink in. "She and I never had sex. I never seduced her, and she never complied with my directives because the whole time, she was playing me. Is that correct?"

"That's correct." Mormo sounded amused.

Duncan didn't often get mad, but when he did, look out. He felt the need to kill, his fangs itching to sink into one smooth, pale neck while he drained her dry.

*Fucking witches.*

He unclenched his fists and let his palms heal from the stinging wounds of his nails. "I'll kill her."

"Right." Mormo looked jolly. "But first, we need you to find Hecate's grimoire. In the witch's hands, it's a danger we can't afford."

"*Hecate's* grimoire? I thought you said it was from Hell." Which didn't sit well with him, but he'd prefer a hellish tome to one belonging to the liminal goddess pulling their strings.

"Well, it's complicated."

"Everything with you is," Duncan muttered, pulling back on his fury, saving it for a sexy redhead who would pay with her life. He'd drain her slowly, enjoy her pain and her fear, seduce the witch past sense, then make her death most agonizing.

The thought cheered him up.

"Hmm. I guess you do need some background for reference."

Two of his kin, Khent and Rolf, entered the kitchen, arguing.

"I don't need you telling me what to do with my pets," Khent bit out. An arrogant reaper, he didn't take kindly to anyone telling him anything. And why should he? Khent knew everything about everything. Just ask him.

"I don't think they're pets," Rolf said, winking at Duncan. The only blond vampire among them, the draugr a thoroughly annoying addition to their group, he did his best to take after the trickster god in his homeland. "More like minions. You summon them, after all. And they're technically dead. I mean, I could bring back our enemy. I'm a draugr after all. But mine are more zombie-like. Yours look real."

"They are real," Khent snapped. "And they're not dead. My *pets* are in stasis. They aren't *minions*. I'm not a super villain." He sniffed with disdain.

"Actually, they're dead before you bring them back." Mormo had to have his say. "So they are dead then not dead. But not undead."

"See? Mine are undead," Rolf said. "But not exactly zombies." He grabbed a blood-pop from the freezer. Their human servant had been making them from different donors, and Duncan had to admit the fae-pops tasted best.

Rolf joined them at the island, licking his treat. "Not bad. I think this one is sprite. A nasty one. Yum."

Khent had opened his mouth to argue, then closed it. "Fae? Oh, are there any more?"

He found another and joined Rolf, both of them sucking down frozen treats. "So what are we talking about?" he asked Mormo.

"We're talking about Duncan's new task. But he— Oh, good. Orion, we need you."

"We really don't," Duncan muttered, ignored Rolf's laughter, and waited for the massive *vrykolakas*, a vampire from the Greek island of Santorini, to join them.

"What? You're eating without me?"

"Where's Kraft?" Duncan asked. "I don't see your shadow near."

Orion growled. "He's not my shadow."

Yet the two vampires had gravitated toward each other like long-lost kin. It helped that the vryko and *nachzehrer* had similar abilities, both strong as fuck and aggressive. Kraft, the youngest of them all at just under a century, had a German accent and an ability to get under Orion's skin. Duncan thought him amusing. And troublesome. But he had a feeling Orion thought of him as a true brother, one in need of looking after.

"Kraft is on a break," Mormo said. "He'll be joining Rolf and Khent tomorrow on a hunt for a certain mage I need to talk to."

"We're back to policing rogues?" Khent sighed. "Isn't that what MEC is for?"

Mormo narrowed his eyes. "MEC has their objectives and I have mine. First and foremost, we do as the mistress bids."

"And just what might that be?" Duncan asked. Hecate had an

uncanny manner about her. As a goddess, she had real clout. But vampires worshipped no one but themselves. Gods and goddesses had no power over them.

Unfortunately, Hecate hadn't gotten the memo.

He did know she had something shifty going on in the basement. He'd seen his share of otherworldly creatures down there. And speaking of shifty... "Oy, Mormo, what happened with Onvyr?"

At the dusk elf's name, everyone stilled and looked around. Duncan shared in the all-body cringe they tried to suppress.

The brother to Varu's mate, Onvyr was a bit barmy. He'd been held prisoner by a master vampire, and torture could do funny things to the mind. Duncan didn't fault the dusk elf for his trauma, but the big bastard was a lot stronger than a fae warrior should be. His daily psychotic breaks made the nights a constant adventure. It broke the tedium, but sometimes Duncan just wanted to relax in his new home. Always prepared to protect himself from a beheading got old. Fast.

"He's out shopping with Bella," Mormo informed them.

Orion shared a glance with Duncan. "Is that such a good idea?"

Bella, their human housekeeper slash servant, had beauty and brains and a decent temperament. She tolerated the lot of them well enough and had taken to Onvyr, for some reason. But Duncan didn't think the dusk elf was good for her. Too scattered, too prone to attract trouble.

"It is what it is," Mormo said in response. "Good or bad, as Hecate wills it."

Behind him, Khent rolled his eyes.

"I saw that." Mormo frowned at Duncan.

He scowled. "What did I do?"

Mormo didn't answer. "So Khent and Rolf, and when Kraft

gets back tomorrow, Kraft. You three will track down my mage and bring him back. Mostly unharmed."

Rolf brightened. "That we can do."

"Intact," Mormo emphasized to Khent. "Don't chop anything off. I need him in one piece."

"Right."

"We'll give Varu and Fara until Wednesday to return. They deserve a little honeymoon, after all." Mormo nodded to Duncan and Orion. "You two need to come with me. To my office." He left them to follow.

Orion shrugged. "Time to see what all the mystery is about. I'm game." He left the others after flipping off Rolf.

Khent was watching Duncan with an odd look on his face.

"What?"

Khent shook his head. "Something a little bird told me."

"Want to share?"

"You'll do best learning on your own." Khent moved to the freezer. "Oh good, there's a lycan-pop in here."

"Mine," Rolf called it.

"You can have the human one."

"Gross. They taste terrible frozen. I want the lycan."

Khent snarled, "Touch my food and I'll rip your fangs out."

"You and what army, bro?"

"I'm not a bro, you moron," said with arched disdain. "I'm one of the Sons of Osiris."

"You *were* a son. Now you're a Night Bloode, my brother."

"Shut up and die."

"Bite me."

Duncan left the pair arguing and followed Orion into the forbidden zone. Duncan had scouted the entire house dozens of times in the eleven months they'd been living together. Not once had he been able to find his way up to Mormo's floor, always deterred by magical means.

And now he had a personal invitation to the promised land.

With a snort, he let himself climb the stairs. *It's all a means to an end,* he told himself. *Just a few more steps on my path to killing the witch.*

"Burn, baby, burn." He smiled and joined the others with happy thoughts.

## CHAPTER FOUR

Wednesday night, Macy shivered, as though someone had walked over her grave. The dive bar where she'd previously met Duncan had a weird vibe, likely from the sucky band playing in the back. Yet despite an odd sense of unease, she actually felt pretty good. Well, better than she'd felt Sunday night.

Her conversation with Cho had been both good and bad. She'd been relieved to unburden herself of such a huge secret but scared at what she'd allowed herself to do. She wanted to advance in MEC, sure, but she didn't have a death wish.

Rational people didn't interact with vampires. Especially not witches, who knew better than to literally stick their necks out to predators predisposed to sucking down blood and magic, which she'd done with Duncan, a vampire of inestimable power. Then she'd done it *again* with that upir in Greenbelt Park. Granted, both vamps had been under a spell at the time, but she hadn't been a hundred percent sure either would work.

None of that was like her. A rule-follower, always doing the right thing for the right reasons, Macy didn't like living in shades of gray. Rules existed for a reason.

She couldn't explain why it had felt so good lately to be breaking them.

Cho, always having her back, had insisted on turning her foolishness into something positive. To do that, they'd have to find a way to share her information on the Night Bloode with her bosses without letting on that she'd gone against protocol, using an ancient grimoire to boost her power. Or that she'd been looking for vampires without permission.

Partners on this roller coaster adventure that would surely lead to someone's death—they were hunting vampires, after all—she and Cho would either advance together at MEC or die together fighting blood-drinkers.

Macy wiped down the bar counter and kept an eye on the growing crowd, swaying to the music that hadn't gotten any better but had subtly infected her into tapping her toes. She fingered the pendant at her throat, confident it would keep her identity and location a secret from MEC. Unless they spotted her with their own eyes, of course.

She adjusted the sleeveless leather vest she wore, conscious it was all she had on to clothe her upper body, her jeans so tight you could ride the crack in her ass with a look. But the outfit was in keeping with what folks expected to see in this rundown, sleazy bar.

For his part, her backup, Cho, wore grungy jeans, black boots, and a stained tee with some rock band on it. With his hair unkempt and his attitude piss-poor, he looked as if he belonged in the place. Since her last visit over a month ago, the dive had attracted more magir than she might have expected. Before, she'd seen a lot more collegiate types and older, skeevy men hoping to get lucky.

Tonight, she noticed a group of lycans, a water sprite, four mages and a witch mixed with the humans dancing to awful music. The sound wanted to have a beat but felt off, jarring somehow. She didn't know the new band, but she didn't think the owner should book them again. They were horrible.

Cho sat at the end of the bar and raised his empty glass.

She reached him. "Want another?"

"Hit me."

For the third time, she refilled his gin and coke minus the gin. Cho hated alcohol so she pretended to make his drinks strong while giving him nothing but the fizz.

"You come here often?" he asked with a fake leer.

"You're not very good at this."

"Are you Wi-Fi? Cause I'm totally feeling a connection."

She tried not to laugh. "Stop."

He patted his chest and pockets. "I seem to have lost my phone number. Can I have yours?"

She burst out laughing just as a pair of scantily dressed twins sat on either side of him, grinning.

The brunette on the left slid her hand to his shoulder. "You sure can have mine, handsome."

"And mine," her sister added with a wink.

Unlike the other magir, the twins had masked their magic, and Macy had to focus hard to identify Cho's admirers.

Minor muses. Oh boy.

Cho lit up like the fourth of July. "Ladies, it would be my pleasure. Let's grab a booth. And something to drink?" he asked them.

"Long Island iced tea," they said together and left to grab an open table.

More people streamed inside, drawn to the loud noise, Macy guessed. Surely not the atmosphere.

She fixed the twins' drinks and slid them to Cho. "I hope you know what you're doing. One muse is bad enough. But you have two waiting on your sorry butt."

He leaned closer. "Twins, Macy. Gorgeous *twins*."

Macy knew she'd lost him. "Go on."

"Nothing had better happen tonight," he growled. "I'm still on the clock for you. But hellfire, look at them. And it's not even my birthday."

She had to laugh. "Just try to keep your clothes on until you get home. Better yet, go back to their place. Don't invite muses to yours. You'll never get them to leave."

"That's just mean."

"But true."

He grinned and left to join his new friends while she served up more drinks in between ignoring her partner behind the bar, a tall, sketchy human who kept trying to pat her ass and stare down her cleavage whenever he passed. Just like the last time she'd tended bar here. If it weren't for the fact she needed to get more information on Duncan and his clan, she'd never have set foot back in the place.

Warmth unfurled in her chest, a flush of energy, excitement, and nerves as the band changed the tune. The sound grew louder. More customers crowded the small dance floor, shifting tables to make room to groove. A few started kissing while others threw punches. The music grew louder, until it wasn't just the dancers getting aggressive.

What the heck?

She turned to see Cho kissing one of the twins. Then the other while her sister got naked. To her left, a customer tried to climb up her date's torso. A few human women took their tops off, attracting the lycans, who broke into an all out brawl with each other. Not laughing about it, but snarling with challenge, likely not far from shifting into fur and scaring humans.

Macy needed to call MEC. The potential for magir to out themselves was always a daily threat, and right now looking like a possibility. She'd have to set the place on lockdown and hope Duncan had no intention to show up tonight. She didn't want to lose the only connection she had to him, but she didn't want MEC to know they'd previously met.

Swearing under her breath, she sent a quick text to Enforcement, including a disaster code and the address.

*Affirmative. There in ten.*

Before she could move toward Cho, the bartender drew her in for an unwelcome lip-lock. She would have shoved him aside, but he disappeared. A stranger had grabbed him by the neck and tossed him down the bar, so that he crashed into the bottles along the wall.

"Th-thanks?" Macy glanced up, and up, into the eyes of someone not human, for sure.

He smiled, showing a hint of sharp teeth, but nothing vamplike. "My pleasure." He had to be at least a foot taller than her. He leaned forward, his blue eyes shining, his blond hair long and luxurious over one shoulder. "And aren't you so pretty and dark. Like the cover of night without stars."

His deep voice captivated her, but something shimmering around his aura gave her pause.

"Who are you?" Her truthsense sputtered, something blocking her fix on the man.

He smiled, and a flash of black overtook the whites of his eyes. "Someone who's intrigued by your power and beauty. I absolutely *love* your hair." He had the nerve to take a strand off her shoulder and rub it between his fingers, which ended in neat black nails. Not claws, but normal nails painted black. At least, she thought they were painted. He lifted her hair to study it. "I'd call this hellfire-red."

She stared back at him, intrigued. "Hellhound?" Many magir had the ability to shapeshift into human form, letting them blend in with the majority of the population.

"One might think, but no." He inhaled then sighed. "You are tempting, aren't you? What is that smell?" He moved closer, and she wanted to jerk back, instinctively sensing danger, but she couldn't, frozen, captured by his powerful gaze. "Ah, I smell lies. Temptation." He licked his lips. "Delicious."

She drew down hard on her power, trying to free herself from the trap she hadn't sensed. But now that she looked with her second sight, she saw bands of shadow twining around her, pushing from the ends of his fingers still touching her hair. Desperate, she glanced for Cho but no longer saw him with the twins, the booth now empty. Great.

"MEC is on the way," she said with a calm she didn't feel, the press of violence and raging lust in the bar circling but not touching her or the man holding her with his will. "I'd advise you to run while you still can."

He surprised her by releasing her, his magic there one moment and gone the next. "Nicely played. But I'll be back to... *talk*... later. You and I have a great deal in common." He kissed the back of her hand, though she hadn't seen him move to take it, leaving behind a jolt of sensation that traveled throughout her body, feeling like an all-over orgasm ending in a bite.

Breathless, she asked, "Wh-what the hell did you just do?"

He winked. "You have such a way with words, Macy Bishop-Dunwich."

The bastard knew her name. Not good.

He continued to stare into her eyes, his now completely black and freaky as all get-out, hers no doubt a glaring brown. "But perhaps you should save your charm for the revenant." He jerked his head toward the front doorway, where a pair of vampires entered.

She felt the powerful bloode energy—the grimoire having enhanced her senses to identify darkness—spotted them, and tensed.

There he stood, the vampire who starred in her nightly dreams that ended in nightmares. Duncan of the Night Bloode.

Looking at both males, one might think them nothing more than extremely handsome humans. Duncan with his sophisticated manner, chiseled features, and deep, dark eyes. His partner stood a good head taller, jacked with muscle, his features coarser but no less attractive.

Regardless of their looks, both broadcast danger. And they'd focused on her and her weird new friend right away. She swallowed her nerves, unable to stop a tremor of fear.

"I'll be seeing you soon," the blond male promised, tamping down his aura, coming across like a weak magir once more. The darkness shielding his eyes vanished, and she could see the whites and blue irises once more. He bowed his head then walked away. Not toward the vampires, no. He instead managed to thread through the chaos all around.

Macy gasped. *Jesus.* While the blond weirdo had been chatting with her, the rest of the bar had erupted in a lot of naked people punching and grinding against each other.

The vampires watched the blond leave without expression. Duncan said something to his friend, who nodded and trailed after the guy, tossing people out of his way with ease. Then Duncan's eyes turned to her.

She'd swear they burned a bright, blood-red.

SHE WAS HERE. *Perfect.* Duncan didn't like the feel of the yellow-haired magir with her, but before he could pinpoint what it was about the male that bothered him, he left.

"Orion, trail him. But be careful."

"I got it. But I have to say, this place is rocking." Orion mowed through the battling humans and magir as if they were nothing, trailing the threat Duncan could all but feel.

He saw the busty redhead eye him with trepidation and smiled. He slowly approached, shoving several men aside, nudging two gropy females away, and found his witch behind the bar.

"Quite an exciting place you have, here." He gave her another grin, pleased beyond measure when she swallowed audibly. On guard this time, he'd know if she tried any magic on him.

"There's something wrong with the band. I think their music started it. You don't feel it?"

"It takes a lot to affect my kind." He looked her up and down. "I'm impressed you managed it."

"Ah, I have no idea what you mean."

Furious but not willing to show it, he nodded. "I thought you'd play it that way."

A lycan slammed into him from behind and knocked his belly into the bar. "Don't go anywhere, Sarah," he threatened her. "But of course, Sarah's not your real name, is it?" He didn't like her, but he admired her ability to lie with a straight face.

"Sure it is." She smiled a little too brightly.

Duncan turned and faced the lycan, who sniffed, realized what he was up against, and roared for his pack to back him up. Duncan needed to vent his rage, not wanting to turn it all on the witch he planned to take his time with, and threw the lycan across the room, knocking several people over in the process.

Two other lycans came after him, and Duncan laughed. "You need more than a few puppies to deal with me."

"We'll kill you, death-bringer," one of them growled, flinging blood from his cheek.

"Kid, you're just an appetizer," Duncan said before kicking him into his friend. They were fast and strong but provided little in the way of a challenge. The ice mage behind them put up more of a fight, and Duncan found himself slipping on the ice that formed out of nowhere, joining several others nearby who swore as they fought to remain on their feet.

"Not bad." He darted faster than the magir could see and

grabbed the ice mage, yanked his neck back, and took a long drag of magir blood before settling the male on the ground. *Out cold.* He laughed at his bad pun.

The jolt of blood infused with magic made him tingle and gave him a slight boost of power. Not that Duncan needed it, but the reward felt nice. After all he'd been through thanks to this blasted witch, he deserved a little bit of fun. The battle, though minor, had stirred his excitement.

But the witch, ah, she stirred a bit more.

Unlike others of his kind, Duncan had always enjoyed his bedsport, treating females like the delights they were. Revenants were known for their power of seduction. The more attracted the human or magir was to his form, the easier it was to overpower them.

Sarah had been a real treat, or so he'd thought. The attraction had definitely raged between them. He still had a tough time believing she'd bespelled him. Something no fledgling witch could do. She would pay for that, but not right away. Not until he'd had his fill of her.

Bollocks, but she was fine. She wore a dark vest that showed off her toned arms and lovely chest. Full breasts with a nice bit of cleavage, and that dark, witchy red hair frothing over her shoulders. He could just imagine gripping it tight while he thrust inside her.

Duncan turned to make sure she'd stayed where he'd left her and saw her being dragged away by a tall, dark-haired human. They disappeared down a back hallway.

With a grin, Duncan trailed after them, maneuvering through moaning couples and too many naked older men. *Excited* older men. Bloody hell. Now that he hadn't needed to see.

He exited to find Orion walking across the parking lot toward him, appearing annoyed.

"I'm on the hunt." Duncan nodded toward the pair disappearing into car that turned down the alley, then out of sight.

A lot of screaming engines neared, likely closing in on the bar.

"MEC's coming." Orion cracked his neck. "I'll keep an eye out from above. Go on." So saying, Orion shapeshifted into a raven and flew inside the bar, no doubt planning to hide out in the rafters and keep watch.

Duncan seconded the notion, shapeshifted into a raven himself, and launched into the night sky. He found his quarry easily enough and glided on currents of wind, content to do what he did best.

Capture wayward prey and demand answers. The hard way.

# CHAPTER FIVE

Corson Westhell watched the vampires split up, the larger one going back inside the bar, the other following the vehicle with the witch and her interesting friend. Not quite human, that one. But not a threat either. Not like those Of the Bloode.

*My lord?* he tried again, eager to reconnect with his master. But after a few moments of silence, he gave up. His master would call when he needed something.

Corson would have followed the woman but realized he didn't need to. The dark power would call to her, and like those before her, she'd be helpless to refuse it.

To refuse *Him.*

He smiled. After over seven hundred years in exile, he had a way to return. To find the blessed book, set his master free, and kill the thrice-damned goddess who'd stolen it in the first place.

For too many years, he'd been adrift, raging, desperate to return to his kingdom and mete justice on the undeserving bitch who'd gotten him into such a mess.

Witches. It always came back to them.

The coven had made a blood bargain of their own free will,

severing their link to Hecate and forging a new one to Corson. In doing so, their terrestrial magic had shifted into a darker thirst, turning them into warlocks. A true triumph he'd been proud to have accomplished.

Thirteen new warlocks for Corson's kingdom, giving him a new entryway into the human plane. Truly, a feat that would have seen him talked about for years.

Until Hecate decided to interfere.

Since when were the damned her provenance? But she'd made some kind of bargain with Hades, who had some kind of connection to Azamoth, Ashtaroth's cursed offspring. As the Grand Duke of Hell, Ashtaroth ruled *the* Hell plane. Not to be confused with the Greek and Roman Underworld, the Norse Niflheim, the Sumerian afterlife of Kur, or any of the other human religious depictions of the mundane hereafter.

Hell was a special place created to serve a higher—or lower, depending upon one's opinion—purpose. Darkness needed souls to feed it. And humanity had some of the tastiest souls around. Unfortunately, every pantheon in existence had its hand in the pot.

The splinters of the underworld allied themselves for fear of returning to the utter chaos that had once been. A primordial soup of malevolence no one really cared for. Even Corson preferred their new way of existing, each pantheon adhering to territories and castes within.

But that meant holding to pledges and bargains. *Not* giving souls back without due recompense, which Azamoth had, the puking whelp. So eager not to offend, to impress his father, the hellish sycophant worshipped only those with power. And though a king of Hell, Corson hadn't been powerful enough to defeat divinity.

So he'd lost the warlocks, but not before one of them had stolen a special grimoire Corson had been charged to protect. And so, seven hundred and fifty two years later, he continued to search, banished from returning to his home.

*I miss the haze of blackness so very, fucking much.* He sighed and entered a bar down the block. With a much more upscale clientele and pricier drinks, the place would do for his present needs. Thronged with patrons organized into small groups, making visibility clear despite the darkened room, the bar seemed to have plenty of attractive customers. But Corson needed the right one.

Ah, there. That one might be workable.

He neared the crowded bar and put a hand on one man's shoulder to get him to leave.

The human turned to argue and seized, frozen by Corson's gaze. The man's eyes remained wide, haunted, even. But he smiled and said, "Please, have my seat."

"Thank you."

The man covered his mouth and raced away.

"Jonathan? Where are you going?" asked his lovely companion.

Corson watched Jonathan reach the wall then pause to lean over and vomit blood, causing a lovely commotion. He then hurried into the hallway, disappearing until others would find him bleeding from every orifice in his body.

"Huh. That's weird," the attractive blond woman next to him said.

Corson ordered a bottle of expensive Scotch and drank a healthy shot, followed by another, feeling nothing but a slight burn down his parched throat.

The pretty blond next to him smiled. "I'll have one if you don't mind."

Corson motioned to the bartender, who added a glass for the woman. In her mid-twenties, attractive, and used to getting what she wanted, she glowed with the need for attention. He could see the vanity shining in her dark eyes.

She drank down the shot he poured her and held her glass out for another. Greedy too. He liked that.

"See anything you like?" She leaned toward him, showing off an attractive figure while taking in his expensive suit and styled hair. Sophisticated, wealthy, and powerful—the look he'd been going for.

"I do." He winked at her.

"Oh, aren't you a charmer." She giggled and sipped her drink while Corson allowed himself to tap into her desires. A simple creature, she wanted sex and power, and he could appreciate her aims. She liked knowing most men would do anything for her and wielded her authority like a whip.

Corson grinned, flashing a wad of bills as he laid down a hefty tip for the bartender. He slid his long, golden hair behind his ear, attracting the weak human. Just as he'd months ago attracted a few arrogant fae, and before that, some annoying mages. All had fed his appetite for revenge and destruction.

As he'd earlier enamored the redheaded witch.

He could almost taste her blood on his tongue, knowing it would spice his tedious existence.

Now that one he'd have to take his time with.

Macy Bishop-Dunwich. A Magir Enforcement Command agent, a witch with real power wearing the perfume of the damned. An aura of Doom, the whisper of his master in her blood.

He grew aroused and pushed the half-full bottle aside. His companion glanced down at him and smiled. "Shall we?" he asked, holding out his elbow.

She put her hand on his arm, and the connection snapped into place.

She tugged him with her outside. "Got someplace we can go?"

"I do." He guided her into the alley next door and pulled her close, sealing her mouth with a kiss. He teleported them to a suite in one of the city's most expensive hotels. The guests currently there gaped at him, and he snapped his fingers, setting the older couple aflame, burning so fast they left nothing but a trace of ash. He would have banished them to Hell, but that ability had been taken from him when he'd been excised.

He couldn't even damn people anymore.

It almost made life not worth living. But then, he had a new friend, didn't he?

She blinked and pulled back. "Wh-where are we?"

"My place. Don't think, just act. Whatever you want, it's yours." He held out his arms and waited.

As expected, she didn't consider more than her own needs. Humans and their terrible choices. He chuckled and gazed hungrily at her mouth.

"Oh, yes." She yanked him to her and kissed him. "You're so strong."

"And hungry," he growled, took off their clothes, and gave her what she thought she wanted. A few quick and fast orgasms.

After her third time, he waited for her to shake off the drugging euphoria of pleasure and sighed when she smiled at him. For a human, she did have pretty features, he supposed. Though she lacked the horns, wings, and tail he dearly missed.

"Oh my God." She panted. "That was the best sex I've ever had in my life, and I don't even know your name."

"Sweetheart, we're not done."

"No, you'll kill me." She put a hand over her heart.

He chuckled. *If only.* Unfortunately, human sacrifices brought too much attention. "Now why would I do that? Why ruin such a gorgeous creature when we have so much more to get to?"

She laughed and put her arms around his neck.

He leaned in and kissed her, gratified that despite what she'd said, her impatient response told him otherwise. She pushed her tongue into his mouth, and he moaned, pulling her closer to him, needing a repeat of the pleasure they'd just shared.

Once again inside her, he caught her tongue, stroked it with his.

Then bit it off.

Drinking down her pain, terror, and blood, he fed her his own flesh, letting his tongue fuse with the stump of hers, creating a new muscular organ through which *he* could now speak.

He pulled his tongue back, letting it reshape, and let her body squeeze his into an orgasm, feeding the once great King of Lust some of his lost power. Too fading, but still, it revived that missing part of him.

The consummation of their new bargain gave her more pleasure, painful though it might feel at first, while she gave him leave to use her as a mouthpiece. He withdrew from her flesh and stood with her in his arms.

The mess of her gave him a feeling of affection. She seemed to be in shock, holding a hand over her bloody mouth, staring at him in horror.

Corson stroked her cheek. "You are so lovely like that." He wouldn't have minded another go, thought even of filling her belly with a youngling. It had been some time since he'd procreated, and he was due. But having half-human progeny was tacky for a demon of his stature. Now, Macy Bishop-Dunwich, on the other hand, would make a decent breeder. Plenty of his kind took witches to bear strong, powerful young.

Hmm. Something to keep in mind.

Corson helped the female into the shower and washed her off, pleased when she continued to tremble before him, even after being clean and dressed. "Now, lovely. Let's talk about how you can help me. I know you want to."

"I do," she said, his tongue telling him exactly what he wanted to hear.

Her eyes wide, she clapped her hands over her mouth.

"No, no. Let's not hide that perfect face."

Her hands slowly returned to her sides. "Whatever you wish. I'm yours, my king."

"Aw, so kind of you to say so."

Tears streamed down her cheeks, and he wanted to hug her. Such a giver, she was.

"What's your name?"

"Lucy Driver."

"You need a better name than that, don't you think? A secret name just for us to share. What do you think?"

She nodded. "I want to be useful."

"Of course you do. I think we'll call you Lilith because you remind me of a girl I once knew. Now let's see what we can do about introducing you to witchcraft. And getting you the help you need to control your talent."

Something those at MEC took pride in, helping the uninitiated.

Lilith would be the perfect vehicle to moving him closer to his clever little witch.

*Oh, Macy. What wonderful fun we're going to have together. I just know you're going to love it in Hell.*

🐦

DUNCAN HAD FOLLOWED the witch and her friend back to a cottage in Fremont. He waited, wondering if he should go inside. Wondering if she and the male were more than platonic friends. Wondering if he would need to kill him as well.

He crouched on a tree limb that gave him full view through the front window.

Until she closed the drapes.

Bemused, he circled the house in the air, the wind kissing his feathers with a lover's affection. The moon overhead wouldn't allow him to hide in the shadows. He'd have to go inside, but he'd be careful. He'd underestimated her once. He wouldn't let it happen again.

He called on the power of his tribe, using the speed and skill of a revenant to its fullest. Known to be fast, Duncan was more than just a quick-moving vampire. He could move between spells. Not fast enough to unlock the secrets of time itself, but he could skate along its edges, working between the seams of before and now and after.

Pushing through one such seam in the ward's lines—so she *had* warded the house after all—

he let himself in through an open window on the second floor.

And came face to face with the dark-haired bloke who jumped back.

"What the hell?"

Duncan let out a gurgling croak and settled on the ground, wondering if the man would be stupid enough to think him nothing more than a bird. He cocked his head, studying the human, sensing something more in him.

A vampire, Duncan didn't have truthsense. But he could sometimes tell when magir hid themselves under a human-seeming. This male definitely concealed a well of power despite looking human enough.

"How did you get in here?" the man asked and rubbed his temples. "Damn. My head's killing me."

"Cho, I told you not to... " The witch stopped behind him and stared down at Duncan. "What is this?"

Duncan encouraged the man to talk by giving him another gurgle.

The man—Cho—shrugged. "Looks like a crow to me."

She frowned. "No, it's a raven. Crows caw, and he didn't caw. See the wedge shaped tail feather? Yeah, that's a Common Raven."

"Someone studied up on her corvids." Cho sighed and rubbed his temples some more.

"I'm a witch. Duh." She rolled her eyes but kept her attention on Duncan.

"I'm in so much pain," the man continued to whine.

"Oh my gosh. Hold on." She put a finger to his temple and hummed.

Duncan couldn't see it, but he felt a well of magic passing from the witch to Cho.

"Much better. Thanks." Cho sighed. "That stupid band had some messed up magic. Really hurt my brain. But not yours?"

"No." She kept looking at Duncan, and he waited to see if she might realize who he was.

Just how powerful was she?

"I think that weird blond guy was with the band," the witch said, her hair looking so soft and shiny against her shoulders. "Or he'd influenced them in some way. The music started to affect me a little too at first, but when he came to talk to me, it passed over us both."

"What was he?"

"I don't know. Not human. His eyes turned black." She grimaced. "I'm thinking some kind of hell-beast."

"My kind of people." Cho grinned, and horns formed at his temples, pointing up.

Ah, a demon of some kind. Duncan fluffed his wings, pleased to have been right about the male having power. Fascinating. His first demon.

The witch frowned at him. "I just reinforced your wards. How did he get in here?"

"I keep out magir, not wildlife, Macy."

Macy, not Sarah. Satisfied to have that much, Duncan knew he wanted more than her name. He launched himself up and landed on her shoulder before she could protest.

She froze.

Cho laughed. "I think you have a new friend." He shut the window. "We'll keep out the other wildlife for now. Hey, little raven, be nice to Macy. I'd hate to have to fry you."

Duncan wondered if pecking her eyes out would be out of order. Then again, they were a lovely shade of brown, ringed with a lighter amber. It would be a crime to destroy her beauty. He glanced down, noticed the full chest exposed by her clothing, and decided to take his time before torturing her. Of course, he meant to seduce her either way, but he didn't need physical force to break her down.

He pecked at her hair and nuzzled her cheek.

She sucked in a breath. "Man, that's a big beak."

Cho snickered. "That's what we guys love to hear."

"Shut up, Cho." But she laughed. "Where did your muses go?"

As they chatted, Duncan was surprised to find her demon friend amusing. Known to be devious, cruel, and strong, demons often made for challenging foes. It had been a while since Duncan had even heard of a demon living close, as they tended to favor pockets of older magic in northern Europe and Asia.

Macy moved, and he flapped to keep his balance and remain on her shoulder. Time for some reconnaissance before he took her back to headquarters—Hecate's house. He didn't think of it as home, exactly, but it had become much more than a lair in the eleven months he'd been living there.

Hell, he'd almost come to think of the bloode bastards he lived with as real kin.

Then he had a thought and paused. Taking a witch back to Hecate might not be in his best interest. What if Hecate refused to allow him to kill her?

Before he could decide what to do, noise from outside the house warned its residents to beware.

Cho looked through the window at the front yard. "Why is MEC outside?"

She joined him. "Crap. That's not just MEC."

Duncan leaned closer to see what had them both in a dither. A nondescript brown vehicle parked in their driveway, a sigil—visible only to those with magic—atop the vehicle glowing. Two large males got out, one likely a witch or mage, the other moving too smoothly to be anything but some kind of shifting magir. Often those who could shapeshift moved with a nuanced speed and gait, which Duncan had been trained to recognize.

Gathering intelligence was his forte, after all. Something he'd done for the Tizan Clan for over a century. Which reminded him, he'd need to call his uncle soon.

The men pushed through the ward as if it were made of water and banged on the front door.

Macy glanced at Cho, who had paled. "I think they know."

"No way. They can't know we were there."

"Cho, I know you were there," one of the men roared.

"Macy, open up," the other man said, as if standing right next to them, though he remained a floor below and outside.

Macy let out a loud breath and followed Cho, rushing down the steps. Duncan continued to ride her shoulder, enjoying the entertainment. But not sure if the males at the door would know him for what he was, he let out a few clicks of warning and flew into the nearby kitchen to perch atop the refrigerator. Then he pulled on his ability to blend into the shadows and sat tight.

"Hell, even the bird knows better than to confront the demon at the door." Cho opened the door and groaned. "Hey, Dad."

Macy suffered the hug from the other man holding her tight. "Dad, you're squeezing too hard."

Duncan laughed to himself, committing the other men's faces to memory. More leverage to hold over Macy *when*, not if, she disobeyed him. Then he sat back to watch and wait.

# CHAPTER SIX

Macy groaned. "Dad, it wasn't that big a deal." She kept repeating herself while he chastised her for being in harm's way.

"Which you'll have to explain to your boss tomorrow at work." He looked stern. "You had no business not sticking around to report on the disturbance."

"We totally will, Uncle Will. Ha. Get it?" Cho chuckled and had his dad, and hers, grinning.

Sure, *Cho* could be pleasant and funny. His dad had been congratulating him for managing two frisky muses while her father had given her outfit a critical onceover before complaining about her working outside the scope of an S&I agent.

Rule-follower that she was, she still felt a heap of guilt for keeping her self-appointed vampire mission a secret. But she'd tell her dad and MEC when she knew more. Not now, when they'd definitely pull her off the case.

"Rules are there for a reason," he said, for the millionth time. She'd grown up hearing about "the rules." She'd had regulations at school, guidelines for growing up with chores and a clean room, how to do magic, how to interact with other witches and magir. Her whole life, Macy had been following someone else's mandates, and lately, it had begun to grate on her.

Hence her involvement with one of the deadliest creatures on the planet.

And speaking of which, how had Duncan taken her disappearing with Cho? She shivered just thinking about it. He wouldn't be pleased.

She stared at her dad, knowing he'd move heaven and earth to shield her from any and all danger. Heck, he'd initially been against her joining MEC. He'd only relaxed his stance because he thought she'd be protected working in Spells & Incantations. Spellcasters were an asset to safeguard. *Not* the group to put on the front line. Cho liked to call her people the magical geek group, and she had to admit, it fit.

Yet, as much as her dad's protectiveness annoyed her, she warmed, knowing he did it out of love.

Technically her stepfather, Grand (Mind) Mage William Dunwich had married her mother when Macy had been young. He'd loved and cared for as his own from the beginning, and his daughter from a previous marriage had become a true sister as well.

Unlike her biological human father, Noah the Shithead, whom she couldn't stand. Not a witch and unable to deal with being married to a woman stronger than him, he'd dumped his wife *and* his daughter and perpetually lived on the wrong side of the law. Last she'd heard, he'd been working for a local lycan pack, running interference for them with law enforcement. She hadn't wanted to know any more and let the matter of Noah drop.

So she endured her *real* dad's concern and did her best to put his mind at ease. "I'm sorry. We had to leave because it was getting crazy inside, and I was worried Cho had been affected. I'll let my boss know tomorrow when I see him." *And explain why I was there in the first place, since he never actually assigned me to work there.*

"You do that." Her dad harrumphed.

"And you," Cho's dad said to her. "I expect more from you. You're the brains in this outfit."

"Thanks a lot, Dad." Cho glared.

His dad's image wavered, replaced by a seven-foot-tall demon with pitch black skin, horns, and bright orange eyes. He sighed. "Ah, that feels better. Squeezing into my human form for hours on end is uncomfortable." He glanced at Cho, who continued to glare at him. "What? It's the truth. Macy's the brains."

"Uncle Anton." Macy frowned. "Cho and I worked together on this. He insisted on backing me up, actually. We were just there to see keep an eye out for any vampire action in town. We had no reason to suspect the band had been bespelled. I think the guy with the long blond hair was behind it."

She described him in detail, leaving out the tidbits about his flirting and giving her an ethereal orgasm. She wished she had a better name for it, but so much pleasure followed by an all-body burn seemed to fit the name. She'd thought him a hellhound, but perhaps he'd been part incubus?

Uncle Anton and her dad exchanged a glance before Anton said, "We've been looking for your blond friend for a while. If you see him again, don't engage, but let us know. And definitely call it in to your supervisor."

"I will." Macy nodded. "He freaked me out. I'm just glad he left. Not sure what spooked him, though."

"Vampires," her dad said, giving her an odd look. "You're telling me you couldn't sense them?"

Her truthsense had always been strong, allowing her to know the core of a person with ease. She had seen Duncan and his large friend. Stymied, she tried to come up with an excuse her dad wouldn't read as false. Though *he* had no inherent truthsense, her dad knew all her tells.

"The magic was really strong in there," Cho cut in. "It messed with my head, I can tell you. And she was dealing with the blond guy, who worked his own magic."

"You're sure you're okay?" her dad asked.

"I'm fine. I think he might have been a hellhound, actually. I had the sense he was there to stir up trouble."

"Oh, he's trouble, all right," Anton growled, and a hint of smoke escaped his nose.

Cho frowned. "Dad, please don't set the house on fire again."

"Oh, relax, boy. I'm just annoyed we missed him. Your Uncle Will and I have been looking for that fucker—excuse my language, Macy—for years."

"You'll get him," Macy said, confident in their tenacity. "Though if he's avoided you two for years, that says a lot about him." She'd been right to be wary of the handsome blond.

"We would have had him if we could have left the city," her dad said. "But MEC wants us working here, not internationally."

Anton grunted. "A real pain in the ass, sometimes."

"How did you even know we were there?" Cho asked.

His dad sniffed. "How do you think? I know the scent of my own son."

"I think he means, why were you there?" Macy asked. "Were you tracking the hellhound or was it something else? You didn't exactly say."

"No, we didn't." Her dad smiled. "Okay, we'll let you two be. Are you staying over, Macy? Because after what happened tonight, it might be best if you had company for protection. When you go in tomorrow, we'll fill you in on everything. Corson Westhell is no mere hellhound, so be on your guard."

She and Cho said their goodbyes and waited until their dads left before turning to each other.

"*Mere* hellhound?" Cho asked. "If they consider a hellhound underwhelming, what the heck *is* the guy?"

"I don't think I want to know." She bit her lip. "I didn't tell them all of it."

Cho smacked his forehead. "Or course you didn't."

"That Corson guy came onto me bigtime. Cho, he knew my name."

"Shit."

"And, uh, he pulled some kind of sex-mojo on me. I'm not sure what he did, exactly. Do I look any different to you?"

Cho transformed into his demon form, still in a man's body, maintaining his human skin tone but with black eyes flashing orange, horns, and wings—fully fleshed out. He stared over her. "There's something off about you, but I think it's the lingering effects of that grimoire. You look the same as you did before you met this Westhell guy."

"Well, I guess that's good news."

Cho turned back to full human and looked around.

"What?"

"Where did the raven go?"

Macy wondered how she could have forgotten about the thing in the first place. "I don't know." Unfortunately, she'd never been able to tell the truthsense of an animal. For all she knew, the bird could have been some kind of avian shifter.

They walked around the house but found no trace of it. "Maybe he flew back out the window?" she suggested.

"I thought I'd closed it."

They walked back to the second story window to see it open. Odd. "You did close it. I saw you close it." She paused. "Didn't I?"

"I guess not."

They both stared at the open window as Cho closed then

locked it. He turned back to her and asked what she'd been thinking. "What if that wasn't just a raven?"

"Then what was it?"

A QUESTION that haunted her as she lay in her own bed hours later. "What was it?"

The raven hadn't done anything wrong, exactly. It looked and sounded like a bird. The right size, the right shaped feathers, the right sounds. Yet where had it come from, and where had it gone?

*Just one more thing to worry about.* Macy groaned and rolled over, trying to sleep, as she'd been trying for hours.

But instead of resting, she grew more rest*less*. She had some kind of hell creature that knew her name, a vampire with a grudge, and trouble with S&I coming her way. She'd really need to have a good story to cover the fact she'd been unauthorized to investigate on her own. Not to mention her use of an ancient grimoire people wouldn't understand.

MEC witches had strict regulations about items they were allowed to use. As an S&I agent, Macy was expected to do her work at headquarters. Period. Yet another rule to follow.

She tossed and turned, coming to lie on her stomach and shifted her head on the pillow to look out the window at the moon. The sky looked black, the hour close to—she cast a bleary look at her cell phone—*four in the morning.*

Macy wasn't a morning person, but later today would be especially awful on just a few hours of sleep.

She stared at the bright moon dancing with the shifting clouds and again wondered what she hoped to accomplish at the end of it all. Did she really think she'd be able to nail down Duncan's whereabouts? Would she get him to confess his intentions for being in the city? Did she think she could continue to toy with an ancient grimoire without consequences?

Her eyes grew droopy, and she yawned, still pondering her future.

It could have been seconds or hours later when someone whispered into her ear, "You've been a naughty witch."

She jerked awake but couldn't move, a solid body pressing against her from behind. She lay on her side, spooned by an angry vampire who made her tremble from dread and a crazy sense of excitement. *There is something seriously wrong with me. Oh, of course. I'm not awake.*

Relieved to be in a dream, she smiled and said aloud, "I'm dreaming."

"Yes, keep telling yourself that."

"Right. So, well, why are you here?"

He chuckled and nipped her ear, playfully. Not drawing blood, she hoped. "Where's the grimoire, Macy?"

She pretended ignorance, her heart racing, despite being in a dream. "Grimoire? I'm a second class witch. I don't use a grimoire."

"Try again." He shifted her hair away from her neck and pressed soft kisses along the column of her throat.

Hmm. This didn't feel like a dream.

Her breath hitched, and arousal mixed with fear. Crap. Then something occurred to her. He lay in her bed with her. In her room. He had bypassed the magical wards she always used to shield the house. Duncan had full access to her things, yet he hadn't found the grimoire?

It should have been in her spell room in the basement.

She didn't want to bring attention to her hiding place, but now she had to know. Had he searched and not found it? Or had someone else stolen it when she'd been out?

The idea enraged her on a level she shouldn't be comfortable with. Yet, it belonged to *her!*

Between one breath and the next, Duncan had her flat on her

back under him, and her fury transitioned into something warm and fuzzy. Into something hungry.

"Where is it, Macy, luv? Where's the grimoire?"

Staring back into blood-red eyes, she wanted nothing more than to please him. Though she knew she shouldn't trust him, she did and smiled. "It's in my spell room in the basement."

He frowned. "Come, show me." He lifted her in his arms and gently set down, her feet on the floor, giving her a generous onceover. "Love the nightie."

She flushed. The overlarge tee-shirt showed the body of a hairy gorilla. A past birthday present from Cho. "It's cute."

"Night willing you're not that furry," he muttered and nudged her to precede him.

"I'm not. I shave because I like when my skin feels smooth."

He chuckled. "And isn't that a loaded statement. Onward, girl. Show me the book." He put a hand on her shoulder from behind, steering her down the steps.

She didn't think she should like it, but she enjoyed feeling his control.

So strange.

Once in the basement, she waved a hand, muttered an incantation, and let the magical shields drop and the lanterns turn on, illuminating the small space. A kind of office, the stone floor and wooden walls encased the room in earth. Nothing artificial in the space, just dirt, rock, wood, and the element of air filling the emptiness.

She had a cauldron in the corner on a wheeled dolly for ease of movement. Shelves along the wall were filled with herbs and ingredients for mild potions. Books upon books stacked the bookshelves along the far wall from floor to ceiling. A small, built-in alcove held a statue of Hecate, bordered by foxglove and wolfsbane and two beeswax candles to which she'd added witchbreath and a touch of lavender for scent as well as purification.

She muttered a blessing to Hecate, and despite the presence of danger at her back, Macy felt at home. Welcome.

"I was already in here," Duncan said, his voice tight.

She frowned. "It's right there." The grimoire sitting on the center altar—a converted circular bar table with a dark cloth draped over it ending in dangling beads with the occasional crystal or power gem embedded in the silken lace—shimmered and vanished. "What the heck?"

"What?" Duncan glanced around. "Where is it?"

"You didn't see that? It was right there. Then it vanished." She walked to the table to study it, seeing nothing of the grimoire that had just been there. Even its odd, smoky scent had disappeared. "I don't understand." She turned to him. "Is this some kind of tease? You steal it then punish me anyway?"

"A brilliant idea, but no." He turned to her wearing a menacing expression.

She blinked and was somehow in his arms, off her feet, her back against the wall when just a second ago they'd been standing in the middle of the room.

He stared into her eyes once more. "You want to give me whatever I want, don't you, sweetheart?"

"I do." She wished desperately to help him. Then a thought struck her, and she smiled. "I know what you want."

Duncan nodded, seeming pleased. His chiseled jaw eased, not clenched so tight, and his firm lips quirked into a beautiful smile. "That's a girl. Now where is—"

She yanked his mouth to hers and gave him the kiss she knew he wanted.

# CHAPTER
## SEVEN

Just a heartbeat away from draining the stubborn woman dry, Duncan hadn't been prepared for her to kiss him.

He could have avoided it. Probably *should have* avoided it. But damned if she wasn't right.

He did want the kiss he'd imagined those weeks ago.

But this embrace had nothing on the illusion she'd once crafted. This kiss was nothing but heat and touch and taste. A rich, earthy blend of sexuality and feminine mystery, Macy enthralled him with her strength and enthusiasm. She plastered herself against him, and he felt her heart racing beneath full breasts, her moans for more distracting as hell.

The seducer, Duncan found himself seduced. Especially when she clutched his hair and sucked his tongue deeper into her mouth. His fangs lengthened, passion riding him hard. The savage control he mastered over everything in his life started to leave him, and he knew he needed to pull back or be consumed... and consume her. Literally.

She shifted, and his fang grazed her tongue, dragging a tiny bead of blood. The taste of her exploded in his mouth like the burst of ripe fruit. So sweet, so incredibly addictive.

He had to have more and slid his mouth to her throat, lost to everything but the redhaired witch.

"Do it, yes," she whispered, but her voice sounded deeper, huskier than he'd have imagined.

The temptation to feast on her grew, and he bit into her throat and drank, lost to everything but her.

Duncan didn't know how much time had passed before he came back to himself, but not enough to have harmed Macy. He didn't think.

He withdrew his fangs, uncomfortably erect and not sure why. He typically didn't get hard from eating, though human myth had vampires fucking their dinner in books, movies, in all manner of media. Occasionally, after a fun evening with a woman, he might indulge in a sip or two, but Duncan didn't typically feed from his bedpartners during the actual act.

This anomaly with Macy had to be some kind of magical defense, which had him hurrying to disengage, yanking himself back from her, only to help her regain her balance when she nearly slid to the floor. But once she'd been righted, he darted away again.

He felt unnerved, shaky, and on fire to have her.

She stood with her head back, her long hair licking the column of her throat like flame, so dark red against the creamy white of her neck.

She sighed and fingered the already healing pricks of his fangs. "Holy shit. I came so hard."

He contained a groan. Not what he needed to hear. Something was wrong with him, and she was at the heart of it. But with dawn pressing, he didn't want to be far from safety, and especially not with a grimoire on the loose capable of decimating his kind.

"Macy, where's the grimoire?"

"It should be right there." She blinked her eyes open and

pointed. "But it's not. But you shouldn't be here either. I cast a pretty powerful ward over my house. How are you here?"

"You invited me in, beautiful." A lie, but she didn't need to know he could skirt spells with the proper notice and speed. No one knew what he could really do. Not even Hecate and Mormo. He planned to keep it that way.

"Oh. Right." She watched him with a foggy gaze.

He sighed. "I'm going to leave. You'll forget this ever happened." He took her in his arms and carried her back to her bed, tucking her in and wishing he wanted to drain her more than kiss her. Definitely something off about this witch. But as he stared into her eyes, he knew a sense of satisfaction to have her under his power. "You're going to get that grimoire back, and you're going to bring it to me." He paused in thought. "Your mate, Cho, is—"

"Oh, he's not my mate. He's my friend."

Duncan was confused for a moment before realizing she'd gotten his wording confused. "Right, your chum. So what is he, exactly?"

"Cho? He's my best friend. We've grown up together. And we're both in MEC training to get into Enforcement. Well, I am. Cho's trying to get into SF like his mom and dad."

Duncan grimaced. "SF?" Special Forces. So the guy's father, that giant demon, was a heavyweight with MEC, not just some bumbling investigator. Just great.

"Yep." She smiled, her features relaxed, sleepy.

"Is Cho's father full demon, then?"

"Oh, yeah. Uncle Anton's scary strong. A mutant demon who wants to protect rather than annihilate. He passed that trait onto Cho, who's a half-demon since his mom is mostly human."

"And what about you?"

"I'm a witch." She smiled and hugged the pillow she wasn't

using. "Like my mom. My dad's a mind mage. He's really strong too."

"And MEC, eh? Is that why you were fucking with me at that bar? Because you plan on bringing me in?"

Duncan disliked the Magir Enforcement Command. After having infiltrated the organization years ago in Europe, he'd come to understand them. They made up arbitrary rules and expected everyone to follow them.

Vampires didn't follow anyone. Hecate was the exception, and only because she'd manipulated their loyalty through bloode-debts incurred by their clans.

"I'm tired of rules," Macy said, sounding petulant. And incredibly sexy. "I want to set some fires, play some pranks, destroy some rogues. Why can't a witch have any fun?"

He let himself smile because she wouldn't notice, half asleep as she was. "I agree. You should have fun. But next time, we'll have fun together. Would you like that?" He leaned closer and inhaled at the crook of her neck. The scent of her called to something inside him. He didn't trust it, yet he wanted to drag that scent deep and hold it tight.

He lowered his voice. "Would you like to kiss me again?"

"Oh, yes." She reached up to cup his cheek, and her hand felt uncommonly warm.

"Then find the grimoire for me, sweetheart. And the next time we're together, I'll make sure I'm inside you when you find your pleasure."

"Promise?"

He licked her neck and had to force himself back. "On my bloode, I swear."

DUNCAN LEFT the witch safe in her home. After doing yet another sweep through the place, he found no hint of the grimoire. But something was wrong. With the grimoire, with Macy, and especially with his reaction to her. He returned to the house in Mercer Island twenty minutes before sunrise and found the others already abed. Except for Orion, who sat in the living area on the main floor indulging in television.

Duncan frowned at the jaunty tunes and characters dancing around. "Are you watching a cartoon for children?"

Orion scowled. "Fuck you. It's quality filmmaking. Don't you talk bad about Simba."

Duncan didn't know what he was talking about. "Never mind. What did you find out when MEC arrived on the scene?"

"Plenty. The stupid bastards never look up, I can tell you that." Orion smirked. "Standard enforcers showed up to cast a major forget spell. The humans went under fast. The magir were questioned then let go, but two agents kept asking about the blond guy we saw—Corson Westhell. I got the impression he's a problem for them."

"And maybe for us," Duncan said, annoyed Westhell had been sniffing around his prey.

"What?"

"Did they happen to mention any more about this Westhell? Like what he is, what he might be after?"

"I learned he's a threat level six, while we're level seven." Orion looked pleased by the information. "MEC was trying to tie the Westhell guy to us. Apparently, Eric's people have been talking about the Night Bloode." Orion frowned. "I need to have a conversation with him about that."

Not long ago, back when Varu had been kin and not their leader, Varu had visited with the upir clan and talked to Eric, their lieutenant. Orion had been with him at the time, and according to the vryko, it had been an almost pleasant excursion. No raging battles or bloodbaths, as would normally occur between rival clans. Orion hadn't done more than bash a few heads in and break a few limbs, all because of one of the six legendary Bloode Stones, which allowed vampires to coexist without needing to kill one another.

If MEC had any idea Varu wielded a Bloode Stone, they'd push the Night Bloode into an Apocalyptic Class threat.

Duncan said, "Right. Talk to Eric. It's not that we asked him to keep us a secret, but I'm sure Varu wants us to keep a low profile. Eric's kin shouldn't be talking to MEC anyway. What is he thinking conferring with lesser beings?"

"I know." Orion shook his head. "I might have to beat his ass to remind him of his place in the city."

"You mean, way lower than all of us."

"Of course." They both paused as a catchy tune played, and a cartoon warthog, meerkat, and lion danced around a jungle.

Duncan frowned. "Why are the animals singing about 'no worries'? What language is that?"

"It's Swahili," Orion growled.

"Yet they're speaking in English with those horrid American accents. I'm very confused." Duncan didn't care for much of what passed for televised entertainment, still drawn to the plays and outdoor musical festivals in his youth.

"You're ruining the magic," Orion muttered and muted the television. "Anyway, what did you find out?"

"That the witch is still playing games, and I'm not sure how."

"Why didn't you bring her back here? We could ask her to explain. Hell, I'll be *super* nice about it." Orion grinned, the expression more suited to the psychopath that was Rolf. "I'll hypnotize her into being more cooperative, since your suave looks couldn't seal the deal."

"Fuck you." Annoyed at Orion's sly grin, he explained, "I didn't want to bring her back here because she's a witch."

"And?"

"And she has a shrine to Hecate in her spell room. Hecate's

her patron goddess. If I bring the witch back here, Hecate might just have a problem with my interrogation techniques."

"I... oh. Good point."

"Just because I don't worship her doesn't mean I can't appreciate Hecate's power. Here, with her blessed realms in a house that doesn't obey general physics, she'll be too difficult to go up against."

"You think you could take on Hecate if you were away from the house?" Orion laughed. "Please. Varu, maybe. Or a few of us together, but not you. You're the nice vampire. Our pet revenant. The one we send when we want to seduce an answer out of someone. Not the muscle."

"And I'm fine with that." Duncan smiled through his teeth. "Because brains win over brawn every time." He glanced over Orion's head and frowned. "What—"

As soon as Orion looked where Duncan had, Duncan moved like lightning and confiscated the remote.

"What the...?" Orion glared back at him then looked around for the black controller. "You took the remote."

"Brains over brawn." Duncan waved it at him, laughing. "But I—"

He wasn't prepared for Orion to come at him in force. Hadn't they been joking? The shove was so hard Duncan nearly knocked the TV off the wall. As it was, he left a vampire-sized dent below it into drywall.

A snarl and threats in elvish explained things.

Huh. Orion had actually done him a favor, shoving him out of the path of a deranged elf.

Said out-of-his-mind elf, Onvyr, hissed at him, his claws and fangs on display. Since the sun hadn't yet risen, Onvyr remained in dark elf form, his skin pitch black, his hair white, and his lavender eyes blazing as he raked at Duncan's chest with an impressive speed and reach.

Duncan batted him away, shoving him at the wall, and unfortunately, breaking the large screen television, which now hung, cracked, at a diagonal. Mormo would not be pleased.

Orion swore up a storm. "I wasn't finished watching that! Damn it, Onvyr. At least wait until I'm done my movie." He dodged a strike aimed at his gut. "I thought he was with Bella."

The human female had a calming effect on the dusk elf. But Duncan had read her earlier text. "No, she left him with Rolf because Mormo wanted her to run some stupid errands."

Onvyr continued to threaten in his native tongue then laughed maniacally before tackling Orion to the ground.

Duncan sighed. "Rolf watching him explains why he's unattended and daft as a loon."

Orion swore as he and the dusk elf tussled. Duncan yawned, overcome with stupor as the sun rose. He knew he'd do best to help Orion settle the elf so they could all go to bed. Of the six vampires in the Night Bloode, only Varu didn't feel the pull of the sun, able to withstand its light without bursting immediately into flame.

Conscious of their shared vulnerability, Hecate had cast a spell to allow light to shine through the dining glass doors and kitchen windows during the day, and the UV rays had no effect on their health. Still, Duncan didn't like to leave anything to chance.

He jumped on Onvyr, and between him and Orion, they muscled the elf down the stairs and shoved him into a detention cell, where he could calm the fuck down and they could get some much needed sleep. Just as they shut the cell door, Onvyr's coloring shifted, his skin turning pale and his hair black. Didn't change his snarl or intent to ram at the bars, though.

Orion yawned. "Sun's definitely risen."

As they climbed the stairs, Orion patted him on the shoulder and said, "We need to get that grimoire, Duncan. Mormo told me that it truly has the power to hurt us. And not much in this world does."

Duncan frowned. "That's what bothers me. It's a grimoire, a spell book made with the darkest of magics, yet Mormo said it belongs to Hecate in the same breath he said it was a tome from Hell, with a capital H. So which is it? The goddess's or an artifact from Hell? And why is a class six threat sniffing around my prey? Coincidence? Or is someone else bent on getting that grimoire back?"

"Maybe this Westhell threat has to do with your witch and has nothing to do with the grimoire."

"Maybe." Orion had Duncan yawning. "I'll think it over. We need to make plans later tonight."

"Right. After some sleep." Orion ducked down the hall toward his room, humming that song from the cartoon.

Just looking down the vampires' long hallway, one might think they all had small rooms abutted to their kin's. But the house had passages and rooms and levels that didn't belong on the earthen plane. At least, that's how Duncan rationalized the weird construction of the home.

His suite sat between Rolf's and Khent's, their doorways spaced maybe five feet from each other. But Duncan had more than just a small bedroom. His area accommodated a small sitting room with floor-to-ceiling bookcases off to the side. In the center of the space, he'd angled a king-size bed to face an armoire, with a side table and chairs in one corner and his clothes valet in the other.

The attached lavatory had been set with marble tile, decorated in shades of gray and white with brushed nickel fixtures, a large, standing shower and double sinks with large mirrors—since vampires *did* cast reflections, thank you very much—all complemented by plush, soft towels, expensive soaps, and facial care products made by Hecate herself.

Duncan appreciated the finer things in life. At home, he'd lived in a castle with all the modern amenities, his clan known for their wealth and class. But since moving to Seattle, he'd adapted to a more upscale-casual kind of living. The accommodations didn't seem to bother any of the others though. Even Khent, who acted as if everyone and everything not associated with his old kin were beneath him, seemed to have taken to the house.

Not that it mattered. Duncan didn't intend to spend the rest of his life as a Night Bloode. Not with vampires from other tribes, a magician who didn't fit into the hierarchy, and a goddess, of all creatures. Here, he was the token revenant, fast and useful so long as he obeyed his patriarch.

But he had a place back in England. A purpose he had to fulfill. And especially now. With Bloode Stones resurfacing, the danger to the realm was real. Add to that a grimoire that could bespell vampires? *End* vampires? That bore critical attention, sooner rather than later.

So Duncan, everyone's friend, listened and observed. Biding his time until he could cut the bloode-debt with Hecate and return to his real kin—a family he felt drifting away more and more.

Though most vampires only tolerated their kin, Duncan had liked his. A lot. His uncle and father—fraternal twins—had remained close for more than five centuries. And they'd included Duncan in all their tricks once they'd seem him wield the family power. He missed them. But lately, not as much as he should have.

Mormo, that tricky monster, had done something more than just binding Duncan to the others. Duncan found he... liked... them. And since Varu had taken the Bloode Stone into his keeping, Duncan found his loyalty tested daily. If it came down to his father or his patriarch, whom would he serve?

To his dread, Duncan didn't know anymore.

As he lay down for a good day's sleep, he couldn't help

feeling as if the grimoire and Macy Bishop-Dunwich might provide him with the solution he needed to escape the Night Bloode and return home. Perhaps the grimoire could do more than bespell vampires. Might it also be a way to liberate him?

That was if he could find it. He scowled, needing to get back to the witch and teach her a lesson. No more kissing and a lot more biting. That would get her to talk.

Except when he scented her, when he touched her soft skin and looked into those witch-amber eyes, he wanted to taste her mouth, her breasts, and more, that soft, lovely spot between her legs.

He shifted, annoyed to find himself growing hard, and let the torpor of the sun steal his thoughts.

As he did, he put one complaint to rest and muttered, "I feel you watching, Hecate. Go away. A bloke's allowed some bloody privacy in his own quarters."

But no, even here, Hecate lingered, saturating the walls, the floor, the air he didn't exactly breathe.

Her voice swam through his exhaustion. "We'll talk at sunset." Her voice, a husky timbre, reminded him of Macy. "Sweet dreams, my revenant."

"I'm not yours, Hecate," he felt the need to remind her. "I serve you to fulfill a bloode-debt, like the others." *I won't always be at your beck and call.*

Her chuckle echoed around the room. "No worries, *luv*," she said in an accent that reminded him of home. "I know what you need, and I'm more than happy to give it to you. And to Edward and Brock. I'll be visiting soon."

Concerned at the warmth in her voice when mentioning his father and uncle, he wanted to ask her questions, but sleep overwhelmed him.

And then the dreams came to sweep him away.

## CHAPTER EIGHT

Hecate slid through the walls and down through the floor to find Mormo sitting in the central entertainment section of the basement, waiting for her while he played some type of video game. She'd seen the vampires toy with them but had no interest in killing pixelated creatures when she had so many monsters to deal with in real life.

She took the form of the threefold goddess, her faces blending from one beautiful face to the next, and kept an eye out for trouble moving through her crossroads. With the wave of a hand, the basement became a speakeasy filled with creatures from all walks of life, moving around her and Mormo, still seated on the plush sectional sofa she'd ordered from a catalogue. The humans had many flaws, but interior design wasn't one of them.

Mormo looked around him, sighed, and turned away from her. "Please, Mistress, pick a face. You're making me dizzy."

She grinned and took a new form, this one older and glorious with lined, brown skin and thick, curly, silver hair, her grace a defining aspect of the Crone. Her necklace, a gold chain with a special key, remained safe, settled between her breasts.

Wearing a dark gray dress with flat sandals showing off her

glossy red toenails, she wiggled them and smiled at Mormo. "Better?"

"Yes, thanks." He remained seated and glared at several of Artemis's huntresses slinging back drinks and laughing at a nearby group of Valhalla warriors on their way to being reborn and trying to get lucky. "If arrows start flying, I'm booting them all out. You know as well as I do that one of them always ends up maiming or killing another, and then we have a divine war on our hands."

"True. But it's fun watching it get started." With her other forms that never stopped studying the mortal and divine spheres, she noted some trouble between Poseidon and Isis that wouldn't end well. But as long as they kept the dead from overwhelming the living, she had no say in what happened. Usually not until it was beyond too late.

"Mistress, I'm concerned about Duncan."

She turned to her favorite servant and waited. Mormo's predecessor, the first Mormo—his mother—had been a gift beyond measure. Soft and sweet and willing to do anything to make Hecate's existence easier. Yet her son gave Hecate what she really needed. A clear mind that used reason and affection to create balance, always making sure Hecate never forgot whom she served while loving her unconditionally.

She had made mistakes, and the one she'd made seven hundred and fifty-two years ago had come back to bite her in the ass. Bigtime.

"Duncan, ah, such a bonny lad," she said in Duncan's voice. "He isn't with us, not all the way yet. I hadn't expected any of our vampires would be able to hold onto their pasts, yet he has."

Mormo frowned, his red eyes narrowed in thought. "I hadn't realized they could feel for anyone other than themselves. We know their kind has been growing more bereft of compassion, morals, and fairness over the years."

She sighed. "Apollo royally screwed them over when he cursed their ancestors. I understood at the time, but I had a feeling making them so angry toward each other, to curb their growing power, would only increase their aggression."

Mormo nodded. "I liked Ambrogio, actually."

She smiled, remembering the love story with warmth. "The first vampire, Ambrogio had first been a human explorer and warrior who had the misfortune to fall in love with Selene, Apollo's sister. But Ambrogio hadn't known of her godhood. He'd given the woman his heart and begged her to flee the temple."

"Where he thought she worshipped," Mormo added, being a dear for having heard this story so many times, yet he always encouraged her in the telling of it.

Hecate continued, amused to find a few nymphs, a troll, and two fae-folk listening in while they congregated between realms, "In love with him as well, Selene agreed to leave, only to find her idiot brother had cursed Ambrogio to forever be apart from the sun, a human turned monster. Turned vampire."

"I really hate that prick," the troll muttered to his friend.

"But Selene was a goddess in her own right. She fled to the earth in search of her lover, fed him her divine blood, and became a vampire herself."

"So why are there no female vampires?" A lovely green dryad with shy eyes and a crown of flowers weaved into her bark-like hair twisted her hands in her gown. "I've always wondered."

Mormo said, "Because the vampires' ability to procreate scared the gods even more. They damned them from seeing the sun, stole away the females' ability to possess vampiric traits, and caused them to hate one another, able to exist only in small groups."

Hecate nodded. "I would pity them, but they don't want pity." She smiled. "They think themselves better than the rest of us. Better than gods and demons, humans and beasts."

"But not better than love," Eros said as he passed by with two men and a woman darting around him, staring with passion. "Am I right?"

Several passersby shouted their appreciation. Then someone turned on the disco ball, started the music, and the creatures moved toward a dancefloor in the back, leaving Mormo and Hecate alone once more.

"Our Night Bloode might not think it, but they are my creatures," she said to Mormo. "Death and blood are mine to hold."

"You did bring Fara back from the dead for Varu," Mormo said, stroking his chin. "A mated master vampire is no small thing."

"I know." She felt proud of that one. But then, Varujan had learned an important lesson. Vampires did more than covet and possess. It had only taken losing his mate to learn that.

"Varu is much more settled and satisfied with her by his side," Mormo agreed. "But we have no further leads on the remaining five Bloode Stones."

"That concerns me as well."

"Yes, which is why I'm unsure of your decision to allow Duncan such leeway. Granted, he's got an impressive talent for ferreting out information. But he shares everything he learns with us *and* the Tizona clan."

"I know." Duncan's secret insistence on clinging to past ties intrigued her. The revenant tribe, known for being underhanded, intelligent, and sly, weren't reputed to be giving or caring. The relationship between Duncan's father and uncle had previously intrigued her, as the revenants seemed to care for each other the way humans could, with heart.

Duncan took his so-called affection a step further. Often smiling or teasing his relations, a stable influence to his kin as well. He also genuinely seemed to like females of all kinds. He had a peculiar softness in his emotions. A killer through and through, yet he treated others with compassion, though he'd be horrified to know she thought such.

Hecate wanted that kind of influence for the Night Bloode. But she hadn't counted on that bond to his family continuing, not after using Mormo's magic to create new bonds for their clan here, in the States.

"He's already met the witch," Mormo said. "I talked to Orion briefly. Apparently, the witch says she doesn't have the grimoire."

Hecate admired the gall of one of her own. She could easily have tracked down the grimoire, but it had to be for one Of the Bloode to end the threat to their kind. Besides, Hecate liked Macy. She came from strong stock. Her mother had always impressed Hecate by doing what needed to be done, her only fault poor judgment when it came to men.

But Hecate had her eye on Macy.

"Hold that thought, dearest." She whistled, and everyone in the speakeasy stopped. "Morpheus? A moment of your time?"

The music and laughter started up again. The god of dreams floated over to her, looking as handsome as always, especially with half his muscular torso exposed by that ancient toga he was never without. In a smooth, deep voice, he said, "Ah, goddess of witchcraft and death, how I've missed you."

They air kissed each other, and Hecate did her best not to laugh at the face Mormo made.

Morpheus gave Mormo a thorough onceover and winked. "Stay sexy, you white-haired beast."

"Eat me," Mormo snarled.

"Gladly." Morpheus laughed as Mormo flushed then vanished. "He's so easy."

"You wish." Ha, she still had it. "Look Morphie, I need a favor."

"What do you need?" He tucked a strand of long black hair

behind his ears, his eyes alight with laughter, his smile wicked and wanting.

"Can you manipulate a dreamer for me?"

"Of course I *can*."

"Will you?"

"Ah, my witchy goddess, now *that's* the question."

She sighed. "What do you want?"

"A favor to call in, some time in the future. I won't know until I need it."

"I'm going to regret this," she muttered, but she needed to prod things. With the many fights breaking out among the realms, she needed to put some negative energy to rest while at the same time finding those dangerous Bloode Stones and that stupid grimoire she should have destroyed ages ago. Unfortunately, the demon locked inside it had hidden the book all too well.

"Excellent. Whose dreams do you want to alter?"

"Not alter, exactly. More like prod in the direction I need them to go. One of my witches needs help to deal with one of my vampires. A hunky little revenant."

"Outstanding specimens. They're all bite and brains with a wicked aptitude for bedsport. So you want me to tamper with his dreams?"

She blinked. "I was thinking more of motivating my witch. Vampires don't dream."

He lost his smile. "Yours do. At least, some of them."

"What does that mean?" Vampires didn't dream. Gods couldn't affect them, and neither could most magir. That's what made her group of kin so dangerous. She'd handpicked six unique vampires from different tribes, each with his own strength, to fight in a war that would come no matter how she worked to avoid it.

"Varujan sleeps in the arms of his beloved and dreams of a future every night. And now Duncan has begun dreaming about a certain red-haired witch, though he hasn't remembered those dreams yet. And the big vrykolakas—I know, *big* and *vrykolakas* are redundant—has begun dreaming about his beloved ocean and the bounties she brings. I can't tell you why, but your Night Bloode is Becoming."

"Becoming what?"

"The million dollar question, Hecate." Morpheus ran his hand through his hair and winked at a nymph who passed by. "So who's it to be, the witch or the vampire? A favor for a favor."

She wanted to know what could possibly be swimming through Duncan's mind, but she had a better chance persuading a witch to obey than a vampire.

So she told Morpheus what she had in mind.

"Your wish is my command." Morpheus stood and bowed, showing off his tight shoulders and arms. "And remember, when you get tired of that white-haired hunk of love working for you, send him my way."

"Oh, I'll be sure to let him know he's always got a place with you."

Morpheus laughed. "Don't sell yourself short, honey. I'm an equal opportunity lover."

"Don't you mean dreamer?"

"Yes, I'm dreaming of the day the goddess Hecate welcomes me back to her bed."

He hadn't been half bad. "Mormo could do worse. And yes, I'll be sure to tell him that."

Morpheus grinned. "All right. One witch with a dream coming up."

Hecate left him and walked down the hallway, out of the speakeasy, back into the human plane, where she found Onvyr sleeping on his back on a cot in the cell he was coming to recognize as home.

She shifted into her human incarnation as Bella and disconnected from her other two forms that would continue toward problem areas between the realms. As Bella, a young, attractive woman with honey-brown hair pulled back into a ponytail, Hecate spent time healing the wounded dusk elf, a creature that could very well have an impact on the grand battle to come.

She hadn't seen his future, exactly, but she felt the taste of his magic all around the Night Bloode. She couldn't know if he tied to the others through his sister, Fara—Varu's mate—or if Onvyr actually belonged with the vampires he kept trying to kill. She only knew he'd suffered horribly at the hands of a master vampire now gone from the worlds.

Onvyr moaned and curled into himself, suffering untold horrors from a history he'd wanted no part of. Feeling for him, she opened the cell and sat with him, stroking his dark hair and pointed ear. "It'll work out, Onvyr. Just you wait and see."

Her voice calmed him, as it always did. But when he moaned again and started crying, she let a divine warmth sink into his blood, providing protection. "It will be all right, my brave elf." Because it had to be. Because a world without order, without goodness to balance the bad, could never tolerate humans. And without humans and their worship, Hecate and all her kind would cease to be.

A place and time where vampires and demons wouldn't be the worst thing to contemplate?

A living hell indeed.

MORPHEUS HAD BETTER things to do than fuss over humans. Controlling his army of dream keepers, the Oneiros, was a full-time job. But he liked Hecate, and he had a vested interest in her small clan of death-bringers suddenly starting to dream. Imagine being able to control the uncontrollable.

But first, he had a date with a witch. Calling on the memory Hecate had implanted in his mind, he let himself fall into the ether and searched for Macy Bishop-Dunwich, Keeper of the Kept, Bringer of Noise and Deluge, Eyes and Heart of the Timeless Devourer. Pretty witch with all the best titles, he thought, amused.

He found her dreaming, and not a moment too soon as she started to come up out of REM sleep. Quickly easing into her subconscious, he scrolled back to watch her dreams and found himself caught by something that didn't belong.

"What are you doing here?" he asked.

Before it could respond, Duncan neared and bared his teeth. "What do you do here, dream demon?"

"I'm not a nightmare, fledgling," Morpheus snapped. "Now get out of the way. We've got a problem with your witch."

Duncan huffed, his eyes glowing red, signaling his annoyance. "Not my witch. My *prey*." He studied Morpheus and slowly smiled. A handsome one, this Duncan of the Night Bloode. And a bother.

Morpheus tried to push him aside, needing to get to Macy, who kept using Duncan to keep him away.

Though Morpheus had entered Macy's dream, he sensed she'd picked up on currents from Duncan, allowing for the vampire to exist as an independent construct in her mind. Powerful dreamers could shape their dreams. Macy appeared to be one of those, yet... He didn't like the feel of the shadow filming both her and the revenant.

When he tried to snap Macy out of it, the darkness glommed onto him as well.

Morpheus felt suffocated. "What strange hell is this?"

Macy moved around Duncan just as the scene shifted. The three of them no longer in her bedroom, now they loitered in a basement full of spikes and sharp implements. A stylish torture chamber filled with innards and blood. Ew. *A lot* of blood.

Morpheus's toga turned red at the hem, the liquid slowly creeping up his body. He slowed, bound by the shadow licking his energy. "Enough, Macy. Bring Hecate the grimoire."

She took a step forward, now clad in a black bikini while Duncan wore a pair of leather chaps and a black thong. Kinky witch.

"Hecate?" The name brightened the darkening room and ate at the feeling of misery clamping the three of them tight. "My goddess?"

"She... requests..." Morpheus found it difficult to speak. "Grim-oire. Bring..."

Smothered by the darkness, he struggled to go free, astounded the human witch could have the power to hold him, with or without a vampire by her side.

And then he saw what truly held him, and he knew fear as he hadn't in thousands of years.

## CHAPTER NINE

Macy woke up feeling groggy, and the previous evening rushed before her.

Duncan. Vampire. In her home. *The grimoire.*

She raced first to the bathroom, clutching her neck, and breathed a sigh of relief to find herself free of any marks. Then she hurried downstairs and burst into her spell room, only to see the grimoire sitting on the altar as it had been yesterday, when she'd left for work.

So strange.

She went to Hecate and asked for blessings, then sent out her own good thoughts to protect the defenseless from all evil.

A remnant of her dream lingered, that of herself and Duncan wearing some weird clothes while a sexy guy with long black hair battled a darkness that didn't belong in this plane. Scared, because her nightmares didn't bother her the way they should, she moved to the grimoire and opened it.

She waited, as she typically did, for its pages to blow by, landing on her lesson for the day.

Macy needed protection, but the book wanted her to learn... levitation?

Whatever. She was up for any and all new magical powers. So far, she'd been enhancing her truthsense to the point of concealing her own lies, able to wield a small fireball with precision, and had once teleported from her spell room to her bedroom. That had been beyond thrilling.

But levitation? How cool.

She pricked her finger and let her blood drop into the book, where it greedily absorbed it. A trade for a trade.

A tingle grew on either side of her shoulder blades, and she did her best to reach back and scratch, the position awkward.

*Do it. Reach out, slowly.*

The sibilant voice scared her, until she focused and realized it was the grimoire.

"Oh my gosh. Is that you talking to me?"

*Who else would it be?* "It," as it preferred to be called, chuckled. Nice to know her grimoire had a sense of humor.

She stretched a new muscle out of her back and pushed. And moved off the ground.

But then bottles broke, and her statue of Hecate nearly fell from the wall.

"Shit." Macy panicked and rose higher, bumping her head on the ceiling.

That's when she noticed the sooty wings on either side of her, flapping to keep her aloft, destroying her spell room.

"Wings?" Not levitation, but *wings*.

Simultaneously excited and freaked out, she eased herself down, finally feeling the muscles she'd used to fly, which felt on fire. And then poof. The wings vanished though her back remained sore.

"Was that real?"

*Yes.*

"How did I do that?"

*With my help. Use the phrase and they will come.* The

grimoire shared a foreign phrase she could never have said out loud, not even sure she could make such sounds. But inside her head, she could repeat them. When she did, a neon image of a sigil seared itself inside her and faded.

Definitely a strange form of witchcraft. Old school, she thought, considering the grimoire was over seven hundred years old. Macy felt Hecate's presence behind much of the grimoire's magic.

And something else. Something shadowy and malevolent. She frowned. It felt—

Fun. So much *fun.*

She smiled, laughing as dark energy tickled through her before disappearing.

Now in a good mood, her dreams forgotten, she showered and dressed, grabbed a bite to eat, and drove to MEC. She ran into Cho in the underground parking garage of a nondescript building just north of the University of Washington. They billed themselves as a construction and tech building, accounting for the many businesslike and rough and tumble types who frequented the establishment.

Cho whistled. "Wow. You sure look nice."

"Nice?" She didn't see anything odd about her pencil skirt, blouse, and chic sweater. Her knee length boots felt cute, and though only she knew it, the polish she wore on her toes matched her blouse.

"You're in a skirt above your knees," Cho said. "Not much above them, but still. I can see kneecaps before the boots catch up."

"Ha ha."

"And your hair."

"What about it?" She curled a strand around her finger.

"It's down. No bun or ponytail."

She flushed. "I'm trying to look more my age."

"You do," Cho hurried to say. "I just... You look pretty, Macy. You look good."

She smiled and gripped his forearm, walking with him to the underground transport train. "Of course I look good."

He rolled his eyes. "Forgot who I was talking to for a minute there."

They took their seats across from a pair of fae in human glamours and beside a group of mages debating the incoming cold front.

"I'm telling you, it's a frost giant. That's no normal weather pattern," one of them argued.

"You're full of crap, Johnson. Not every cold snap is due to a frost giant."

Johnson snorted. "It's all fun and games until we get a blizzard, then you idiots will see I'm right."

"Whatever."

A fireball singed one of their beards, which had them all laughing hysterically.

They got off at the stop for the arcane lab, and the elves left at the intelligence stop-off, leaving just Cho and Macy.

"I'm coming with you to make my report," Cho said.

"You don't have to do that." Macy frowned. "I don't need you to back me up."

"You do, because our dads already talked to Ishaan, and he's not pleased with you or me." Cho sighed. "Apparently, my boss didn't like me assigning myself to that bar either, even though I told him I was just there for a drink. He didn't buy it."

"Because you're a terrible liar."

"There is that." Cho tapped his knee with nervous fingers. "Louis called to tell me he's not pleased with me, and he let Dad know too."

"Already?" She checked the time to see it had just reached eight o'clock. "When did our dads check in, anyway?"

"Around six, I think. Dad only needs a few hours of sleep a night, so he's usually at the office when Mom's trying to sleep."

"So that's why they're still married."

He grinned with her.

"Still, I'm sorry you got yelled at before we even got in." She wondered if her dad had heard from her boss, a friend of the family. Although come to think of it, Ishaan was closer to her mom than her dad. But her mom might not know what they'd done last night since she and Cho's mom had been having a brief vacation together, a girls' trip to the Caribbean. Would Ishaan have called to rat her out? Not likely. She hoped.

Her phone beeped. She looked at the text and sighed. "Crap. Dad is yelling at me with emojis, and he said Ishaan isn't real happy with me either. I got us both in trouble, Cho."

"Nah, it's okay. I needed to step out from Dad's shadow anyway."

"But maybe not right before you're trying to get into Special Forces?"

He shrugged. "Either they trust me to make the right decisions or they don't. Our little bar hopping last night isn't going to get me kicked out of MEC."

"Yeah, well, I'm glad you're confident. I hope the estimable Ishaan Varma is more easygoing than I think he's going to be."

He wasn't. After reaming out Cho and sending him to talk to his own department head face-to-face, Ishaan lit into her. A supreme witch with an ability to harness elemental and arcane power, Ishaan was "The Man" in Spells & Incantations as well as her mom's good buddy, so he acted overprotective all the time.

At first, having him near had felt good, as if she had a safety net should she falter. But after three years of him hovering when her mom or dad weren't around, Macy just felt tired. Too bad she couldn't show off her new wings or ability to bespell a vampire.

If she didn't think he'd noticed the grimoire's presence in her efforts, she might have.

"Bad enough you were there last night, in the presence of Westhell," Ishaan said, looking dignified in his black suit and tie, fastidiously dressed, as always. His black and white goatee trimmed, his shoulder-length black mane sleek, not one hair out of place. "But I've been informed you've been milling around the city for weeks, working off-book. Care to explain yourself?"

Dang it. "Who told you that?"

"Is it not true?" Ishaan raised a brow. He had that mature, I-can-see-into-your-soul presence that often discouraged his people from lying to him.

"It's true, but I wasn't doing anything wrong." Not exactly. "I just want to help MEC eliminate threats before they become a problem."

His expression softened. "I know you do. And you're one of our best spellcasters, Macy. A true joy to work with. I have faith in you."

"But...?"

"But being out in the field, where danger lurks in both magic and human form, takes skill. If you want to hunt the monsters, you need to be properly prepared. When Noah told me—"

"Noah Debman." She scowled. "That jerk is just upset I refused to tell my sister about him."

"What?" He frowned.

"Nothing." She fumed. Debman was a weak witch who had a thing for her stepsister. In an effort to protect the sweet girl from that dickhead, she'd warned him to leave Kaia alone. Except she'd used more forceful language and in front of his friends no less. Hmm. Maybe not the smartest choice she could have made at the time. Even four months later, he held a grudge.

"Macy, please." Ishaan left his desk to join her on the other side of it. Through the window that overlooked the S&I department, she could see dozens of witches and mages working spells and incantations. The protective wards around the lab protected MEC from possible experiments gone wrong. Like that fireball that just exploded.

He sighed and sent out a mental notice to the group: *Please, people. Wear your inflammatory suits when practicing with fire.* Then he turned his intense black eyes back to her. "I'm not just your boss. I'm your friend."

"My mentor," she agreed. "And friend because of Mom."

He smiled. "Diane scares me. I'm not too proud to say she does. Are you?"

"No," she muttered.

"This isn't a case of being upset because you didn't get the authorization to be out and about, Macy. This is worry for you getting involved with vampires, which, hell, are beyond even *my* pay grade unless we're attacking en masse. If you aren't worried about that, then something is seriously wrong with you."

She flushed. "I'm worried, okay?" And excited and enthused, but he didn't need to know that. "I wanted to help find the threat, and I did. I got lucky, or unlucky, I guess you could say. I had no idea I'd run into this Westhell guy, that my dad and Anton would freak out over it, or that he'd have vampires with him."

He sighed. "Yes, Corson Westhell. We need to talk about him and about these vampires who might be in league with him." He motioned for her to join him at the seating area and murmured under his breath. A tray of coffee appeared as they sat. "Help yourself."

"I need caffeine for this?" She poured a cup of coffee with cream and sighed. "Good stuff."

"Good. Right. Well, you already know what a threat vampires can be. We're on so-so terms with the Seattle Bloode, but their lieutenant has proven much more amenable than their patriarch." Ishaan frowned. "If I could stake that bastard, I would. In any case, the local clan has been better about using our resources to feed."

"You mean, giving them the criminal element you're not at all sorry to see drained and dried."

"Exactly." He smiled and stroked his beard. She didn't have it in her to tell him he looked more like a criminal mastermind than the head of a MEC department. "They clean up the city their way, and we turn a somewhat blind eye. But when they step out of line, it takes an SF and SI comp unit to remind them we have rules. I'm talking close to fifty of our people to handle one or two rogue vampires. Macy, the threat is real."

"I know."

"The report I received from your father and Anton says two vampires were seen together, entering the bar just after the demon."

"Demon?" She blinked. "You mean Westhell?"

"Yes. The vampires aren't known to be a part of the Seattle Bloode, and the damage just one of them inflicted on a few lycans and mages scares me. Then you have Corson Westhell, a fugitive we've been after for decades. A few centuries, actually. His warrant came out before I was born.

"Agent Novak—Anton, has been assigned to bring Westhell in. Working alongside your father, the pair has nearly managed to do so. It's not a good thing you came into contact with the creature. He's got you in his sights now, and I can only think he means to derail your father's investigation."

"Into what, exactly? What did this Westhell do? What kind of demon is he?"

Ishaan sipped his coffee before setting the cup firmly on the tray. He steepled his fingers and studied her. "What I'm about to tell you can't leave this room. There are only a handful of people in this command who know what he is and what he can do."

"I won't tell." MEC dealt with so many threats to humanity

and the city on a daily basis it was a wonder they had time to sleep. Though they continued to recruit, the entities they faced, just in this section of the country alone, made her wonder how humanity continued to be unaware of the magir living beside them.

"Corson Westhell is a previous king of Hell, a predominant plane most of us associate with pain and suffering. Not just *a* hell, but *the* Hell. He used to be Hell's King of the West, hence the name. But close to eight hundred years ago, he got kicked out. We're not sure why, but rumor has it he's after a grimoire. A spell book from Hell, I don't have to tell you, would be very, very bad in the wrong hands. And his hands are definitely wrong."

Ishaan paused, studying her. "We've been after the book and the demon for years. Then we found a dead book dealer, a mage who had traces of dark magic all over him."

Uh-oh. He was looking at her as if he knew she'd called in the mage's murder.

"Macy," he said softly, "do you have something you wish to share?"

"Um, well, I think that was me. Who called in the dead mage, I mean. I didn't know he was dead, exactly. But I saw him through the window, and he looked not right."

"Did you see the book with him?"

"No." Her ability to lie kept growing. As did Ishaan's frown. She wished she could tell him the truth, but then he'd make her give back the grimoire. She wasn't ready yet. Soon, she knew, she'd have to put the book in safe hands, but not until she'd learned just a little bit more.

*He'll know. Fog his mind.*

"What?"

Ishaan frowned. "Are you sure you didn't see the grimoire, Macy?" He looked at her. "You seem... different."

"Different how?"

*More. Better.* The grimoire seemed to have a smoky laugh at her expense.

*Oh my God! It's talking to me again.*

"You're more confident. You literally let your hair down, and I've been telling you to do that for ages. You seem to be more powerful." He looked concerned. "You're a powerful witch, something you won't believe no matter how much your mother, father, and I tell you."

"So powerful you won't let me practice my spells," she muttered.

"That's my point. You've been powerful enough to create third level spells. That's incredible for a young witch. You use so much magic in crafting them that you have little left to deploy your creations. Not safely. Until now. I sense growth inside you, but it's unnatural."

She scoffed. "Everything we do here is unnatural, if you want to get technical about it. You zapped us a pot of coffee a few minutes ago. Where did it even come from?"

"The kitchen," he answered. "And that's not the point. You make better spells than anyone I've ever met. Even your mother. You are precise and take no shortcuts, and your spells *always* perform. One hundred percent of the time. Not having the magic to power them isn't a bad thing. It just is."

Her mother had tried to explain to her that some witches couldn't do more than make magic for others, and that it was no handicap but Hecate's way of balancing power, so a witch wouldn't take on more than she could handle. She'd hated that explanation then and she hated it now.

"But I want offensive skills," she told her boss.

"And I want to change into a bird and fly, but we all have limits, Macy."

"We shouldn't have to." Annoyed, because deep down, she knew he was right, she remembered instead how it had felt to sprout wings, to cast a spell of dread around the park before bespelling that vampire. So much power. She *craved* it.

*Then take.*

She shouldn't. Ishaan just wanted what was best for her. She knew that.

She also knew she needed more time to study the book and make her changes permanent before giving it back. If Ishaan took the book now, she'd lose all that.

An image of a smoky form coalesced behind Ishaan, a piece of the grimoire made real. She watched it carve new symbols into the air above him.

"Macy?" Ishaan leaned forward. "There's something marring your gift." He narrowed his eyes. "You've used it, haven't you?"

She read the runes inside her mind, and they vanished above her boss. He went still, his body locked tight, his lips frozen. Settling her will over his, she mentally commanded him to forget their conversation about the grimoire, instead, focusing on Corson. That handsome chap she definitely needed to see again. It had been so long, after all.

*Wait. What?*

*Focus,* the grimoire commanded.

When she snapped her fingers, Ishaan eased back in his seat. "As I was saying, Corson Westhell is not someone you want to deal with."

"No, sir."

He nodded. "Very well. I'd like you to keep working on those offensive spells we talked about. And I want you on this detail to find the Night Bloode, a new clan running around the city picking up rogues before we get to them. We need to find out what they're doing here, and why they're grabbing rogues off the street and putting them back."

"I hadn't heard about that." Vampires who weren't killing their prey, but toying with them for some reason?

He nodded. "We're keeping it quiet, obviously. The rogues have no idea of what's been done to them." He frowned. "Except for one who mentioned Hecate. But in my devotions to her, she's said nothing about bloode kin."

"You talk to Hecate?" She gaped. She'd known Ishaan was one of the most powerful witches in MEC. But to have direct access to the goddess?

"Not in conventional sense, but our goddess does occasionally grant blessings. She's far too busy to listen to me." He flushed. "Not when she has to constantly balance the living with the dead."

"Right." A hunger shifted inside her, a need to consume and destroy. She refused to acknowledge it as anything more than an empty stomach. "Say, Ishaan, if we're done here, can I go grab something to eat? The coffee was good, but I need something more."

He nodded. "The bear claws are delicious today. I'd recommend the coffee shop over the cafeteria."

She smiled. "Thanks."

"Keep safe, and let me know if you need my help with anything." He watched her, and she didn't see anything odd in his expression. Just minor concern.

"I will." She walked away. But as she made her way to the Magir Bean on the ground floor, she passed Noah Debman, who sneered and whispered to an equally obnoxious mage. The pair laughed openly, taunting her.

She only smiled.

When she later heard from a few colleagues that Noah Debman had contaminated himself and a fellow mage with a magical plague of lycan-pox, she laughed so hard she cried.

# CHAPTER TEN

"I'm not taking Kraft and Orion," Duncan said calmly as he ate a breakfast of eggs, bacon, and blood at ten in the evening. He had plans to grab the witch later on and figured some human food might ground him, adding a layer of protection from that damnable grimoire. He knew enough about witches from his father, and a vampire had to protect himself from their mischief as best he could.

Human food could counter terrestrial magic when mixed with the right quantity and type of blood.

So he suffered in silence and pretended the eggs weren't absolutely disgusting, the bacon only slightly less so. The blood, however, was perfection, fresh from the neck of an unwilling and divine host, he liked to imagine.

He felt the buzz slide over him while their human servant tried her best to convince him to step into his own version of hell.

"Please, Duncan." Bella batted her pretty lashes at him. She had a woman's way about her. Sandy-brown hair flowing in waves over her shoulders, her jeans framing a lovely ass, her top a pretty blue and set over a healthy bit of curves. Not as fit as Macy, but still, Bella delivered.

He swore at himself for thinking of the witch again, as he'd been unable to stop since he'd woken. Worried that she might have enchanted him without him knowing it, he'd gone to Mormo to doublecheck. The magician's sly chuckle, delivered with a "No, you're just fine," hadn't relieved him the way it should have. Because he didn't trust the bastard.

"Dun-can," Bella dragged his name out. "Orion and Kraft are getting on Onvyr's nerves. Mr. Mormo's too. And I have a ton of work to do tonight."

"Oh? Like what?" He took his dishes to the sink and returned for a healthy drink of water to wash the awful taste of human food from his mouth.

"Well, Khent had an... incident... so I have to bring him the SUV."

"Wait. What incident?"

"He kind of killed an ogre in the vehicle, and now there's green blood and brains stuck in between the seats." She grimaced. "He FaceTimed to show me. It's disgusting."

He coughed to hide a chuckle. "Wait. He killed it *in* the vehicle? How could an ogre even fit in there?"

She scowled. "That's what I was wondering since I've heard they're huge. But when I asked him, he turned the phone around and stared at me like he wanted to tear my throat out."

"He probably did." Khent had less tolerance for mortals than the rest of them .

"Yeah. He keeps telling me how honored I should feel that he's considering reanimating me as a pet." She swallowed. "Mr. Mormo told me not to worry about it, but I'm worrying. Anyway, so I have to drive the SUV out to him then bring the ogre-infested one to that all-night repair and detail shop. Then Rolf is supposed to swing back to get Khent from I don't know where."

Duncan frowned. "Those two are working together. And

they're supposed to have Kraft." Hadn't Mormo said that a few days ago?

"I don't know about that. But from there, Fara and I—"

"Wait. Varu's letting her out without him?" The strigoi had been so possessive of his mate lately. Duncan wouldn't have thought Varu would let Fara out of his sight, especially since she'd only recently come back from the dead.

"Yes, well, he's going to meet us at the repair place and take us shopping at an all-night magir boutique. Then I'm done for the night, only to be right back up in the morning to fetch some demon thing for Mr. Mormo."

"What?" Lately, Duncan was up to his armpits in demon *things*.

"Yeah. The boss wants a copy of a canonical text I'm supposed to pick up from a friend of his."

"I didn't realize Mormo had any friends."

"Neither did I," she murmured. "But supposedly he knows a guy who knows a guy. And I've been tasked to get it for him."

"Sounds like a lot of work."

She groaned. "It really is. If you'd be a sweetie and take Kraft and Orion away for me, I could settle Onvyr then get to all of Mr. Mormo's chores." She perked up. "Or I could leave you with Onvyr and I could—"

"I'll find the vampires." He left before she could try sticking him with dusk elf duty. Though a human, she'd done a fairly decent job of manipulating the vampires to dance to her tune. But being one of the few creatures who could withstand daylight, she was needed. And it did sound as if she had a lot to get done for "Mr. Mormo."

Duncan sought the vrykolakas and the nachzehrer. Despite them being from different tribes and different areas, Orion from Greece and Kraft from Germany, they had a lot in common. Both were larger in size than the others, physically stronger and not as refined. Duncan didn't mean that in any derogatory way either, but the truth was, if left to Orion or Kraft, the pair would spend the majority of their time brawling and bloody with anyone they could get their hands on. Just for fun.

He found the pair wrestling—*ha, called it*—downstairs in the basement, using the gymnasium where they'd first been bound as kin. Five months ago, Mormo had worked Hecate's magic to bond them together. Duncan didn't know how he'd done it, and Rolf, their resident magic user, had no idea either.

But after some wicked bloode magic, Duncan and the others had become family.

And in every family, there were the undesirables. The troublemakers.

He stared at two of them.

Orion had Kraft in a headlock. Instead of taking the fight seriously, Kraft kept insulting Orion's family line while biting his forearm and pulling his hair.

Obviously annoyed, Orion ripped Kraft's teeth from his arm, dislodging a gush of bloode Duncan deftly avoided, not wanting to get his new suit dirty. He leaned against the wall and sighed as Orion slammed Kraft's head into the ground.

Then Kraft twisted and powered up with a harsh uppercut to Orion's face.

Duncan cringed. That had to have broken a cheekbone.

While Duncan would have dodged, struck fast, then dodged again, the brutal vampires before him continued to take the hits before retaliating by punching or kicking back harder. Using unfair tactics, they sparred, each building up steam.

As their wounds healed and they continued to pummel each other, Duncan checked his watch. "Gents, if you could speed this up. We've things to do and it's going on ten-thirty."

"Fuck off," Orion managed before ramming into Kraft's midsection. He laughed and kicked Kraft in the ribs when Kraft moved too slowly to dodge. "There you go, you naive fledgling. Stay down. Bow to your betters."

"Nice. You sounded a bit like Khent there." Duncan nodded in appreciation.

Orion grinned, showing bloody teeth, and missed the sight of Kraft's eyes narrowing then turning a fiery red before he shot off the ground and up into Orion's gut. His momentum propelled both vampires up several feet, not hindered by the gymnasium's expansive ceiling, then turned and crashed down. Hard. With Kraft on top.

The sound resonated, even onto thick gym mats, and Duncan felt for Orion, who groaned loud enough to wake the dead.

"This fledgling just kicked your ass." Kraft looked as if he meant to rip Orion apart, and a wolfish snarl escaped his lips, his fangs growing. Kraft's tribe were known for having a rare few kin who possessed legendary rages, producing a fury that no one had ever been able to match. Surviving against one such enraged nachzehrer meant avoiding them when their blows landed. Period. Even Orion, with all his strength, might not be able to beat Kraft in a hand-to-hand fight.

Something Duncan was dying to see. But not now. "Oy, lads. We have witches to hunt. Tonight. As in, go clean up and meet me in the dining room." When that didn't get either to move, still glaring at each other, Duncan added, "Or you two can stay to babysit Onvyr while I'm out and about."

Kraft moved as if he had a flock of harpies on his tail. "I'll be there. *Fünf Minuten*."

"That's five minutes," Orion explained and stood to crack his vertebrae back in place. "He's an asshole, but wow, when you yank his chain, he gives what-for." Orion grinned, the sorry sod.

"I haven't had a battle like that since we tried killing Varu before we bonded."

Duncan shrugged. "What can you do? Once you become kin, it's tough to get a good fight."

Orion sighed. "I know it." He moved past Duncan, who followed. "We're grabbing your witch tonight?"

Duncan liked the sound of that. *His* witch. "I'm thinking not yet. We need a little more surveillance before I'm comfortable taking her." He'd been toying with something he didn't think Mormo would like but that made sense, strategically. "I want to see if we can get a look inside MEC."

Orion blinked. "You want to infiltrate the Magir Enforcement Command? Damn, Duncan. That takes balls." Orion continued to stare at him and, if Duncan weren't mistaken, he'd say he had the vryko's complete attention. "They have real firepower in there. Stuff that can seriously hurt us. Access to UV weapons, bloode magic. Maybe maim or outright kill us." A crazy light lit Orion's dark eyes. "I'm in."

"Of course you are."

They walked up the stairs, and Duncan waited for the pair out on the outside deck, staring out at the water of Lake Washington. MEC had been a thorn in their sides for a while now. Not a real problem, but filled with magir and strong witches, the command force had been building a not-so-secret task force to deal with them. Word of the new Night Bloode had gotten out, as they'd all known it would. A little sooner than he might have liked, but Varu was seeing to that tonight by meeting with the Seattle Bloode's patriarch.

Frankly, Duncan was eager to get into MEC. He wanted to see what the lesser beings could do.

And knowing Macy's friend was part demon, his father a full-on demon, stirred his appetite to battle. Duncan wouldn't mind a chance to fight hell-spawn. But not before grabbing that stupid grimoire.

He didn't feel good about his last go with the sexy witch. She kept fucking with his head, doing something to him that felt a lot like that shadowy tome.

He also had problems sleeping lately. Not anything he'd admit aloud, but it unnerved him. Vampires didn't dream. When the sun rose, and they fell into their daily stupor, they recovered mentally and physically. Then bam, the sun set and they woke as if they'd never closed their eyes.

There was no in-between, no vulnerable dream state from which a god, demon, or mage might infiltrate and manipulate. No one controlled those Of the Bloode. Even Hecate, calling in a bloode-debt and using Mormo's magic, had only enchanted them because *they'd* allowed it.

A bloode-debt must *always* be repaid.

He still wondered what his father had done to incur the debt, but he'd been told he had no need to know. More power games that his clan loved to play. Knowledge was power—the family motto, advice Duncan usually ascribed to. But being ripped away from his father and uncle had... hurt. He rubbed his chest, annoyed to feel it beating to the rhythm of his new kin.

Sure, he had emotions. Revenants had no problem expressing disdain, hatred, annoyance. But unlike the others, they also expressed pleasure. Varu had acted as if he loathed females before he'd mated Fara. The others seemed to consider females no better than breedmates or the occasional meal. But Duncan liked their softness, the way their hair would curl over their shoulders, their breasts. The way the dark red wound like a flame, like a bead of blood trailing along Macy's neck.

*Ack. That bloody witch.* He grabbed his head and gazed up at the moon, wishing he knew why he was so fascinated with a human. He could appreciate her clever escape, her sly magic, the way she'd tricked him into leaving without killing her or stealing that grimoire. And yes, he wanted her blood and her body, no question.

But when the time came, he planned to kill her. Maybe not so slowly though. He frowned. Should it matter if she felt pain? Not really.

"Okay, we're ready." Kraft said as he and Orion joined him outside.

Duncan turned. "You're wearing that?"

Kraft growled like the wolf he could turn into. "What's wrong with this?"

"Nothing if you're going to a frat house for losers."

Kraft muttered in German, a language Duncan had never considered learning, and plucked at the sweatshirt with a hole in it, his jeans and scarred boots much the same.

Orion chuckled, and Duncan gave him a sour look. "You're no better."

"But I don't care." Orion shoved his hands into jeans, his tee-shirt black and clinging to his large frame, no jacket in sight. Like Kraft, his clothes looked wrinkled and a step above thrift shop wear. "You're a clotheshorse and a snotty prick. He and I are slobs who don't care about fashion. Great. Let's go."

Kraft shot him several dark looks but preceded them out into the garage. Duncan looked from the back of his head to the back of Orion's and grinned. "You two even look alike from behind."

"Shut up," they said at the same time, causing him to laugh.

More muttering, this time in German *and* Greek.

"Ah, now that I understand."

Orion shot a full palm, all five fingers outstretched toward Duncan's face and said what sounded like, "Na."

"And there, a moutza, a big Greek *fuck you.*" Duncan chuckled. Satisfied he'd irked his partners for the evening, getting their attention, finally, he said, "Now, let's go screw with MEC. Do you want to go in the hard way or with stealth?"

At the SUV, Orion and Kraft stopped and looked at each other, then grinned back at him. "Finally, you talk sense," Kraft said.

"The hard way, of course." Orion nodded.

"We're going to need a spell or two for that." Duncan said to Kraft, "Grab the keys. Let's go talk to Ahnessa." His favorite evil sorceress. Again, redundant—evil and sorceress were the same thing.

Kraft frowned. "I don't like her. She makes my fur stand on end."

"Sorceresses are creepy," Orion agreed. "Are you sure we want her help?"

"We need to learn more about Corson Westhell, or at least learn what MEC knows about him. He has something to do with my prey."

At Kraft's confused look, Orion said, "His witch."

"Ah, the pretty one with blood-red hair? Can I have a taste?" he asked Duncan.

"Do what I tell you to and you might."

Kraft nodded, but Orion frowned. "Why are you in charge?"

He had a point. Orion had forty more years of life than Duncan, but Duncan had the skillset for this specific task. "In brutal war or battle, I'd follow you, no doubt." Maybe, but he'd give Orion his due. "But in this, we're relying on stealth, speed, and strategy. Not on the battlefield," he said to forestall the argument he could see brewing. "We'll be dealing with other magir in an academy-like setting. It's like breaking into school, not setting fire to armies. The next time we need to kill everyone at the scene, you're in charge."

Orion shrugged. "Well, when you put it like that, okay."

They got into the SUV after a small skirmish in which Kraft won the keys, then drove toward MEC's "secret" headquarters.

The same place Duncan had visited just a few weeks after setting foot in the city.

No one kept surprises from Duncan. Not MEC and not its agents. And that included a certain sexy witch. One way or the other, he'd tear down her walls.

One bite at a time.

# CHAPTER ELEVEN

The drive to northern Seattle went quickly. They parked a few blocks away from the university, far enough not to draw attention to themselves, just out of range of MEC's hidden sensors.

"Damn, I can feel that power." Orion shook his head at the trees lining a nearby park. "So obvious."

Duncan turned the big vryko in the direction of the hidden scanner under the eave of a tall building. "That's it. The building. The park is a decoy."

"Even I knew that," Kraft said and dodged a swipe from Orion's large fist. He snickered and in a deeper German accent said, "Leave the spying and the stealth to our smaller brother. Let our baby revenant do his job."

"You're calling *me* the baby?" Duncan forced a smile. Sometimes Kraft got on his last nerve, and the screwy bastard knew it. Pretending he didn't care put Duncan in a position of power. "Once you've seen a hundred years, then we'll talk."

Orion chuckled. "He's got you there. What are you, eighty?"

Kraft scowled, his eyes flashing red. "I'm ninety. Almost ninety-one, you fangy merman."

"Oh, words hurt." Orion clutched his chest before giving Kraft the finger.

Kraft wasn't too far from the truth by calling Orion a merman. Vrykos were attuned to the sea and could swim as well as any seafolk Duncan had ever met. Most vampires loathed the ocean, but not the vrykolakas tribe. Too bad they didn't need to deal with MEC agents in Union Bay.

Duncan motioned them to come closer. "Here's the plan. I know what I'm looking for inside."

"How?" Kraft asked, his dark brows narrowing. He had a head of thick, black hair, a bit shorter than Orion's but no less tumbled about. His clothing, though dark, looked worn. He actually blended much better than Duncan did.

But the charms the sorceress had given them, when activated, would allow Duncan and the others to look and smell human until the charms wore out—in another seventy-two hours.

"I've been working on MEC agents for months. I have a general layout of the building and the schematics for Intelligence, the arcane lab, and the S&I wing."

"Seducing mortals is beneath me," Orion said, puffed up with pride.

"Oh please. You can hypnotize, but that isn't as strong as his skill with seduction, and you know it." Kraft nodded to Duncan.

"It's true," Duncan agreed, "but only because seduction implies a willingness to agree in the first place. They want to do what I want them to. Hypnotism, from a human perspective, sounds the same. But in reality, the way you do it, you're stealing their will. It's a complicated magic, actually."

Orion nodded and looked down his nose at Kraft. "Complicated, he said."

"Bah. Just rip their spines out and be done with them."

Duncan shook his head. "Because dead humans are so accommodating."

"They are when Khent's done with them."

Orion turned to him. "He's got a point. Want us to kill a few and bring them back for Khent?"

"We'll see." That was an option, but Duncan didn't like keeping anyone not kin at home. *Not home. The* house. *Hecate's house. Not mine.*

"The plan," he emphasized, needing to bring his own mind back to roost. "You two provide distractions. No killing outright. We need some reports of vampire attacks near the campus. So don't use the charm unless you want them to think you human."

Orion rolled his eyes. "This is the plan? We don't need to huddle up and break, do we? This isn't American football."

"Ech. That doesn't count. Nothing is as grand as human European football." Kraft sounded proud of his opinion, so when both vampires looked at him, he said, "What? The humans are good for more than food. Football, sex, and video games. Right?"

"Eh." Duncan didn't rightly care. "Be back here before five. That should give us plenty of time to then head over to the witch and her friend. I want more information on the demons involved in this grimoire." He paused to share with his kin, "I don't trust Hecate's motives for getting it back. Yes, I do think it has the power to kill us. I felt a lot of evil in that book, mates. But I don't want the goddess getting her hands on it, do you?"

They looked at each other, then at him. "No," Kraft said.

"Good point," Orion agreed. "We need to lock it down and keep it far from Hecate."

"Yes. But first, MEC."

He watched as Orion transformed into a raven and flew away while Kraft walked slowly, adopting a slouch, his look morphing into a wayward young human. A college student, perhaps.

"Shoo." He motioned to Duncan. "Go, little bird."

Duncan scowled even as he shifted into a raven and flew toward MEC's secret entrance. Once there, using his beak, he punched in the code a mage had given him just yesterday. So easy to convince human prey into helping. A handsome man with grand hungers, the wind mage had been his since he'd first fed on him a few months ago.

Just like Ahnessa, a tasty mage gone rogue turned evil sorceress who wanted nothing more than to destroy MEC, humanity, the world, any- and everything. Chaos was her god.

The duality of mage and witch power fascinated him. Mages, born magir, were not human though they shared many traits with humans. When they turned evil, they became sorceri. The same way witches turned into warlocks. But witches didn't have the extended life or energy mages did. They were human, and their magic could and did die out without strong bloodlines. Mages, even with the faintest taint of mage ancestry, had real power. In different levels of course, but there was no diluting a mage's magic.

Truth be told, Duncan preferred witch blood. The spice of human emotion gave it a taste unlike any other. Even better than fae, though he'd never admit that to the others.

Although he only considered one source of blood to be so tempting.

*And there I go thinking about her again.* Duncan entered the building and pulled on the charm to make him look like nothing more than a bird, should the sensors pick up on his entrance. But he flew so fast he didn't think they'd notice.

His night vision allowed him to see clearly in the near pitch-black tunnels of the back entrance into the command center. Such pitiful defenses, really, he thought as he flew toward the arcane laboratory.

Once there, he flew higher and took a break, looking down over the magir still working. Night was a busy time for those who lived to prey on others. Lycans, vampires, ghouls, and the possessed especially loved to roam under a loving moon. He hadn't sensed many ghosts nearby, but that could change when in the vicinity of a cemetery.

He saw the mage he'd been on the lookout for and winged down to a darkened corner, shifting into a human shape in the blink of an eye. Then, peering around the corner, he nabbed a white coat from a nearby hook on the wall and walked toward his prey—a wind mage with thick auburn hair and bright blue eyes, a hint of gnome in the irises.

"Hello there, Ian. Remember me? It's Duncan, the witch you met a few weeks ago at my orientation." He smiled wide, luring Ian closer. Their blood-bond had clicked not long ago, but it never hurt to reinstate it, especially around so much magic. That would also help to make sure Ian remembered Duncan wearing this new face.

Fortunately, no one nearby gave them a second look, intent on working their crystals and material spells. A lot like witchcraft, yet arcane magic worked around objects with minerals attuned to magic. Varu's mate, Fara, a dusk elf who could command power gems and rocks, would have felt right at home in here.

"Oh, hi, Duncan. Hey, I was wondering where you'd gotten to." Ian flushed, a handsome bloke who might have been diverting if Duncan hadn't fancied Macy so much. Which annoyed him to no end.

He forced himself to smile. "Just working hard, as usual." He peered at Ian's desk. "Got time for a break?"

"Yes, please." Ian turned to his coworker across the workspace. "I'll be back in a bit, Colleen. Getting a coffee."

The woman nodded, not paying him much attention as she worked a new spell.

"Busy tonight."

Ian nodded as they left for the main hallway that connected MEC's main branches. From what Duncan knew, they included: Special Forces, Intelligence, Enforcement, Administration,

Weapons, Spells & Incantations, and the arcane lab, which technically fell under S&I.

The command center was huge, but connected by the hallway, one could access the other branches via the carts whizzing by or by magical transport, as many around the place had access to wings and teleportation. Duncan nodded to the stairwell, which would take them down to the subfloor, where a massive cafeteria and the admin branch were located.

Before they moved another step though, he nipped Ian and healed him in the same breath, so that it might look to any overhead camera like they stumbled before righting themselves. The blood-bond refreshed, Ian looked delighted to accompany Duncan down the stairs, quietly telling him everything he wanted to know.

Once he'd purchased two coffees, Duncan left Ian with a promise to see him before he left, adding, "And give that coffee to Colleen. She looked thirsty."

Ian waved and shot him a lingering look before heading back to work.

Armed with new information on where he'd do best to look up what he needed, Duncan headed back upstairs, this time to the Intelligence wing.

Along the way, he passed several offices with blackened out windows, which provided a reflection to see his glamoured self: a handsome blond with dimples wearing a white coat over dark trousers and ugly shoes. Ech.

He hurried, appreciating the time Orion and Kraft were giving him. Supposedly. He frowned, not having heard an alarm. But maybe the lads were going for subtle?

As if he'd conjured it, a blaring alarm went off, and a sudden rush of large magir, the majority of them likely shifters, ran by.

"What's up?" Duncan asked in a boring American accent.

It never hurt to practice being mundane.

A shifter, ursine by the look of him, slowed to answer, "Vampires on the campus."

Duncan tried to look frightened. "More than one? God."

"Yeah. I think we have two of them. Maybe more."

"Good luck."

The shifter grunted and hurried on. *Those idiots better not be messing with my plan.* It had been a rough idea but well grounded. Scare MEC with a vampire presence near university students. How hard was that? But Kraft was supposed to be a student, not a vampire. That way Orion could dart all over the place and keep MEC on their toes while Kraft fit in with his rescuers, watching and studying for future reference. Knowing how they responded to a vampire threat would be ideal.

Now realizing he needed to hurry, Duncan made haste for the Intelligence wing and found the witch in charge—a pretentious human with white hair in a bun, glasses perched on the bridge of her nose, and the scent of a domestic canine. Ah, there, a chihuahua sitting in a dog bed under her desk. Not good.

Would the animal know what he was?

It growled as he entered the office after knocking and being told to come in. But it soon lay back down in its bed and went to sleep.

Duncan turned on the charm. "I'm sorry to bother you, but I need access to the vampire files. We've got one on the loose."

"I heard." The woman narrowed her eyes on him. "You're new."

He smiled wide. "Yes, Ma'am. Connor MacLeod." *There can be only one.* A reference to an older movie he'd recently seen and liked, and, oddly enough, recommended by Mormo. Well, the magician had to be good for something.

"Hmm. That name seems familiar." She pursed her lips, and he glanced at the nameplate on her desk. Dr. Margery Brown.

He didn't want to chance anything, so he looked into her eyes and waited. Her desire for youth made him that much more attractive, and he played on it, letting her see herself through his eyes while he kissed the back of her hand—taking her blood. Just a small dab, painless and unnoticeable.

He didn't want to alert such a powerful witch to his presence.

He straightened and dropped her hand. "Your perfume is a delight."

She tittered. "Thank you, young man."

He smiled. "Do you think we could talk about Corson Westhell? Is it safe to talk here? In this room?"

"Of course, dear. We're warded." She blinked, and her eyes lit up with an ethereal, neon blue, as did a net of flashing lights around the room. She frowned at him, so he *pulled* on her, seducing with all she might desire. Power, wealth, fame. Typical human yearnings.

Her eyes faded back to their normal color. "Right. Warded." She cleared her throat. "Corson Westhell is the King of the West in the Hell plane. Or he was."

"A demon king?" That didn't bode well.

"Yes. He's been banished from Hell for over seven hundred years, and on our books for the past three hundred. We've had a task force after him for centuries, but here at MEC we have to do our best to patrol the Pacific Northwest. We haven't been able to chase him all around the globe, though we've had plenty of agents who've wanted to." She sighed. "Two of our finest are are currently on his tail." She laughed. "I do mean literally. We almost had him at a downtown bar last night, but he got away thanks to the vampires we think he's been working with."

And what a horrible bar it had been. "Vampires and a demon?"

"I know. A lethal combination. Trust me. We're ready for them."

"Oh?"

She frowned. "I, well...." She fingered her temples.

*She's a supreme witch, the strongest of her kind. I admit, I'm impressed.* He tapped the amulet under his shirt, staying human, while he tugged again on the seductive power of his revenant ability. "Tell me, Dr. Brown. How will you combat vampires and demon? What does the demon want, anyway? Why is he here now?"

She blew out a breath. "The demon wants an ancient grimoire. But while we think he only wants it to get back to his kingdom, we also think the grimoire is a part of something bigger. It's been holding something dark inside it for a very long time."

"What's it been holding?"

"We're not sure, but the MEC coven has a meeting with Hecate Saturday night to discuss it."

"She's coming *here?*"

Dr. Brown blushed. "Oh, she doesn't ever manifest, dear. She's a goddess with responsibilities. But she does gives us signs and portents. We study and we do her will, and in return, she protects us from all evil."

"Then why is the grimoire not under lock and key?" he asked, annoyed with Hecate all over again.

"It was. Do you know the story?"

"No, please. Tell me."

"Would you like to hear it before or after we stake you, vampire?"

A net came down and burned like the devil himself had set Duncan on fire. It seemed to settle into his skin, the power severe and sizzling against his bloode. But thanks to the charm he wore, the effects weren't visible.

Dr. Brown pointed at him while the blue surrounding the office lit up once more. Two dozen magir suddenly appeared around him, weapons aimed at his head and his heart.

But Duncan only smiled, as human as could be under the

charm. "I do think you've mistaken me for someone a lot more fangy." He felt as if his bloode would boil but refused to let these lesser beings see him in pain.

The intelligence maven frowned. "Not a vampire?"

"Madame, I'm many things, but a blood-drinker isn't one of them." No, because he savored the bloode, he reveled in it. Blood-*drinker* was too tame a word for the likes of him.

"He's telling the truth," a man standing back, behind the others, said. "Not a blood-drinker, and he's not burning."

Dr. Brown sighed and waved her hand, and as the net disappeared, the burning inside him vanished.

Duncan didn't move, acting confused even while he did his best not to show how much it hurt while he recovered. "I'm supposed to be a vampire? In *MEC?* I thought they couldn't breach the walls. Can they?"

"I wouldn't think so," the man said, staring at Duncan. As he came closer, Duncan realized he'd seen this magir before.

"But we've been wrong before," a deeper voice said as he and his partner approached.

The two agents he'd seen just the other night at Cho's house. Macy's father and a big-ass demon in the flesh. Huge, with horns, a tail, wings, and skin as black as pitch.

Duncan could only stare, wide-eyed, and hope humans weren't used to seeing demons, because he had a tough time looking away being this close to the creature. The other magir continued to focus on Duncan, their weapons still at the ready even as they stepped back to allow the demon and the mage to approach Dr. Brown.

Anton, the demon, emanated danger. Will, the mage, was steely-eyed and powered up, his fingers glowing with a golden magic. With the firepower centered around Duncan, in addition to a demon, a mage of Will Dunwich's caliber, and Dr. Brown, one might come to the conclusion that a vampire would be outnumbered and outgunned.

But Duncan knew nothing but the pleasure to be had in outthinking his opponents.

He smiled, deliberately showing a fang should the sorceress's magic not be as strong as she'd promised.

But no one fired, and the silence around them made Duncan want to laugh... and lunge and cut a bitch. That too.

Hmm. What was a revenant to do?

# CHAPTER TWELVE

Orion wanted to gut the smarmy bastard.

Duncan sat, surrounded by a host of problems—a demon, a powerful mage, a powerful witch, plenty of magir ready to fire enough rounds into the stupid vampire to cut his head clear off, and more backup just waiting around the Intelligence director's office.

Yet Duncan sat looking pleased with a cheery grin on his face.

The magir surrounding him had to know the idiot was a vampire. Hell, Orion had watched him lick the blood off the woman's wrist. Although, come to think of it, he had been fast about it. Perhaps they hadn't realized what he'd done. Or were they playing games with him?

Orion kept himself still, his talons clutching the railing above the witch's office. Such feeble humans. How tough was it to have a ceiling with security? At least at home, Mormo and Hecate made sure to protect the house from flying enemies.

He wanted to call out to Duncan, but instead he sat and watched while Kraft was out leading a stealth attack on cute coeds at the university. Their plan to distract MEC had worked for a while, but Orion had been too good at hiding, apparently, and the morons at MEC had left for a threat inside the compound.

*Great work, Duncan, you arrogant ass.*

Below him, Duncan shifted in his seat, and everyone around him tensed. "You're right. I'm not a part of MEC. Not this one, anyway. I'm part of a secret unit doing its best to track down Corson Westhell. I should apologize for using my compulsion talent on you, but we know someone has been helping the demon skirt authority. And we think it's someone in law enforcement."

Orion was impressed. Duncan seemed sincere. The big liar.

The powerful witch eased into a seat across from him. "What's your real name?"

"Not important."

The demon chuckled, and Orion wanted to get closer. Now *that* winged beast would take a decent beating and likely give one in return. The creature growled, "You don't get to break into our command and issue orders. Talk or lose a lung."

"And an eye." The mage next to the demon called forth more golden light into his palm.

Orion didn't like its brightness. Duncan had to be worried. Could he regenerate an eye? Varu could regrow whole limbs, but Orion could only heal flesh wounds and minimal bone breaks without a healing spell. Duncan had always been closemouthed about his abilities, and Orion had a feeling they didn't know the half of what the shifty revenant could do.

"I'm only here for information," Duncan said without looking worried about all the guns still pointed his way. "If I'd wanted to harm or kill anyone, I could have done so. Instead, I walked in here, in good faith. Once I determined your director was not in cahoots with the demon, I would have exchanged information."

*Cahoots?* Orion rolled his eyes.

The director exchanged a look with her agents.

The mage extinguished the golden glow in his hand and turned to the enforcers. "Clear out."

The demon added, "Head over to the university. We've got more problems."

The director's eyes widened, and she touched her ear. Hmm. A hidden earpiece. Perhaps those at MEC weren't as pathetic as they appeared. "We've got a lycan pack running amok and a vampire leaving bloody bodies behind. No, two—*three*—vampires. Damn it. Get it contained, Major."

One of the soldiers nodded. "Yes, ma'am. Enforcers, on me."

As one, the group with guns vanished, leaving Duncan alone with the demon, mage, and witch.

"You seem busy," Duncan said, unrushed, unbothered.

The demon's long tail flicked in agitation, the pointed end coming perilously close to Duncan's face. "You seem undaunted."

"I'm not your enemy." Duncan sighed, and Orion had to hand it to him. The bastard could deceive like a champ. "I want what you want—Corson Westhell gone from this plane."

"Tell us what you know."

"And you'll tell me what else *you* know that you haven't already shared?" At the witch's nod, Duncan shrugged. "Fine. I've been after Westhell for ten years. He's elusive, and he never stays longer than a few weeks in any given place. I have other cases. He's not my only one, but he's the one I just can't close."

"I know the feeling," the mage said and leaned against the director's desk. "He's always a few steps ahead of us."

The demon nodded.

"Who do you work for?" the witch asked.

"EuroMEC. I'm in their SO division."

Orion had heard of them. He wondered how far Duncan planned to take his story. Were Orion to be in charge of this intelligence gathering mission, he'd have killed everyone but the witch then made her tell him everything he wanted to know while ripping her limbs off. But no, Duncan had to do things the long, hard way.

Shifting his claws to ease his perch, Orion noticed the demon give a cautious look around. *Huh. Guy's got pretty good hearing.*

The witch considered Duncan. "You said SO. You're Special Operations?"

"No. I don't exist." Duncan smiled.

"You're human," the mage said.

"Am I?"

"You're no vamp," the demon said, but he didn't sound convinced.

"If I were a typical vampire, I'd have already gutted you and drank down the mage and the witch." But Duncan was anything but typical. "Yes, we study up on our vampires. I've primarily dealt with nachzehrers and revenants, the occasional strigoi. But things have settled down at home, where they're intent only on killing each other. And with the new strigoi master in power, things have definitely changed for the better."

The MEC heavies stared at him.

"What? You haven't heard that Atanase of the Crimson Veil is gone for good? Yep. And good riddance."

Nice way to let everyone know, Orion thought.

The magir looked shaken.

"Who killed him?" the witch asked.

"We're not sure, but we think Mihai of the Crimson Veil intends to announce his ascendancy soon. He's a lot more level-headed than Atanase."

The mage nodded. "That's for sure."

"So while *our* vampire problems are settling, here, you've apparently got trouble." Duncan paused. "Especially if you have rogue lycan packs and vampires killing human students."

The mage sighed. "Trust me. This is new. Our local clan is fairly young. Close to forty upir who keep to themselves, mostly.

But the lycans have been getting restless. In fact, a lot of typically peaceful factions have been having trouble lately." After a glance at the demon, who nodded, the mage added, "We think their behavior might be tied into the grimoire."

"We saw the same about five years ago." Duncan shook his head. "Rumors of a dark book circulated. Then it vanished, as did our troubles. Only to hear it's started up again, here. I want that demon gone." Duncan gave a dramatic pause, looking grief-stricken. "He killed a partner of mine."

Orion wanted to give him a standing ovation for his theatrics.

The others looked moved. Well, the mage and witch did.

The demon looked as if he couldn't care less. "Yeah, well, life goes on. Now who are you?"

"He said his name is Connor MacLeod," the witch said.

The mage bit back a grin. "You mean, the lead character from *Highlander*, the movie?"

The witch scowled. "I knew I'd heard that name before."

Duncan and the demon had been staring into each other's eyes, and even from his perch some distance away, Orion could feel the hostility building. Then Duncan smirked and said, "You can call me Duncan. Now, I'd like to know what you know of the demon making a mess of this town, causing a disturbance at a local bar last night using chaos and lust to blind the crowd."

The witch shook her head. "You shouldn't know about that. We bespelled the crowd to keep that quiet."

"Not quiet enough." Duncan slowly crossed his ankle over his knee, looking as if he didn't have a care in the world. "Your city is going to shit."

"Nice mouth," the demon snarled.

"Truth hurts." Duncan turned to the mage. "Look, I just want the demon king and the grimoire." He paused. "It's got a convoluted provenance. Some say it belongs in Hell, others say it belongs to Hecate."

The witch perked up. "Hecate, you say?"

Duncan nodded. "But I haven't been able to confirm that. Can you?"

She glanced at the mage, and Orion wondered if they communicated telepathically. The demon kept his focus on Duncan, his wings rustling, his tail whipping about as he snarled, showing some pretty big fangs.

The witch said, "As I told you before, we have a scheduled circle for this Saturday, when we'd hoped to get something more from Hecate. The High Coven has been having visions of the grimoire, so we know Hecate is involved in this mess somehow." She paused. "But how did *you* come by this information?"

An armed guard burst into the office. "Dr. Brown! Reports of an all out vampire-lycan battle on the campus! We're doing our best to contain the threat of exposure, but it's chaos. We can't tell why the vampires are fighting each other *and* the lycans, but if we don't shut it down soon, we'll have no chance of keeping this out of the local news."

He darted away, and the witch glared down at Duncan.

He held up his hands. "This isn't any of my doing."

"Wait here. Anton, Will, watch him. I'll be back." Her eyes turned a blinding blue before she vanished.

Then what she'd said penetrated. Vampires fighting lycans could be easily explained, but not vampires fighting other vampires. Kraft had to be attacking the locals. But what the hell were they doing on the campus in the first place?

Duncan looked from the mage to the demon. "Sounds like you have a real problem. Better go take care of it before it gets any worse."

Words directed to *him,* he knew. Orion huffed and shot away, hoping to find Kraft in one piece so he could take him apart, limb by limb. What a dick. How had a simple plan to distract MEC turned into a blood bath?

And why hadn't Kraft waited for Orion before starting any heavy shit?

---

Duncan waited for Orion to fly away, his attempt at stealth pathetic.

As the demon clearly noticed. "Now that Dr. Brown and your feathery friend are gone, how about you get real with us?" He murmured something in another language to the mage, who nodded and smiled down at Duncan.

That smile didn't reach the mage's eyes. "Yes, *Duncan.* Now it's time for some truth." The lights in his hands glowed, the magic pure, powerful, and dangerous.

Duncan looked to both males and braced his hands on the arms of his chair. "May I?"

The demon nodded.

Duncan made sure to rise very slowly. Once on his feet, he looked up at both men. Huh. The mage hadn't seemed so tall when back at Cho's house. "Gentlemen, as much as I'd like to school you in the fine art of battle, I have somewhere I need to be, a grimoire to find, and a demon to fuck with."

They tensed.

Well aware of the containment spell the witch had left behind, Duncan had been subtly looking for time fissures to slide between while he'd been interrogated. And now that he had them, he knew where to push through.

"What are you?" the mage asked, not looking at all like his daughter. Too big and brutish, not at all delicate or pretty. "I know you're not the human you appear to be. Are you fae of some kind?"

"I don't care." The demon snarled. "Tell us what we want to know or—"

Duncan vanished, now on the other side of the barrier, in the hallway outside her office.

"Fuck. Brown is not going to be pleased," he heard the mage say.

The demon swore. The smell of smoke and brimstone swelled past the office, and Duncan laughed to himself as he hurried to find out what the hell Kraft had been up to.

All in all, the night wasn't a total waste. He'd seen MEC up close, had reestablished his bond with Ian and made a new one with Dr. Brown, should he need those bonds later, and had taken an odd little stone from the corner of Brown's desk on his way out. Something important to her, just one more item to enforce the blood-bond Duncan had created.

He clutched it tight, letting its sharp edge cut into him, letting his bloode soak into the stone before healing himself. The stone vibrated with pleasure, and though it wasn't a Bloode Stone, he liked its response to him. He'd have to ask Fara about it when he saw her again.

*After* he'd settled a few things with the local upir pack.

Really? Brawling in public?

What he found when he encountered Kraft and Orion, though, was way worse than he could have predicted.

## CHAPTER THIRTEEN

Orion held the rabid lycans back while MEC took care of their berserkers, the overlarge direwolf hybrids currently decimating two dozen humans while to the side, Kraft battled four upir, punching and kicking as if in a human-looking grudge match. At least the upir had the sense not to show themselves as bloodsuckers.

Duncan motioned for Kraft to stop dicking around with them, looking like a mass murderer in his human form, covered head to toe in blood. Yeah, so Kraft would need to explain all that blood later.

Kraft nodded to a shaded area under a large tree, far enough away from the many cameras aimed at a pack of "wild dogs" attacking students and MEC, posing as armed security.

"It's crazy," Kraft said quietly, watching as the stubborn group of upir refused to let him go. They shifted out of sight and subtly stalked him, once again battling under the cover of darkness and the overhead tree. They continued to throw themselves at him one at a time or in pairs, and Kraft kept tossing them back, careful not to overly damage them.

Duncan stood back to watch him work, impressed despite himself. "What's going on?"

"I was out here picking a fight with some lycans, all of us in human form. Just jerking them around." Kraft didn't even sound winded while knocking around the upir. "Then this weird darkness crept over the courtyard." He nodded to where the massive fight continued, some distance away in a courtyard bordered by tall buildings. "The lycans shifted—out in front of everyone. Then they started attacking. Now, I understand the need to feed, but not out in the open. And so sloppy." He motioned to himself. "This is human blood, by the way. Not my fault one of the lycans ripped a few students apart and then tackled me in the entrails."

Duncan saw more than a few mauled humans behind him. "When did the upir show?"

"About ten minutes ago. At first, it was just a pair of them. We were dancing and having fun together, looking like brawling humans. Then the stupid ones showed up and forgot to blend."

"Fucker." One of them hissed. "You broke my foot *and* my arm."

"You're still alive aren't you?" Kraft snorted. "You're welcome." He kicked the rushing upir in the face, breaking his nose, then tossed the vampire away from the carnage, as if launching a shotput. He turned back to Duncan as the other upir gathered their wounded, cursed Kraft back to hell, and quietly escaped. "I didn't feel a need to crush them," he said, sounding surprised. "Still don't. Varu's hold over our clan is secure."

That the upir were leaving without a slaughter was also a good sign. That meant either their patriarch had them in hand or Varu did. It was a very good thing Varu had no urge to rule or annihilate everyone in his path, or Duncan and his kin would soon be ruling the city.

"Varu is a decent patriarch," Duncan admitted. "But *some* of his clan have issues." He shot Kraft a look the nachzehrer couldn't mistake.

"Hey, I did my part."

"Oh? You were supposed to be a small distraction to get MEC out here, not start a vampire-lycan war."

Kraft shoved his bloody hair back, a thick hank of red-stained yellow lumped on top of his head. He did nothing to wipe it from his face, though, and Duncan thought about handing over his handkerchief but didn't want it ruined.

"I honestly don't know what happened," Kraft growled. "Orion started out distracting MEC, but they got bored and left. Then he left. So I tried to distract the humans by attacking —nicely—

and having MEC come out again. When the lycans shifted and started eating people, MEC left me alone. Then the upir showed, and I engaged them until one of the lycans butted in. More upir came, and it turned into a vampire-lycan-MEC battle. It was like a giant free-for-all for a while." He grinned, but seeing Duncan's sober expression, wiped the smile from his face. "It wasn't natural. That shadow I mentioned? It stirred the rage I keep buried deep inside me. Duncan, that should never come out when it's not controlled."

"I agree. But you're feeling all right now?"

"I had to pull back, away from the lycans. They're..." He said something in German. "I think something has infected them."

"Something magical." Duncan had felt a similar pull to the wildness with Macy.

Who had the grimoire.

"I need to grab the witch."

Orion appeared, wiping bloody claws on his jeans. "We need to go, *now*. MEC spotted me and will soon be on my tail. I'm all for killing them but you said not to."

"No."

"We have to talk to Mormo and Varu about what happened. One of the upir got lost."

Duncan frowned. "Lost?"

"As in, he lost his fucking head. The lycans devoured him. He's true-dead."

The three of them looked back at the cluster bombs of magic MEC was launching over the area, where at least a dozen humans lay unmoving on the ground, covered in blood, some missing body parts. He only saw a few lycans on the ground, most now rounded up and contained.

Duncan nodded. "Let's go." The three of them raced to the SUV, got in, and drove away. "First stop, Ahnessa's." Duncan fiddled with the charm under his shirt, taking it out to crush it. "Let's make sure we didn't inadvertently cause this." With a sneaky malevolent spell tied to the illusion charm. He didn't think it was dirty, but it paid to be safe.

Orion and Kraft destroyed their charms as well, reverting back into their true forms. Vampires, not humans.

When they reached Ahnessa's place of business, it looked normal on the outside. A small, plain, brick building with a psychic sign over the door. Inside, they found it empty. And by empty, devoid of *everything* but thick smoke and a smear of black ash in the shape of a person lying on the floor.

"What the fuck is going on?" Kraft gaped. "Who had the power to take her out?"

"Or the balls?" Orion asked. "She had protection agreements with the upir clan, the lycans, and the mage guild. This weird cloud of death magic hurts my nose." He grimaced. "It stinks."

A strong, crafty sorceress, Ahnessa had expressed caution only around Mormo, or so she said.

Duncan glanced around. "What do you two smell?"

"Nothing but smoke." Kraft sneezed. "Ah, that's a little better. Ash?" Kraft cocked his head. "Cinnamon."

Both Orion and Duncan said as one, "Brimstone." Hidden under a muting spell.

Duncan added, "I think we found our demon's trail. What say we follow it?"

Kraft snarled and shifted into a large black wolf with blazing red eyes.

"After you find him, come back and let us know."

Kraft left. Duncan and Orion waited, looking through what remained of Ahnessa's things. The sorceress had a healthy respect for Mormo's power, so she did occasional work for him. Never on the up and up, she worked for the underbelly of the city's magir. MEC only left her alone because they'd never been able to tie her to illegal activities. Ahnessa was—had been—that good. Orion went upstairs while Duncan remained on the first floor.

In the back room, books had been ripped or burned, potions askew, pools of magical substances on the floor and spattering the walls. Glass and rock crunched underfoot.

Orion returned. "It's just like this. Nothing up there." He paused at the landing by the staircase.

Close by, something moved.

As one, Duncan and Orion followed the tiny scuffle to an open, triangular space under the stairwell, where they found glowing green eyes and a hissing, spitting surprise in the darkness there.

Orion crouched to look closer, and as Duncan's eyes adjusted, he watched a slight, nasty-tempered feline spit and strike out at Orion with sharp, curved claws. Smudged black fur matted with blood and a foul gunk covered the small cat, its only burst of color its bright green eyes. It looked almost unreal, cartoonish in its cuteness marred with a mess of deadly intent.

He frowned. "Is it a kitten? Or some kind of illusion maybe?"

Orion stuck his hand close and pulled back bloody scratches.

"No, it's real." And it stood its ground in front of two large vampires.

"It looks too small to be an adult cat," Duncan said, wary. The last feline he'd seen had fortunately disappeared the past week. A feline larger than a Siberian tiger, with black and white stripes and a bad attitude, had taken to strolling through Hecate's house on Mercer like it owned it. Or rather, like *she* owned it. Because, yeah, their crazy dusk elf thought he could communicate with animals. According to Onvyr, *she* didn't like Duncan much.

Orion stared at the kitten, predator to predator. "It's very angry." Instead of being afraid, the kitten snarled, its back arched to make it look bigger. Orion hissed at it, and it hissed back.

"Take care of it," Duncan said. "But be careful. It's probably infected with the same stuff that's in the lycans. I'll go wait for Kraft by the vehicle."

Orion flexed his fingers and let his nails lengthen into steel-hard claws. "I won't be long."

WHEN KRAFT RETURNED, he got in the back behind Orion, and Duncan put the car in drive and pulled away from the curb. With any luck, the blood on his clothing had dried, because if not, Bella would not be pleased about more car detailing.

"I lost him." Kraft swore. "But that scent was definitely not human or magir. It was the same smell as what settled over the lycans. Disappeared into thin air." He paused. "Why do I smell blood?"

He leaned forward to see Orion cradling a bloody mess of fur on his lap.

Duncan sighed. "We can't keep it."

Orion lifted the bloody ball of fluff to his face, ignoring the paw on his cheek as he licked the kitten's wound clean. "He had a massive splinter in his back paw. That's why he was so mean, weren't you, little fella?" He rubbed his nose against the kitten's, who gave another hiss, but this one a pathetic whisper of warning.

"Oh, I want to hold it." But when Kraft stuck his hand closer, the kitten sliced a long scratch along his finger. "Damn it."

Duncan chuckled.

"He smells the dog on you," Orion explained and tucked the kitten against his chest, his hand as big as the thing's body.

"It's not dog. It's wolf," Kraft growled. "And forget about petting it. Now I want to eat it."

Orion gasped. "Never. He's mine. You eat him, I'll eat you."

Duncan let them bicker, amused to see the kitten curl up against Orion's chest and close its eyes. If only every wild thing they found was so easy to tame.

Heat curled inside him, a need to check on Macy—his prey—eating at him. "We should grab the witch tonight. Now."

"Feeling possessive, eh?" Kraft grinned, showing a lot of teeth in the rearview mirror.

Duncan didn't care. He had a bad feeling that leaving Macy until the next night might prove too late.

He drove them to her home and parked in front. "Wait here."

"Wait. Go. Sit." Kraft sighed. "Now I feel like a dog."

"Told you." Orion laid his head back.

"Shut up."

"Just wait here," Duncan said again. "I'll be right back."

Orion waved him away.

Duncan hurried, rushing through Macy's ward and getting a shock because of it. He found her in her spell room, looking tired, leafing through that damn grimoire. "Witch, let's go."

She shrieked and jumped back. "You!"

The grimoire vanished right before Duncan's eyes.

"Not again." He didn't have the patience for nonsense. "Bring the book."

"I— Where did it go?" She looked all around then turned

back to see him staring at her legs, visible from ankle to ass, not covered by her overlarge yet still too-short-to-be-decent sleep shirt.

"We don't have time for games." He scowled. "Corson West-hell. He's here."

"In my house?" she gasped. "No way in hell."

"No pun intended, I'm sure."

"What? Oh, ah, no."

Duncan pinched the bridge of his nose. "We have to go."

"Wait. Why are you all dressed up?" She looked over his suit, and he had to admit, he did wear it well. "Where do you think you're taking me? I won't go. I'll scream."

"Go ahead." He crossed his arms over his chest, giving the appearance of boredom. "Still waiting."

"Ass."

"Oh, that hurt. Got anything stronger, witch?" He really liked the look of her, all lean lines and curves where it counted. And that glorious hair. Kraft had been right earlier. It was the color of bloode, not fire, the red dusted with magic.

"Blood-sucking, dumbass, sun-hating motherfucker. How about that?" she spat.

A lot like the kitten but with sharper claws.

He smiled.

Her expression darkened. "If you tell me I'm beautiful when I'm angry, I will honest to Hecate castrate you."

He laughed and sank his fangs into her neck before she could cast so much as a whisper.

# CHAPTER
# FOURTEEN

The taste of her made Duncan forget his own name. But only for a moment. Having to tamp down his sudden erection, however, took a bit longer to control. "Witch," he murmured and nuzzled Macy's neck, licking away the wound before kissing his way to her mouth.

Duncan hadn't intended to actually kiss her on the lips. She was too dangerous, nearly naked and soft and sweet. "Time to go, luv."

Except Macy put him under *her* spell by yanking him close and kissing the ability to reason right out of him.

She moaned into his mouth, her hands everywhere and suddenly down his trousers, gripping *his cock* with the strength of a war maiden. She started pumping him, and his mind blanked.

Duncan had no idea how to combat the rush of desire overtaking his senses.

"Lust and love, fear and fire, mine to take," she murmured and in seconds had him coming into her hand in one of the hardest, most explosive climaxes he'd ever in his life experienced.

Duncan's moan turned into a growl of shock and rage that once more morphed into need as she rubbed her hand on his belly, under his shirt. The feel of her warm hand on his flesh was like the rush of first blood down his throat after a fast.

Macy stared into his eyes as she pulled her hand free and sucked her forefinger clean. "Yum."

Licking his seed into her mouth. He felt himself trembling, his hunger for her a raging storm.

As much as she had claimed him, by taking his essence inside her, she'd allowed him to claim her right back. He felt stronger.

And aroused once more.

She blinked, stared from her hand to his strong erection, and darted away from him up the stairs, yelling about possession.

Duncan sighed, stared down at his open trousers, and put himself to rights once more. "I guess I won't be getting a round two anytime soon." Then he smiled as he climbed after her. "Well, not tonight, at least. But tomorrow night, we'll definitely try again."

MACY COULDN'T BELIEVE she'd been so forward. Had he hexed her? No, vampires didn't hex. He had to have seduced her with his vampy powers. The cocky bastard. She rushed around her room, trying to figure out what to do. How to get rid of him so she wouldn't be tempted to throw herself at him. He'd felt so good, so right against her. *Gah. At this rate I'll be begging to become his permanent mattress and let him bounce all over me.*

Perhaps a spell? Though she'd gotten much stronger since using the grimoire, she still needed to think and plan, storing reserves before casting for maximum power.

But the wings might work. If she could concentrate, leap out of the house, and fly away before he caught her.

"Can we go now?" he asked from right beside her.

She screamed in fright.

He winced. "Can you stop doing that?"

"Stop sneaking up on me!"

"Unless you want to make friends with Westhell in that tee-shirt that shows off your lovely arse, we should leave. Bring the book."

"I don't know where it is, I swear."

"You were downstairs paging through it." He frowned. "I saw you."

"I was, I just can't remember how I got from sleeping in my bed to being downstairs, apparently learning new spells." She saw new sigils in her mind's eye that slowly vanished. A spell to heal. A spell to sunder. And another to steal blood. What the heck?

"Macy Bishop-Dunwich, it's time to go."

She forced herself to look at him, begrudgingly mesmerized by his trademark smirk despite wanting to smack him for his arrogance. "I dreamed you came to visit me again, and then there you were." Was he ever. Her fingers—and other parts—tingled from the memory of having held him. "I kissed you."

"And took me to bliss with that graceful hand." He smiled.

She did her best not to gape, because when Duncan smiled, he looked like a fallen angel, too beautiful to be human, too wicked to be saintly. And he did it all while wearing a suit and tie and designer shoes.

"You made me touch you," she accused.

He snorted. "I came to take you back. You're the one who shoved your hand down my trousers. Not that I'm complaining."

Crap. He had no reason to lie, and though a little hazy about the details, she just knew she'd been on fire to have him. There had been power in the taste of his seed. But what did that mean, exactly? Because she wanted him still.

He cocked his head. "Time's up." He *moved.*

Before she knew it, she was tossed and belted into a large SUV outside her home. Plunked next to a large vampire with dark, shaggy hair, covered in blood—*gross*—and wearing a bad attitude that changed into a delighted one as the door closed her in with him.

"Ah, dinner."

"Touch her and die," Duncan said in a conversational tone from the driver's seat.

She noticed his friend from the bar sitting up front beside him. The big guy turned to look her over and sneered. "She smells like you. No wonder it took you so long to come back."

"Didn't take him long at all, I'll bet," Kraft said with smirk.

Which had Orion and Duncan, surprisingly, laughing. And dang it all, then Macy was joining in, because that was funny.

By the time she caught her breath, they'd already pulled away. "Wait. Where are we going?" *And where can I get some pants? And why am I not completely freaked out about being near death-bringers?*

"Someone wants to talk to you about the grimoire," Duncan said, and she met his gaze in the rearview mirror. "She's not happy."

"She? Who's she? And who gives a shit if she's happy or not?"

"I like this one," the vamp next to her said with a smile. "I'm Kraft. The fun, good-looking predator among his pathetic kin."

The big vampire next to Duncan snorted. "You mean the dumbass who can't keep his sorry ass out of trouble."

"'Dumbass' and 'ass' are repetitive." Kraft shook his head. "Stupid? That would be Orion," Kraft leaned closer to whisper in a charming German accent, "Don't worry about him. He has performance issues."

Duncan choked.

Orion snarled. "When we get back to the house, rematch."

"Fine. That's if you're recovered from fighting all those big bad lycans." Kraft snorted. "No wonder you like the feline." He paused. "Pussy."

"I will make your eyes bleed," Orion promised and continued with threats of bodily harm.

She met Duncan's gaze in the rearview again and saw him roll his eyes as the threats turned to insults about fang size and kill counts.

Though she knew she should have been terrified, surrounded by powerful vampires, who, for all she knew, had come to the city to kill everyone, she sat back and smiled.

---

CORSON WATCHED from his position down the street, Lucy—his Lilith—standing with him. It had taken her some time to stop crying, shouting, and dry-heaving with panic, which had devolved into demands he kill her quickly, and if not, to just fuck off.

He liked her spine. But he'd liked her even better when she'd asked what she was to get out of their little deal. Just to see her response, he'd mentioned riches beyond imagining. Her eyes had grown wide. After he'd told her she'd need to bring him one measly human as a sacrifice, she'd graciously accepted. Under her pretty looks beat a greedy, self-obsessed heart.

"Ah, my Lilith. You complete me." He snickered and kissed her, absorbing her will and leaving her shell empty for the moment. Corson would return her consciousness when needed. By Lucifer's Star, she was a delight.

Humans. Such a pleasure working with them. Or rather, working them over.

*Master, do I get the grimoire now? Shall I free you, finally?* he mentally called out, desperate to free his liege. *I'm happy to track down the witch and feed her to you piece by piece.*

He waited, as he'd been waiting for centuries for an answer but not expecting one.

Disappointed, he pulled Lucy with him into the witch's house, looking for traces of stolen magic. Nothing but the scent of lust in her spell room, a taste of the vampire lingering in the air.

Corson inhaled, committing the scent to memory. A vampire would do as much, if not more, to feed his master than the witch bloated on Hell-power. Hmm. Something he'd been considering, but this tie of vampire to witch was an added bonus.

Should he feed more of her blood to the book in hopes his master might be reborn?

A haze filled his mind, and a prickling weight sat on his chest. *Not yet.*

Overjoyed to experience the tremor of fear that always accompanied his master's presence, he quivered with anticipation. *Whatever you need, it's yours, Master.*

Dark laughter filled him, a muddled essence of decay and power. *So much* power.

*Wait and watch.* A pause, then his master added with smoky satisfaction, *I'm right where I want to be.*

# CHAPTER FIFTEEN

Macy had listened and observed all through the drive to Mercer Island, watching with shock as they pulled the vehicle toward a mansion along the water. She had a short burst of panic, her mind and body on fire for the brief seconds it took to pass through a protective shield of some kind, a magical gloss of Hecate, if she weren't mistaken.

But then a soothing balm of welcome eased her pain, and she felt better than she had in months as they parked in a multicar garage filled with high-end vehicles.

She sat there, still trying to process that pain against her bornagain wellness when the car door opened.

"Come." Duncan waited.

She wondered what he'd do if she— "*Oof.*"

Duncan hefted her over his shoulder and entered the house, following the other two vampires.

"Hey. Let me down." *My ass is hanging out in panties with hearts and kittens on them. Oh man.*

"Nice ass," Kraft said.

"True," Orion agreed and added a "*Meow*" that had Kraft roaring with laughter.

Yep. He'd seen the panties. Fuming, embarrassed, yet also vainly pleased by the "nice ass" compliment, she hung over Mr. Fussy's shoulder, trying to decide what to do. Duncan only gripped her tighter.

Keen to see their residence, she wasn't prepared for vampires to be living it rich, having expected a cave or underground lair filled with coffins. And yes, she knew she was stereotyping, especially after seeing Duncan fill out that designer suit. She pushed up against the small of his back and looked around.

They passed through a long hallway of cream colored walls decorated in art that would do the Seattle Art Museum proud, over marble tiled floors into an open living space. Ahead of her was a large dining table and beyond that what appeared to be a state-of-the-art kitchen. To the left of the open dining room, a large, leather sectional sofa faced a center partition of shelving and a huge television mounted on the wall. And behind the sectional, another wall of shelving filled with books and knickknacks teeming with magic.

The center wall created a definite living space while also making a dedicated walkway from the front door through to the dining space and beyond, outside to a grand porch overlooking Lake Washington.

Huh. Vampires had floor-to-ceiling glass doors overlooking a gorgeous water view. Glass doors that would too easily let the sun shine through. That didn't seem very smart.

"Look what we found," Kraft said as he walked into the kitchen.

A small *meow* made her blink. And no, that time wasn't Orion, but an actual feline.

"What is that?" a cultured voice asked, smooth and full of power.

She shifted on Duncan to try to see and gaped at the men

standing around the large kitchen island. Duncan set her on her feet, and she took a good, hard look.

Two menacing looking heart-throbs, one with dark hair and fangs, the other wearing a smirk and thick blond hair, braided at one temple. Hmm. A Viking warrior, maybe? Next to them, another hottie wore a long white robe to match his long white hair. He had slightly pointed ears and red eyes. A fae?

She'd seen only a handful of fae while working at MEC, and none of them looked like the beautiful, graceful characters from *The Lord of the Rings*.

"Well, well, what have we here?" the vampire with dark hair, dusky skin, and intense, black eyes asked, his tone arrogant, his posture combative. With a more slender build, not short on muscle but not as bulky as Orion or Kraft, he had a dignified air about him.

"That's Khent," Kraft said. "He's a reaper and a bit of a dick."

"Fuck off."

"A big dick, you mean," Orion muttered.

Khent glowered.

Kraft continued, "The blond draugr is Rolf. Gandalf the White isn't one of us, but we're tolerating him until Hecate says we can eat him."

Khent looked confused and asked Kraft, "Why are you talking to dinner?"

"I'm not dinner," Macy hurried to say at the same time the white-haired guy said, "She's not dinner."

Thank goodness.

"She's in big trouble though," the white-haired guy continued. "Training with a grimoire is a no-no, even for a Bloode Witch."

Hmm. She heard capital letters there, but she'd never heard of a blood witch before. Or did he mean they'd suck her blood? Like, a witch who served others *her own* blood? She took a step closer to Duncan.

"I wasn't training with it, exactly." Puzzled, because Macy suddenly remembered looking through the book, rifling through spells and concentrating on certain ones. "I don't think I was." Why had she been doing that? She'd never tamper with dark craft. She was no warlock and had no desire to become one.

Duncan crossed his arms over his chest, and his arm brushed hers. "She says she lost it again, Mormo."

Macy frowned, angry and frightened to recall a loss of control around the grimoire. "*She* has a name."

The blond man moved closer, his dark eyes twinkling. "*She* smells like Duncan."

Macy flushed. What had she been thinking to give Duncan a handjob? Not like she was dead below the waste—the guy was better looking than any man she'd ever seen. But sex with a *vampire?*

Duncan nodded. "She's my prey."

His... prey? "Now hold on a minute."

The blond smiled, and she felt as if her heart stopped beating. He had fangs, and his eyes turned red. A blond vampire.

She'd never heard of any vampire not being dark-eyed and dark-haired. "Kraft called you a draugr." A vampire tribe commonly found in Scandinavia.

"*Ja,* he's right." Rolf winked at Kraft, who kept glaring at Orion. Then Rolf turned to Orion. "You brought me a kitten?" He seemed to go from scary vamp to softie in seconds.

"No, he's mine. I rescued him. He's my fur-buddy." As if to prove his point, Orion held the kitten toward Rolf and watched it swipe and hiss at the draugr.

"Aw, that's adorable." Rolf showed way too many teeth.

Kraft nodded. "It scratched me. Those little claws are sharp."

Khent crossed his arms over his chest. His wise eyes and dark sweater and jeans gave him an odd dichotomy of ancient being and contemporary male.

"You're a reaper?" she asked.

He ignored her. "I don't want a cat in the house. I'm allergic."

Orion snarled. "Liar. You just don't like the fact this one is mine."

"Yes, Khent's a reaper," Duncan said as he leaned back against the kitchen counter, watching everyone with a narrow-eyed stare. "He's also, as Kraft said, a dick."

Khent said something in a language Macy didn't understand, but she knew it hadn't been nice.

Duncan only grinned.

Macy had always thought of reapers as closer to necromancers, since they could raise the dead. Many of them occupied territories in southern Asia and Africa, though the odd clan would appear in other parts of the human world. True to his reputation, Khent seemed abominably arrogant.

"But don't worry," the white-haired male, Mormo, said to her. "I won't let him kill and reanimate you. Not as long as you tell us where the grimoire is."

Silence settled over the kitchen as all eyes turned to her.

"Um, well, I'm not sure where it goes when it disappears. Seriously." She shrugged, beseeching them to believer her.

Mormo frowned. "She seems to be telling the truth."

Rolf yawned. "She probably is. If the grimoire is what I think it is, it's attached to her. Probably inside her right now. We should drink her down to find out."

"What? No!" She tried to back away, but Duncan wrapped his arms around her middle from behind, chaining her with muscles made of iron.

"No one's drinking Macy down." His accent was sharp though his tone remained mild. "I've got her under watch."

"I'll bet you do," Orion murmured, and Kraft chuckled. Fighting one minute, friendly the next.

Duncan ignored them. "It's late, and we're tired."

"And you three have Bloode Stones to find." Mormo pointed to Khent, Rolf, and Kraft.

"Aw, come on, Mormo," Kraft complained. "I'm working with Orion and Duncan."

"You *were,* you mean." Mormo stood straighter, and he looked *pissed.* "How about you explain to me why MEC is putting out alerts, and the Seattle Bloode *and* Bloode Empire are requesting meetings and issuing threats. Something about a problem at the university, I believe."

Duncan subtly started inching toward the dining area.

"You, revenant," Mormo barked. "Don't move."

Rolf and Khent looked at each other then made some lame excuses and left in a hurry. Orion followed on the pretense of needing to care for his new kitten, which Macy thought pretty clever.

"No," Mormo said. "Orion, I need to hear your account of what occurred tonight. Kraft, you start."

Kraft groaned and explained a complicated mess that led back to Corson Westhell and the grimoire she couldn't control. Orion then added what he'd seen, including an interesting accounting of Macy's dad, Uncle Anton, and Dr. Brown, the head of Intelligence. Talk about a shit storm at MEC that she'd missed. Wow.

Mormo studied Duncan, who finally shifted so that he stood next to Macy and not directly behind her. Way too close. "So you pushed through silver?"

Duncan shrugged. "A silver laced spell, maybe. It hurt like blazes. The witch was strong but nothing I couldn't handle."

Macy turned to him, her mouth open. "Dr. Brown is one of the highest ranked witches on the West Coast. She's supreme."

"Supremely pedantic," Duncan said.

Kraft said to Orion, "Pedantic means obnoxiously learned, stodgy or stuffy about what you know."

"I know what it means," Orion growled.

"No," Macy said. "She's the highest rated witch in all of Seattle. In all of MEC."

"And she bows to Hecate," Duncan said. "Whom I do not serve."

Mormo raised a brow. "Oh?"

Duncan flashed a fang in annoyance. "I'm repaying a debt. I'm not owned by the goddess." He nodded to Macy. "Not like this one."

"I'm not owned by anyone."

That had the vampires laughing at her.

"I'm not! I give tribute to Hecate because my goddess is just and powerful."

Mormo seemed to soften. "She truly is. She's a miracle."

"She's a pain in my ass," another vampire said, joining them. This one had short dark hair, an aristocratic appearance, and emanated waves of power. Uncomfortably strong and scary. When he settled his dark eyes on her, she couldn't stop herself from taking a step back.

He didn't react except to say, "The stone feels its presence, but its faint."

Mormo raised a brow. "The stone feels it?"

Feels what, she wondered. The grimoire?

"Yes," the new vampire said, and for a moment she thought he'd been talking to her. His focus remained on Mormo, though. "Don't ask. I can't explain half the things it feels or says."

"Hmm." Mormo cupped his chin, lost in thought.

Macy wanted to leave. Bad enough to be surrounded by vampires wearing nothing more than a sleep shirt. Orion and Kraft were big and dangerous, Duncan even more so because of his speed and frankly, because she found him too appealing. At least the other two, who considered her dinner, had left. But this guy put her back up.

He had to be their leader. The patriarch.

Unfortunately, she couldn't outrun this group, and she didn't have the power to cast a spell over them either, not in this house. It felt of Hecate and something else. Something that muted her skill with magic. So weird.

She yawned and noticed the others yawning as well, except for Mormo and the new guy.

A ray of sunlight filtered through the windows, brightening into day. But since Macy had been up all night, she needed sleep. And escape, but she'd take sleep if only to rest her reserves so she could escape later.

The scary vampire shook his head. "Weak and useless," he growled, and Macy cringed when he stalked to Orion. "What the hell is that?"

The kitten backed into Orion's chest and gave a frightened mew.

"Stop bullying my new fur-buddy."

"Would you stop calling it that?" Kraft snorted. "You vryko are so weak with your sentiment." Kraft glared at Varu. "Yeah, you too, strigoi. Getting a mate. Varu, what were you thinking?"

"That she's mine?" Varu—scary vamp—smiled, showing sharp fangs. He turned to Macy and looked from her to Duncan. "Who is this?"

"My prey," Duncan didn't hesitate to say.

Varu only nodded. Macy would have protested being called prey, but she didn't want to draw more attention to herself. "Keep her under watch. She's your responsibility." He sniffed and turned away, but Macy could have sworn she saw his lips quirk into a small smile.

To Mormo, he said, "We have a new lead on a stone."

Mormo's eyes brightened. "Outstanding. Fill me in." He turned to the others. "I expect you three back here at sunset. And Macy, my dear, I think you'd better locate that grimoire for us.

Fast. There are worse things than vampires, and a few of those are attached to that book."

She swallowed. "If I had it, I'd give it to you right now."

"I can make her tell us," Varu said. His words were all the more terrifying for the blandness with which he uttered them. No hint of threat or promise of power. It was just there.

"I'll get her to talk," Duncan said and tugged her with him. "After rest."

"Weak." Varu shook his head.

Duncan, to her shock, flipped off the vampire. "Go drain a fae."

Varu laughed, surprising her anew.

Orion and Kraft left, walking down a hall off the main living area. Duncan followed, pulling her along with him.

"Where are we going?"

He looked at her but didn't answer.

"Hey, fang-boy. I'm talking to you." Not smart to antagonize him, but Macy didn't like feeling so vulnerable.

The vampires ahead of them turned and watched, a smirk on Orion's face.

Duncan just sighed, which had the others laughing before they disappeared behind doors. Duncan opened one across the hall from them, entered with Macy, and closed it behind them. The snick of the door closing sounded overly loud in the sudden silence.

"The loo's through there if you need it."

She looked at the bathroom doorway then back to him. "I, ah, can I shower?"

Duncan's hooded stare as he looked her over told her nothing. "Go ahead."

She rushed to the door and locked it behind her. Hearing his low chuckle didn't help her feel secure.

Not like a locked door could keep out a vampire if he wanted to get in, but locking it made her feel better. She took her time, letting herself escape the crazy danger of her situation by enjoying the incredible spa bathroom.

After a long, hot shower, she dried herself off and used a hairdryer to dry her hair, surprised Duncan would have one. But she didn't used his brush, not wanting to leave any hair behind that might be used in a spell. So finger-combing was the best she could do. She stared at her sleep shirt and panties on the floor, not wanting to put dirty clothes back on.

Instead, she grabbed a plush robe from the back of the door and sighed at its luxurious feel. Black and soft and overly large, it even smelled like Duncan, a subtle mix of power and sandalwood, like his soap.

She felt funny, close to him, oddly enough, and after grabbing her dirty clothes, let herself out of the bathroom to see him wearing nothing but a pair of dark lounge pants, lying in bed.

He had his hands behind his head on the pillow, looking sleepy and gorgeous in the middle of crisp white sheets, a blanket and duvet pushed to the end of the bed.

"That's my robe," he said in a husky voice.

"I don't have any clean clothes."

He glanced at what she had crumpled in hand and nodded to a side table, where a stack of clothing sat. "Bella brought some things for you."

"Bella?"

"She works for Mormo. She's human."

"Oh." Honestly, Macy wanted to keep wearing the robe. She took the clean clothes and ducked back in the bathroom. A tank top and boxer-like shorts to sleep in. Jersey cotton, the clothing was soft against her skin. But the top clung to her, showing she wore no bra quite clearly.

Should she keep the robe over her clothes?

"Hurry up, witch. I'm tired." Duncan sounded cranky.

She didn't want to annoy him more than she already had, so she hurried to hang up the robe and returned to the bedroom, kicking her dirty clothes into the corner on the floor. He patted the spot next to him on the bed.

She eyed it with trepidation. "Where do I sleep?"

"Right next to me. Or we can put you in the guest room, all tied up, and let Khent watch over you. And if he happens to take a bite, oh well."

Her heart raced. "But you wont?"

"Luv, I'll drink from you for certain. But not now. I need sleep, not food."

It bothered her to be considered food, making her less than human. Or rather, less than a "person" to a vampire.

"You won't touch me, will you?" She swallowed loudly. "I mean, no kissing or ah, anything else while I'm sleeping?"

He huffed. "Rape has never appealed to me. And in any case, I don't need to seduce women to get sex. They come to me like bees to honey."

"More like flies to dung."

"Mouthy witch." His lips twitched. "Either get to bed or I'll think you'd rather be doing something else right now."

Which she would. But Macy knew better. Just because he had sex appeal didn't mean he wasn't a stone cold killer. He was a *vampire,* for heaven's sake.

She needed to get her mind right around him. "Do I have to sleep next to you?"

He didn't show how he felt about her clingy top or shorts. "Yes. And know I'm a light sleeper. You try anything, I'll kill you. I don't want to, but if it's a choice between my life and yours, I'm picking mine."

She swallowed.

"All we want is the grimoire. But there are so many ways to get that information, Macy." The truth in that statement terrified her. "I'd rather we just got some sleep, so you can make better decisions when we wake. Ones where you give us what we want and no one has to get hurt."

He sounded sincere, but she couldn't trust him. Still, what were her choices? Lying next to Duncan in a big, fancy bed or being vulnerable around other vampires who wanted to eat her for dinner.

She slid next to him and pulled the blanket up over her, a pathetic buffer between her and the revenant. Turning her head on the pillow, she saw him staring at her, his eyes so close she could detect bursts of red in his irises. He said nothing, only smiled, then turned his head away and relaxed into sleep.

Macy slowly relaxed with him, her heart easing into a comfortable rhythm as she let herself fall into slumber, warm and oddly happy. And not sure why.

# CHAPTER SIXTEEN

Duncan frowned, alarmed by the clothing he would never in a million years have been caught wearing—a thong under a pair of leather chaps? He moved around, comfortable despite the horrible fashion. But then, what did he care while a nearly naked Macy stood by his side in the middle of... nothing.

His environment disturbed him on every level, yet he was drawn to Macy and the two scraps of fabric barely covering her body. Though he very much appreciated the form-fitting tank and shorts she'd worn to bed, the tiger striped bikini she wore left even less to the imagination, highlighting her full breasts and toned stomach. He thought she looked especially witchy with her wide, amber eyes. Staring beyond him?

He turned to see a large, malevolent shadow under the glare of a bright moon.

Huh. The area all around had been a vague gray, yet now Duncan saw them standing in a drab field surrounded by trees, the moon high overhead. Some distance away, the shadow congealed into a creature grappling with an injured man with long, dark hair.

The creature had the look of a satyr with the legs and ears of a horse, yet it differed in that its muscular torso and arms were covered in gray fur not flesh, its face that of a monster, part goat, part man—all demon—with massive horns curving in spirals toward its head, its eyes overly large, the pupils white and shaped like diamonds against black orbs. All of the hell-beast was covered in black horse hair and gray fur, with coloring to blend into the night.

It seemed to speak to the injured man in a jumble of barks, roars, and a language Duncan didn't understand, hampered by the creature's sharp teeth. Like looking into a shark's mouth, except seeing serrated black teeth in multiple rows.

Macy vanished and appeared right next to it, the man now lying on the ground next to Duncan, the two having apparently switched places.

The hell-beast had a white tongue that flickered as it tried to taste Macy, something she refused to allow, dancing away anytime it grew near.

Annoyed and yes, worried, Duncan tried to go to her, not conscious of anything more important that getting his prey away from a dangerous predator.

Except someone grabbed his ankle.

He blinked down at the man on the ground, flattening the already short grass. He had long, proportionate limbs and a muscular torso and wore a ripped garment wrapped around his waist, what had once been white linen now streaked with smears of gold-colored blood, from the scent of it. That liquid gold put him in mind of eternal rest and unending power. Duncan thought he might be looking down at a god.

The man had long black hair and eyes that brightened into a glowing white, overtaking his irises and pupils. Definitely a deity of some kind.

"I have been waiting long enough," he boomed and pulled himself to his feet using Duncan's body like a ladder. Though Duncan tried to move back, he found himself stuck in place. He scowled, readying to eat the arrogant bastard touching him without permission.

Macy and the beast turned as one, watching Duncan and his new "friend," who continued to grow until he stood twice as tall as he'd been, making him into a giant.

Duncan finally shook off his temporary paralysis and stalked toward Macy. "What are you—"

Before he could finish, the giant jerked him out of the way and leaped at the hell-beast. "Try to capture *me,* will you?" He wound golden bands of power around the beast while they raged at each other, until the creature grew to the size of the giant and laughed while setting him *on fire.*

Definitely time to go.

Macy hurried to Duncan and threw herself into his arms.

Well now, his night was looking up, finally. He patted her back, trying to calm her, enamored with the scent of bloodlust that grew between them. She shoved her face into his neck, and he stroked her hair, aroused and growing more desperate to have her.

Then she struck, biting his neck and sucking down his bloode.

He moaned and ground against her slender body, taken with the scent of her twining around him.

"Out, now," the god snarled and pointed at Duncan and Macy as if *they* were to blame for his predicament, being devoured by the hell-beast. He accompanied the command with a blast that launched them far away. They eventually landed in a raging river, until Duncan could only see the fight as a spec in the distance. But before he and Macy toppled over the waterfall, he swore he heard dark laughter and the promise of eternal damnation.

DUNCAN BLINKED AWAKE, staring at the ceiling in his bedroom while Macy lay on top of him, somehow having gotten under his guard. He should have woken the moment she touched him. Her flat teeth nibbled at his neck, not drawing blood or doing more than making him crazed to have her.

He wrapped an arm around her to hold her in place, pulling her down by the small of her back until his erection found a firm spot, notched between her thighs. As if their thin clothes weren't there, their bodies touched in all the best ways. The sweet scent of her need flowered, and he rolled them over, so that she lay under him.

Her eyes remained closed, and he had an uneasy notion that she didn't know what she was doing, trapped in a spell of someone's making. Witchcraft? A curse?

She opened her eyes and stared at him. "Duncan?" She glanced down at herself. "Oh man. What the heck was I wearing?" Then she looked him over. "And what were *you* wearing?"

He froze. "What?"

"You were wearing chaps, and I was in a bikini, and the god of sleep was battling with a demon. Who won?"

He recalled seeing those same things in his mind's eye, a vision that returned in force, stunning him silent.

"Duncan?"

"You dreamed that?"

"Yes. It was really weird."

"Do you normally dream?"

"Well, yes. I'm human."

"I'm not. Yet I shared a vision with you in a dreamstate." He scowled down at her. "Did you put a spell on me, witch?" She shifted under him, effectively distracting him from being angry. "Do you make me want you like this?"

"Like what?" she asked, breathless, and stared at his mouth. She licked her lips. "I feel you against me."

He glanced between them and saw her nipples through her tank. "I feel you as well." He braced himself on his elbows to keep the majority of his weight from her while pushing more firmly between her legs.

She gasped. "Wh-what are you doing?"

"Giving you what you want." He nipped his lip with a fang, drawing bloode, then leaned down to kiss her. "Taste me." Their mouths met, and after a brief kiss, he pulled back. "Lick it off." The way she'd once licked off his seed.

She stared up at him, the gold flecks in her brown eyes magical. Her tongue darted out to clean the bloode from her mouth. The bond between them snapped taut. He had her, but he didn't want to just take. The seduction would be all the more powerful if she instigated it.

"You taste like chocolate." She blinked at him in shock. "I just drank you. Like in the dream."

"Where you bit me, suckling from my throat. And then you wrapped your magic around me to hold me close." He sat over her, straddling her waist, his erection impossible to miss. "I think it's time you paid the price."

"Price?" she whispered, staring at his crotch, up his torso, and landing on his face. "I don't think I can afford you."

He smiled, pleased with the tricky witch. "Lift your arms."

She did, but slowly, as if unsure about obeying. He tugged her tank top off her, displaying a perfect set of breasts. Pale in color with rose-red areolas stiff with need. He shifted over her and leaned down, watching her expression before he took one peak in his mouth.

Macy cried out, tangling her fingers in his hair, and froze.

He loved that she had to find her control after losing it. He moaned and sucked her nipple, nibbling the sweet flesh and scenting the deepening of her lust. He switched his attention to the other breast, sucking while molding her with his hands. By the Night, she was exquisite, her shape, her softness, drawing him in.

Pulled by need, connected by bloode and blood, he had to

have her. But she was already pushing her shorts down, exposing her sex covered only by a thin strip of dark red hair. Duncan moved down her body and parted her thighs, kicking off his lounge pants as he did so. His dick throbbed, weighted with an urgent need to possess, to pour himself into her.

"Macy Bishop-Dunwich," he said in a low voice, caught in the honeyed trap of her body, the essence of her magic. Her rebellious attitude and the way she refused to give in to fear around him made her so very, very tempting. And he was done waiting.

"Duncan, er, I don't know your last name," she managed, breathing hard as he caressed the insides of her thighs. "Ah, you're touching me."

"And kissing you." He planted kisses along her thighs, sliding his fingers along her slick folds, pleased to find her wet and ready for him. But not ready enough. He pulled back, stroking her sex and watching her. The slumbrous slant of her eyes, the full parted lips, and the rapid beat of her heart entranced him.

"Duncan, please."

"Please what, *witch?*" The word not so much a curse as an invocation of all that was pleasure and desire.

"In me," she whispered and arched up when he thrust a finger inside her.

Duncan had never seen a woman so beautiful, embracing her desire as she gave herself to him. He massaged her clit while pushing his fingers in and out of her. But wanting to do more, he lowered to suck her nipple, tonguing the erect flesh and grazing with the edge of his teeth.

She cried out, coming around his fingers, but it wasn't nearly enough.

"God, yes, oh, Duncan," she moaned and reached for him.

He never rushed, always taking his time with a bedmate. But the urge to fill her stole his ability to restrain himself. He blanketed her body, edging her thighs wider, and kissed her luscious mouth. He hadn't meant to, but seeing her parted pink lips invited the need.

She stole reason and control, spurring only a hunger as she ravaged him as thoroughly as he ravaged her. Duncan couldn't slow down, couldn't wait, and when she wrapped her legs around his waist and dug into his back with her heels, he let himself go.

He thrust deeply inside her and felt absolute bliss. He wanted to savor it, to keep still and let her body hug him tight, but he had to move. He pulled back then shoved deeper inside. In and out. With his cock and his tongue, he possessed her, the feel of her smooth skin against his an all-body caress.

"More, harder," she said on a gasp when he moved to her throat, his only conscious need to appease his thirst. "Bite me," she ordered and dug her fingers into his hair.

Lost, Duncan thrust once more and bit her neck, coming even as he drank down her magic, the very essence of Macy herself.

He dimly heard her shout as she convulsed around him again, lost in the throes of passion.

But he had no awareness of anything but her taste and touch, the blood of his witch more satisfying than life itself.

It took him some time to come back to himself, and when he did, he found himself still hard inside Macy, his fangs no longer buried in her flesh as he kissed her neck and cheek, then her mouth.

She opened for him, her hands stroking his shoulders, the nape of his neck. She shifted and sucked in a breath. "Duncan, you're still hard."

Something that shocked him as well, for even vampires needed a short respite. Usually. With one or two exceptions he didn't want to consider right now. Instead, he rolled over so that she lay on top. Macy pushed herself up, giving him the perfect view of her breasts. He reached up to catch them when they swayed as she shifted to bring her knees under her, still straddling his body, his cock buried inside her.

In this position, he felt thicker, gripped harder. She must have felt it as well, for her eyes widened and she clutched his chest. "Duncan, you feel *huge*."

He grinned. "Is that a statement or question?"

"But how?"

"I'm a vampire. And a worlds-class lover. Yes, I said *worlds*."

She huffed, a hint of humor in the quirk of her mouth and warm eyes. "No lack of ego in you."

"Ah, I see."

"What?"

"You haven't been properly pleasured yet." The thought of filling her once more overwhelmed him.

"Your eyes are *red*."

"I'm in lust, and you're making it difficult to remember why I shouldn't kill you for putting a spell on me." He barely knew what he was saying, enamored with his red-haired witch—no, his prey. He had to remember... Her breasts moved, and he dragged her down to take a plump nipple in his mouth.

"Duncan," she moaned. "No spell. This is just chemistry."

He growled, felt her shiver, and surged up, trying to get deeper inside her.

Macy gasped and squirmed over him, then pulled back and began riding him, up and down. She put her hands in her hair, holding that waterfall of fire back, her throat bare and unmarked, and the sight of that pale canvas bothered him. His fangs should be there, marking her, that no one might mistake her for anything but his.

Duncan reached between them to massage her sex, finding the hard little bud and working his own magic, needing her desperate, on fire. For him.

She moved faster, slamming down harder, and he snarled,

losing himself to the dance, a passion he'd never before felt now all-consuming. He committed his senses to memory—the sight of her body, the scent of her passion, the taste of her cream over his lips, the sounds of her desire as she cried his name.

He rocked up and came, jetting into her as she squeezed him tight. With a roar, he sat up and held her in his arms, still coming, and thrust his elongated fangs into her neck. The decadent flavor of witch and lover mingled with his bloode, and he drank until full.

Duncan retracted his fangs and laid his head on her racing heart, beating in time with his own, he realized. Odd but not unknown between trusting partners.

But they weren't that. Not yet?

He had no words and hugged her to him, conscious of the mess he'd made. He wouldn't have gotten her with child unless intent on the deed, and he'd been about nothing but passion. The need to possess her had been a desperation to satisfy carnal hungers. Nothing more.

So he told himself. And when she hugged him back and sighed his name, he convinced himself the spark of warmth in his heart had nothing to do with affection and everything to do with satisfaction. Maybe he'd keep the witch for a while after they got the grimoire.

Yes, he would. Because this was the start of a passion he craved. And the quench of a thirst he'd had for a very, very long time.

# CHAPTER SEVENTEEN

Macy didn't know what to think as they finally disentangled. Duncan lifted her in his arms and took her to the bathroom. She would have complained about being able to walk herself in, but she liked a man holding her. Even if said man wasn't a man at all, but a vampire.

Curious, she held herself back to see what he might do.

He said little, just small commands telling her to turn or close her eyes while he soaped up her hair. He used his shampoo and soap on her, and knowing she'd smell like him after getting clean gave her butterflies.

*I'm not crushing on a vampire,* she told herself. She barely knew the guy. So they'd shared some hot times and a dream. No biggie, right?

Macy didn't do insta-love. Heck, she barely dated. And this situation had her all backward. Acting fierce, using a freaking grimoire, taunting vampires. It was like she didn't know herself anymore.

Warm lips caressed her shoulder, a hungry vampire at her back.

He whispered her name, and she shivered.

"Macy, the dream.... That's our little secret, hmm?"

"Sure," she said, her head bent forward as the water sluiced over her and his hands ran a washcloth in circles over her back and belly. In his arms, she did as she was told, feeling cared for despite, or maybe because of, what he was. The warm spray of water from above and mist from the side jets felt soothing. He turned her to face the wall and nudged her ankles wider, brushing against her backside with a thick cock.

Everything inside her screamed *Hell, yes.*

"Good little witch," he said with a chuckle and pushed inside her again, feeling huge from behind. "Oh, luv, you're so warm." He raked sharp teeth over her shoulder but didn't tear her skin, only made her more sensitive to every brush of his body against hers. "So tight."

He continued to saw in and out of her. This a fast, determined taking. "Touch yourself," he growled. "Come all over me."

She rubbed and he thrust, their harmony perfectly in sync. Before she could blink, she was coming, and he was spilling inside her, his grip on her waist bound to leave bruises. He'd made her insatiable. She'd had sex a bunch of times and it had to be just past sunrise.

*No. Sunset. You're with vampires now.*

She flushed, tingling from the kisses he pressed over her throat and cheek, turning her head to meet his mouth.

Duncan satisfied her as no man ever had. What did that say about Macy that she preferred vampires to humans? She didn't care at the moment, missing him when he withdrew then set to cleaning them both all over again.

Much later, she found a set of clothing in her size on the bed and dressed in it, conscious of Duncan watching her slither into the white lace bra and panties with interest.

"You can't possibly want to have sex again?"

He just smiled, and she laughed, finding him charming despite what she knew of his kind. Duncan seemed so different. Was it all an act?

"What's that look, witch?"

She flushed, trying to ignore the way "witch" sounded like a term of endearment coming from his lips. "You. You're confusing."

"Ah." He smiled but said nothing more.

"Your fangs seem to grow then recess." She stared at him. "But they're always there."

"They get longer when I'm hungry." He smiled. "Or aroused by a beautiful witch."

"You're charming me. On purpose."

"Of course."

"The others would have threatened or bitten me. You could have seduced me." Her eyes narrowed. No, he hadn't vamped her with his innate power. His allure was on the up and up and came not from any revenant ability, but from Duncan himself.

"I could have but didn't. Because you seduced me first. Be honest, Macy, you want me."

"Sure. Why not?"

He cocked his head, now studying her.

"What?"

"You're a tough one to make out." He pursed his lips. "First you run from me. Then you put a spell on me. Then you kiss me like you're dying and I'm all that's left between you and life. What's a gent to do but see to what a lady wants?"

She snorted. "You're no gentleman."

"And you're no lady." He buttoned up his shirt and tucked it into jeans, which should have made him look goofy. Instead, he paired the jeans with loafers, no socks, and a black sportscoat and looked like a million bucks. "But that's why I like you."

"I'm no lady?" Why didn't she feel insulted?

"Gor, no." His accent thickened. "Luv, I'd rather drain a woman with conviction than a lady out for nothing but fashion and flitting about on the arm of a man." He sighed. "Although hunting was a lot easier a hundred years ago. But not so much a challenge. Not like today." He grinned. "And there's nothing quite like taking a witch from behind and coming hard inside a warm quim."

She flushed, having read enough historical romances to know quim and pussy meant the same thing. "Nice mouth."

"Not nearly as nice as yours." He chuckled, and she saw a flash of fang that, for some reason, she now thought of as sexy. *Gah. I'm losing my mind! We had sex. That's it. Get over it.*

"Are you done?"

"You know, for a redhead, you look good with a blush."

She let him lead her out of his room and down the hall. "Wait. So you're saying redheads look terrible when blushing?" Talk about insulting.

"Yeah, sometimes." He took her to the kitchen, passing the glassed doors of the dining area, through which she saw the moon hiding behind clouds.

"Hey, Duncan. Why do you have all this glass around? It lets in the light."

"We're protected from sunlight by a spell. A powerful spell," he warned. "So don't try to fry me with sunlight. Hecate crafted the spells on the house."

"You think I'd try to kill you after—after before?"

"After before. If I didn't know your context, I might be confused. And yeah, sure, you'd try to gank me no matter how great the sex was. I'm a vampire. A greater species. Your kind has always wanted to eradicate its betters."

She studied him, watching as he grabbed a glass of something from the refrigerator. "You don't seem bothered I might want to kill you."

"Why would I be? Death is kind of my calling card." He winked at her. "Hungry?"

Death and breakfast. What the hell, why not? "Got any yogurt? Or maybe some eggs and bacon?"

"Sure." He reached into the fridge again and pulled out a plate of scrambled eggs and bacon with a cup on yogurt on the side. He set the plate in front of her and added silverware.

Though the plate came out of the refrigerator, the eggs and bacon were both hot and delicious. She didn't speak until she'd finished it all. Great sex made her hungry, apparently. "Don't tell me, magic," she said as she pushed the plate aside and accepted an orange juice from Duncan. "Thank you."

"You're welcome." He paused. "Juice is especially helpful for blood donors. Drink up, buttercup."

"Ass."

He smiled wider, and she had the feeling he liked her being aggravated with him. What a contrary vampire.

She sipped and watched him watching her, the two of them battling a visual duel she was determined to win. Until a creature from legend walked into the kitchen with a pretty young woman and distracted her.

"Hi. You must be Macy. I'm Bella. I run things around here for Mr. Mormo." The pleasant woman looked to be about Macy's age, if a few years younger. Tall, lively, and human. "This is Onvyr."

"Hello." Onvyr nodded at her with a smile, opened the oven—that wasn't on—and withdrew a platter of meat and vegetables that sizzled. He stood a little taller than Duncan, wore jeans and a tee-shirt that clung to his broad chest, and looked completely alien. Black skin the color of night, long white hair, purple eyes with arched brows, and fine, handsome features capped with high-set, pointed ears said *elf*.

"Dark elf." He pointed to himself. "But this is my nighttime look. I'm a dusk elf. Never seen one of us before?"

She noticed Duncan frowning but didn't care. "I'm so sorry to stare. But no, I haven't seen an elf before. A few fae at work, but not much more than that. Sprites and an elemental, I think."

"Ah." He nodded. "Fun but nothing to write home about."

She blinked.

Bella grinned. "He's funny. You should see him do tricks."

"Oh? Like what?" Duncan asked and moved closer to Macy.

"I'm working on card tricks." The elf patted his back pocket. "But I forgot the deck downstairs. Hey, what's the deal with rumors that someone found a kitten?"

"He also talks to animals," Bella confided to Macy. "It's so cute."

"It's just adorable," Duncan drawled, "when he's not trying to chop our heads off."

Onvyr sighed, the huge, broad-shouldered male with large, graceful hands looking not as pathetic as he might have wished. "I —" He leaned closer to Macy, looked at Duncan, and laughed. "Ah, I see." Then his laughter vanished and he asked, "Do you want me to kill him?"

She blinked. "Kill who?"

"The revenant. If he bothers you, let me know and I'll rip his head off."

"Um, thanks. Will do." She smiled when he patted her on the shoulder.

Bella cleared her throat, and Onvyr turned to her. "Yes?"

She pointed at his platter. "Your food's going to get cold."

"Oh, right." His good mood restored, the dark elf—dusk elf—tucked into his plate, eating enough for a family of four.

"He's not actually dark all the time," Bella said as she sat across from Macy at the kitchen island. "He's a dusk elf. That means he's both dark and light. When the sun rises, his skin turns white and his hair black. It's pretty cool to see."

Onvyr didn't react, continuing to eat with a smile on his face.

Duncan scooted Macy farther from the happy eater, keeping a wary eye on the fae. Because he might be jealous or he worried about Onvyr's danger? Obviously the latter. *A vampire get jealous? Get real.*

"So, what are you two up to today?" Bella asked after brewing a pot of coffee.

"I have to get to work." Crap. She'd missed her workday, and she hadn't checked in with Cho. "We might have a problem."

Duncan shrugged. "Nothing we can't handle."

"I work for MEC," she said plainly, something he already knew.

"And?"

"And they know about you guys."

"Again, and?"

She frowned. "You should be a little concerned. We police all the magir in the city and are headquarters for all MEC concerns in the Pacific Northwest."

"Still not impressed."

Onvyr chuckled. "Not much bothers Duncan. He's the chillest vampire in the clan if you don't count Rolf. And Rolf isn't exactly chill. More like silly."

That was a first. A silly vampire?

"He's a goofball." Bella nodded. "Plays a ton of pranks and can do magic. It's a lose-lose situation with him."

"Oh?" No. She refused to get distracted. "Hold on. Duncan, MEC should concern you."

"Why? We rule the players in this town," Duncan said.

Mormo appeared out of nowhere and scared her half to death, not having expected *Gandalf* to appear in front of her with no warning.

"Hi there, Macy. Nice to see Duncan has been taking care of you."

"He's been such a gracious host, not devouring me yet."

"Well, there's eating and there's devouring, but we'll get there soon. I swear," Duncan said with a sly grin.

"Real mature," she snapped, knowing her cheeks likely looked as red as a tomato.

Bella coughed. Onvyr snickered.

Mormo rolled his eyes. "Do you see what I have to deal with on a daily basis?" He motioned to Duncan. "In my office."

"Seriously? Another invitation to the most holy of places?" Duncan snorted. "I spent nearly a year trying to see where you work."

"With no success, I know. We have things to talk about." Mormo looked to Macy. "Well? Let's go." He nodded for Duncan to join him, and the two left the kitchen, talking in low voices.

Macy stood and gratefully took the coffee Bella handed her. "Thanks."

"I put some hazelnut creamer in there too." She added in a whisper, "Helps to have a bit of sweet when dealing with Mr. Mormo."

"I heard that," Mormo called back. "Let's go, Macy."

She hurried toward them, her coffee in hand, and ignored Duncan's raised brow. Following Mormo and his long white robe, she walked down another corridor and upstairs, wondering at what didn't seem to fit.

When they reached a large landing, opening to a wide space broken up only by occasional pieces of furniture, she realized what bothered her. "This shouldn't be here."

"Oh?" Mormo led them to a long table covered with ancient books and scattered papers.

"This level. The house has a main level with the lower level even with the ground. There is no second floor. Technically, a main floor and basement, right?"

Mormo grinned. "In my mistress's domain, anything is possible."

"Your mistress?" She wanted to hear it from him.

"Hecate. Your goddess."

"Is that why I feel so at ease here?"

He nodded. "That and Hecate broke your link to the grimoire. At least, partially."

"What?" she and Duncan asked at the same time.

Macy frowned and asked, "Is that why I've been acting unlike myself?"

"How so?" Mormo shuffled a few papers aside and sat at the table.

Across from him, Macy sat as well, and Duncan sat beside her.

"I'm not a super aggressive person."

Duncan snorted.

"I'm not," she said. "I'm great at casting spells and making incantations, but I don't use them much. I make them for other people."

"Why?" Duncan frowned. "You have the power."

"Now I do. But before the grimoire, I was just a big reservoir of energy. By the time I craft something, that energy is tapped and needs time to rebuild. So I can't power my spells."

Mormo studied her, his dark pupils circled with bands of silver and gold. "That's very odd. Something I've rarely encountered with witches."

"My parents tried for a long time to fix me, but nothing worked until I found the grimoire."

Mormo leaned forward. "How did you find it?"

She'd wanted so many times before to share with Cho and hadn't. Or couldn't. Now that she thought about it, her mind and spirit felt freer here. Unshackled, in fact. "I share everything with my best friend. But I couldn't share this before."

"The grimoire is a power unto itself. Its current occupant has a definite way about him."

"Huh?"

"How did you find it?" Duncan asked. "We need to know."

She shrugged. "I was walking to meet friends after work one day. A few months ago. I don't know. I felt a pull to check out this antique store downtown. But when I went in, the owner, an older mage, was being robbed by a human. The mage was shot just as I managed to throw an emergency charm at the thief. So the human saw nothing. But the mage... The book absorbed his blood. I knew it was bad news. He tried to get me to take it away, but then he freaked out. I don't think he wanted me to have it."

Mormo watched her. "Did your blood mix with the book?"

"Yes. I was wearing a scarf, and when I took it off to stop the mage's bleeding, I managed to prick my finger with my scarf pin. In the craziness, it was just one more thing that happened. But then the book took my blood too. Just a drop." She looked at the finger where she'd been pricked. "I tucked the book in my bag and left. Outside the shop, I managed to call MEC and warned them about a dead body. But I never told them about the book or handed it over." She frowned. "And then I started using it."

"To do what, exactly?" Mormo asked.

She swallowed and refused to look at Duncan. "Just learning at first. Then the book seemed to push me toward certain pages. I used it to bespell Duncan." She sighed and turned to him. "I'm sorry. I just wanted to get out of S&I, to get into Enforcement or something better than being a magic nerd. Bringing them information on vampires seemed just the thing for a promotion."

He didn't respond with a smile, as she'd hoped. He just looked at her with a flat gaze.

She swallowed. "You guys are a big deal. New vamps in

town? If I can get info back to MEC, I'll advance. Probably." She ran a hand through her hair, agitated because her plans didn't seem to be working. "Then, before I knew it, I was using the grimoire more often. To make better, stronger spells. To create a well of my own, so I could use some of the spells I'd drafted. Like this really cool dread spell, that..." she tapered off.

Neither Mormo nor Duncan looked impressed.

"Then, um, I used it to fog a upir's memory a few days ago. And I did it again Wednesday night with my boss. He's a pretty powerful witch, but he forgot everything I told him to. And wings," she added, liking that spell. "The book wanted me to learn to levitate, but instead I grew wings."

Duncan's eyes narrowed. "Is that why you have that tattoo on your back? I thought it looked a little like wings, but then, from a different angle, the ink looks like Enochian script."

"*What?*" Her heart threatened to beat out of her chest. "I don't have any tattoos."

"Yes, you do." Duncan turned her back toward Mormo and lifted her shirt up.

"Ah, I see. You've been marked by the resident in the grimoire."

That was the second mention of something living in the book, but it would have to wait. She had *a tattoo?* "What are you talking about? I thought Enochian was a made-up language. Something a bunch of ignorant sixteenth century religious folks created."

Mormo nodded. "Yes and no. In 1581, Dr. John Dee wrote in his journals that God had sent him 'good angels' to communicate directly with prophets. The next year, he teamed up with a seer named Edward Kelly to scry for him. Together, they established a language of the occult—the Enochian alphabet."

He paused. "However, what *really* happened is a bunch of drunk angels and demons got together to screw with humans.

They gave Dee a few actual insights into communicating with the Hell and Heavenly realms along with some mish-mashed characters."

"By mish-mashed, you mean pretend letters," Duncan clarified.

"Yes. But a few of those letters were real and did connect humans with magic to other realms. The letters on Macy's back reveal real Enochian script and spell a certain name."

"Do I want to know?" she asked, terrified to be marked by something evil.

"Probably not, but you should." Mormo sighed. "It's Abaddon."

"Wait. *What?*" she screeched.

"I hate when you do that." Duncan wiggled a finger in his ear.

"Duncan, Mr. Mormo said 'Abaddon.' Do you have any idea who that is?"

"First of all, it's just Mormo. No 'mister' needed."

"Hey." Mormo frowned. "I like the mister."

"Secondly, yes. I know of Abaddon. He's a supposed heavy-hitter of a hell realm, and his presence is a portent of doom. So what?"

Macy just stared at him, conscious Mormo was looking at Duncan with real interest. She enunciated in case he'd misunderstood. "He's a bringer of *doom,* Duncan. Torture, damnation, destruction."

"Chaos." Mormo nodded.

"Yeah, he's a bad guy." She worked to hold back the tears. "And he put his mark on my body."

"He's just a demon. He's not a vampire." Duncan shrugged. His lack of concern stunned her.

"Duncan, I don't think you understand."

"He's got a magic book we need to get rid of. That's what I understand." He stood. "I'm going to grab Varu. Together, we'll smite this fucker, free you from his tyranny, and stake me a new pet." He rubbed his hands and smiled down at her. "Relax, luv. You're in good hands. I take the best care of my things." He shot Mormo a warning look. "Mine." He nodded at Macy then left.

She didn't know what had happened. "Does he not understand who we're up against? Abaddon is bad news. Mormo, the things I can do with that book are unnatural and likely destructive beyond measure."

Mormo groaned. "My dear, what you don't yet understand is that vampires consider the rest of us beneath them."

"No, I get that." She frowned. Did Duncan still think her a lesser being even after their mind-bending sex? He couldn't, could he?

"To Duncan and the others, Abaddon will represent a challenge they assume they'll overcome. Pain and violence are second nature to them." The magician watched her carefully. "They are a possessive, territorial, violent species. And they hold tightly to what they consider theirs."

"I get that." She thought over what Duncan had said. "Um, when Duncan mentioned a new pet, what was he talking about, exactly?" Had he referred to her as a "thing" he'd take care of? No, she had to be wrong about that.

Mormo just looked at her. "You know."

"He thinks I'm going to agree to be *a pet?*" To her surprise, she felt more insulted over that than scared of battling a demon of Abaddon's caliber.

"To Duncan, there is no choice to be had. I believe he already considers you his." Mormo's lips quirked.

"You've got to be fucking kidding me."

"Yep. Never a dull moment around here living with vampires."

## CHAPTER EIGHTEEN

Duncan finally had a handle on things. They had to kick a demon lord's ass, then, bam, success and he'd get to keep his witch until he tired of her. The perfect ending to this mess with the grimoire. He liked things neat and tidy. And speaking of which, he really needed to talk to his uncle about certain spells affecting vampires.

He found Varu having a discussion with Fara about her brother.

"Onvyr means well," Fara was saying. She sat in the room she'd turned into her laboratory. With pale gray skin, dark hair, and fine, pretty features, she looked the way he'd picture a dusk elf to look, like a combination of her parents. An elf who specialized in power gems, she was also an expert when it came to nature, anything fae, and rocks of all kinds. Her brother, though, needed some time in one of those human hospitals to heal the mind. One far away from here.

He knew Varu felt the same, but the sorry sod would do anything for his mate, to include counting a bloody dusk elf warrior as kin. A mate, Duncan understood. The mate's brother? Not so much.

"He's a menace, Fara, and you know it."

"Well, yes. He's an elven warrior. They're all a menace."

Varu's lips twitched. "Okay, that's true."

"I promise. He's getting better."

"What happened?" Duncan asked as he entered the lab filled with plants and natural woods, the light tan walls making the space brighter, the paths of stone set in the floor a kind of massage for the feet that also promoted clearer reflection. He thought it nonsense, but Fara practically lived in the place when not tied to Varu.

Fara flushed, her pale gray cheeks turning a shade of lavender that looked lovely. Almost as pretty as a certain red-haired witch. "Onvyr accidentally—"

"Purposefully," Varu growled.

"—kind of almost chopped Khent's arm off."

"That's all?" Duncan leaned against the wall, growing more amused as Varu growled and Fara offered excuses for her kooky brother.

"He didn't mean to." Fara glared at her mate. "He was aiming for Khent's dead birds. And you know Khent keeps siccing them on Onvyr. Khent started it."

"He wasn't aiming for Khent's arm. He was aiming for Khent's neck, but Khent moved at the last minute."

"Well, there, see?" Duncan nodded to Fara. "It's Khent's fault for not having better awareness. Lesson learned."

Fara beamed at him, and Duncan smiled back, feeling a debt to the dusk elf he could never repay. Because of her, they'd been able to kill Varu's father, a nightmare of a beast who would have destroyed the world if left to it. Fara had sacrificed herself for kin, and no one ever did that. She had earned her place in the Night Bloode and deserved the most powerful among them as a mate.

Which also meant dealing with Varu's lofty attitude and inability to relax, the poor girl.

Duncan sighed. "Varu, take the stick out of your arse—"

"Don't you mean ass?" Fara teased.

"—ass, thank you, and leave your mate and her brother be. We've got a demon problem."

Varu scowled. "You're not very deferential."

None of them were. Unlike most vampires, who clung to tradition and treated their lieutenants, patriarchs, and masters with reverence, none of the Night Bloode were of the same tribe, and all of them had a cheeky attitude they carried from their respective homes.

Duncan, though the most affable, still had no intention of treating Varu like a god. He huffed. Gods—and goddesses—were *such* a headache. "Bite me, Hecate," he muttered as they walked out of Fara's room.

"What's that?" Varu asked.

"Nothing." But Duncan swore he heard an echo of laughter trail them to Mormo's landing.

Once there, he spotted Macy sitting backwards in her chair, facing away from Mormo, her shirt hiked up her back to expose her tattoos.

Mormo waved them over when he spotted them. "See this? It looks like an Enochian 'Veh' overlying an 'Ur,' but the symbol is actually a signature. A blending of 'Geyh,' 'Nuv,' and 'Ptset'."

"I've never heard of those letters."

"Because they're real, not doctored by John Dee and Edward Kelly." Mormo traced his finger over the marks, and Macy hissed in pain.

Duncan moved between them in a flash and growled at Mormo. "What the hell are you doing?"

Varu looked from Duncan to Macy and narrowed his eyes but remained quiet.

"That shouldn't hurt her. I didn't rip open her flesh." Mormo held up a finger, showing no blood or claw, just a short, sharp nail. "It's my binding to Hecate that causes her pain."

"But I'm bound to my goddess," Macy said, her breath hitching.

Duncan didn't understand. "I think you need to tell us exactly what happened with this grimoire, Hecate, and Abaddon."

"Yes, please do explain," Varu said.

Mormo glanced at him. "It's not exactly my story to tell."

"Before that, how about healing her?" Duncan insisted, pointing at Macy's back. The markings looked enflamed.

"How about you heal her?" Mormo suggested.

"Fine."

"Uh, Duncan?" Macy tried to pull her shirt down.

Duncan wasn't having it. He lifted her in his arms and sped down to his room, closing them in privacy. He settled her face-down on the bed, careful not to hurt her. That her creamy skin might be marred didn't bear thinking about. Enraged and trying to figure out why, he stared at the raised welts starting to fade, and kissed the marks.

He used his saliva to heal, planting gentle kisses all along her back until nothing but those tattooed glyphs remained. Then he tugged her shirt down.

She slowly turned over and stared at him with wide eyes, her hair mussed around her face.

He couldn't look away.

"Thank you." She gave him a half-smile.

He nodded. "My pleasure."

She sat up, and he waited for a kiss. Maybe a quickie out of gratitude. More soft words?

The slap across his face shocked him speechless.

"If you think I'll ever let a man call me his pet, or be treated as some stupid lesser being, you are seriously in for a world of hurt." She seethed, her eyes glowing, and stormed out of the room in a blaze of righteous anger.

He just stared, awed at her temerity, amused, and charmed, by all that was bloode. He laughed as he made his way back up the stairs to Mormo's den. But when he got there, he couldn't look anywhere but at the witch who'd slapped him. Not his pet, she'd said.

*We'll see about that.*

MORMO SIGHED. "I *said* it's not my story to tell." He waited.

Varu studied Macy, who glared at Duncan, who grinned at her like an idiot.

"She smells like you," Varu said to Duncan.

"She's mine."

"I am *not*," Macy growled.

Varu considered her. "She's right."

Macy nodded.

"We should see if the others bond with her. Give her to Khent. He's been dying to bring a witch back to life."

Duncan smirked. "But he's already got enough pets."

"True." Varu seemed to ignore Macy's obvious anger toward the revenant. If looks could kill, Duncan would be one true-dead vampire right about now. "Maybe Rolf could use her in ritual sacrifice. He keeps trying to make some deals with the gods in his lands, but Loki's not talking to him. Something about a prank gone wrong."

Both vampires sighed. Mormo felt for them. Everyone had had enough of the draugr's practical jokes. Though Kraft hitting himself in the face with whipped cream a few weeks ago had been inspired.

Macy, listening to the vampires, looked a little less annoyed.

"How about Orion?" Duncan asked Varu. "He thinks she's attractive and isn't that messy a feeder. I'm sure he could keep her alive for a few months, at least."

"Not a bad idea."

Macy scowled. "Oh, shut up. Duncan claimed me. I'm his." She wiped a finger across her throat and pointed at Duncan. "For now."

"So feisty. Must be the demon inside you." He paused, and a self-satisfied grin lit him up like a star. "Or the demon that *was* inside you."

Varu turned to hide a smile.

Mormo blinked in shock. Now Varu was smiling? Showing emotion? Talk about the positive effects of a mate. Just like the way Duncan was starting to thaw with his kin, accepting the others more even if he didn't yet realize it. Mormo could feel his heart warming to them.

"Shut it, blabbermouth. What are you, twelve?" Macy muttered, bright red.

"More like two hundred and two." He coughed to hide a grin.

A godly warmth unfurled within Mormo, a feeling of peace and belonging. Mixed with a sizzle of witchcraft and death.

*Finally.*

A spark of light lit the corner of his grand office, and Hecate appeared, wearing an often used form. Tonight, the threefold goddess of witchcraft—Maiden, Mother, and Crone—took the form of the crone, a wizened woman with long braided hair, threaded with white, skin aged with spots and wrinkles, her body stooped, the beauty of her wisdom shining in her eyes and overtaking the decay of age in her body. She wore a dark robe with a circlet over her forehead, the stone missing.

"Duncan, sweetheart, you have something that belongs to me and mine." The crone smiled and held out a hand.

He reached into his pocket and pulled out a golden stone Mormo hadn't seen before. "I wasn't going to keep it." To Mormo he said, "I found it in the supreme witch's office at MEC."

Mormo watched him and knew Duncan was lying. He'd totally meant to keep it.

"Of course not." Hecate delivered the stone to her crown, where it must have belonged.

Macy, who stood with her mouth open, watched Hecate with awe and reverence.

She had tears in her eyes and bowed. "Hecate, my goddess, I—"

"Relax, child. I'm here to help and to visit my boys."

Macy straightened and stared, dumbstruck.

Next to him, Varu scowled. Duncan broadcast the same irritation.

"Not yours, you old bat," Varu said, causing Macy and Mormo to gasp.

Hecate only grinned, showing a missing tooth. She had the nerve to cackle like the witch goddess she was. "See what I mean, Macy? Aren't they cute?"

Showboating. Mormo tsked.

Duncan coughed. "While it's always lovely to have you visiting above the basement, mind telling us what the fuck is going on with the grimoire and the demon trapped inside it?"

"Abaddon." Mormo nodded. "He's already marked her."

"I knew it. First Bloode Witch in centuries." Hecate rubbed her hands together, the joints gnarled, the nails yellowed with age. "Have a seat, my lovelies. Tea?"

Duncan didn't seem to mind this turn of events. "Why, yes, please."

"So polite." She said in an overloud voice, "You're my favorite."

"Christ, can we get on with this?" Varu sat at the table Mormo had cleared.

Macy tried to hide a chuckle, but Duncan saw it. And the sparkle in the revenant's eyes meant that Mormo's plan was coming together very well. *Better than I'd thought it might,* he sent to Hecate.

*I told you so. Now hush so I can watch this play out.*

DUNCAN STARED AT MACY, enchanted with her attitude. That she could sit with such powerful creatures and not be scared out of her mind, that she could challenge *him*, Duncan of the Night Bloode, son of Edward of the Tizona Clan, impressed the hell out of him. And she'd thought herself weak before the demon book found her?

As if she'd read his mind, she asked Hecate, "Am I me? Or have I been possessed since getting the grimoire?"

They paused as Bella arrived to deliver a tray of tea and cookies. She smiled at everyone but gave Hecate a special wave.

"Such a sweet girl," Hecate said as Bella left, taking Macy's cold coffee with her. "Duncan, be a dear and pour."

He poured them all cups of tea, conscious the teapot never felt lighter or ran out, and that the biscuits, scones, and clotted cream continued to remain on the tray, no matter how many they served Mormo and Macy.

Varu didn't take any. Duncan, however, wanted a scone. It had been a while since he'd eaten one. To his surprised, it tasted scrummy.

"Why are you eating?" Varu asked.

"Reminds me of home." What *used* to be home. He glanced at Macy.

"This is fabulous," she said with her mouth full. "What kind of tea is this?" She took it with two cubes of sugar and a dollop of milk.

"Earl Grey," Duncan said. "My favorite."

"Oh? Not blood tea? Or virgin tears tea? How about a brew of death and dismemberment?" she asked, snarky as hell.

He grinned. "Why? Know any virgins who might cry for me?"

"You're so full of yourself."

"Of course I am. I'm Duncan of the Night Bloode." Odd how easily his ties to his clan rolled off his tongue. *New* clan, he reminded himself.

Hecate cleared her throat. "To answer your question, Macy, you've always been you. Until you memorized spells from the grimoire. Then that was Abaddon, working through you. He wants your body."

"Don't we all," Duncan murmured.

Macy flipped him off, which caused Varu to cough, suddenly. "As a vessel? He wants to possess me and use me?"

"Yes. Kind of." Mormo poured Hecate a new cup of tea, since she'd finished her first. "He's a powerful demon who wants more than anything to cause chaos."

Varu looked from Mormo to Hecate and sat straighter in his seat. "Chaos, eh? Is this like the Darkness you keep talking about, Mormo?"

"A part, surely." He nodded. "You know we gathered you six for a reason. The Darkness that comes wants to create chaos, which will ensure a mass extermination of humanity and magir, throwing us into a new Dark Age. The last time this happened, the gods created new gods and heroes to vanquish Chaos. And now the Darkness takes many forms to work its way into the weakest of all the realms—the human plane."

"Wait a minute." Macy paled. "Hold on. I thought we were talking about Abaddon and the grimoire. This all sounds a lot more complicated than markings on my back."

Hecate nodded, her eyes sad. But she looked at Duncan, not Macy, when she said, "Oh, it's very complicated. Change is coming, and it's not going to be good. Bonds are breaking, lights are dimming, and love is the most fragile link of all. Without a strong chain to hold us tight, we will break. And we will fall."

# CHAPTER NINETEEN

Macy looked from the vampires to Mormo and Hecate, confused and starting to feel the heaviness of what she was hearing. They said meeting your idols never turned out well, but she couldn't remember ever feeling so warm and loved as she did right now. To Hecate, she'd pledged her heart and soul. And she continued to feel the right of that pledge.

She trembled, still not believing she'd met *Hecate*. And Mormo, who served his mistress. *The* Mormo? She'd thought the name a coincidence, but he existed. In this plane. It boggled the mind.

But all this talk of chaos and bad stuff coming was too heavy to handle.

As if sensing her distress, Duncan put a hand on her shoulder, and damned if she didn't feel better, which made little sense.

"Let's start at the beginning," Varu suggested.

She nodded with the others, though she didn't know how she felt about their patriarch. Of all the vampires she'd met, Varu truly frightened her. So much power in that inhuman gaze that seemed to see everything. She had no doubt he'd kill her in a heartbeat if he deemed it necessary, and he wouldn't feel badly about it either.

How could MEC hope to police creatures without conscience? Who didn't heed goddesses? Yet Hecate seemed to like them well enough.

"Ah, the beginning." Hecate settled back in her chair. "Quick recap—our universe exists across several planes. The fae live in a world apart from valkyries, and they live in a realm apart from the Amazons, who live in yet another realm apart from the gods, and so on and so on. We have hell worlds, fae worlds, magic worlds, places where the dead are more common than the living. But they're all connected. I guard the doorways, the crossover passages, and I keep peace between the living and the dead."

Mormo nodded. "My mistress is order, a system that connects and makes right the balance. Now, there are many deities who do as much to make the balance even, but they do not understand the essence that is magic and death. Not like Hecate."

"We all have our roles to play. My part is to monitor the Between. I have done so for thousands of years, after the first battle, when Chaos came and took everything apart. We succeeded in throwing the Darkness far from us. But it's coming back, and it uses our own hands to do the most damage."

Varu nodded. "Vampires were created a long time ago, a result of gods cursing a mortal. For years, we had no one to rein us in, and we flourished."

"And grew too powerful." Duncan shrugged. "We're a race born of violence and death. Our hearts beat to circulate the magic in our bloode, but we don't draw breath, and we can sustain damage that most living creatures cannot. Some of us can even live through a beheading."

Macy's jaw dropped when Duncan glanced at Varu.

"We were drawn here for a reason," Varu continued, looking

at Macy. "To find and contain the danger of the Bloode Stones. So the Darkness can't use us."

"The what? I've heard you all talking about them. But I've never heard of them."

"You might know them as Ambrogio's Tears," Varu said.

She frowned. "You mean, Ambrogio, the ancestor of the vampires? The guy who got kicked out of the divine plane for falling in love with the wrong girl? She turned out to be Apollo's sister, and when her love fell, she fell with him, shared her blood, then created a race of monsters." She blushed. "Sorry, I meant, a race of vampires."

"Monsters, yes." Varu added, "The vampires grew too strong, so Apollo and a bunch of other gods cursed our kind to never get along except in small groups, and to make nothing but male vampires, to limit our abilities to pass on genetic traits."

"Correct." Duncan nodded. "And I quote, 'And when the great Ambrogio first fell upon the earth, bereft of his mate, whom he'd thought he'd never see again, he cried. And his tears fell as bloode upon the earth, and six stones burst forth.'"

Mormo frowned. "It was drops of bloode, not tears."

"But it's so much more romantic if he was crying for his mate, dearest." Hecate smiled.

Varu talked over them. "And the stories go that with those six stones, peace will fall upon the vampire race. The Blood Empire will unite and rule the worlds."

"Worlds?" Macy blinked.

Duncan gave her a dark smile. "Yes. Not just the human one, but eventually we'll consume the others as well."

"The first wave of chaos," Hecate said softly. "But we're on to that plan, and we're doing our best to stop it from happening."

"Are you serious?" Macy thought of the horrors that would befall the world if vampires started working together. They were bad enough in small numbers.

"Very." Hecate swirled the tea in her cup. "That's a threat we're still working to contain. But the threads of Darkness are constantly moving, weaving, creating new drama. And in comes Doom, the great demon lord Abaddon.

"Several centuries ago, I learned of a book. It was guarded in the Hell plane, a grimoire capable of such evil, such power. The King of the West guarded it, well away from any who might take it to use against those in his world.

"I sent a coven in to retrieve it. And retrieve it they did. When the guardian of that book learned he'd lost it, he swore vengeance on me and mine." She sighed. "I'll admit I cheated. Corson thought he was getting a new circle of warlocks. Instead, the witches he'd turned got their souls back in addition to the book that cost him everything."

Mormo took over. "Corson Westhell, the previous King of the West, has been looking for that grimoire for nearly eight hundred years. Because not only did he lose it, but then Hecate and a few of her friends locked a naughty demon lord inside it."

"Abaddon." Macy cringed. None of this was looking good for her.

"That's him." Hecate sighed. "We needed something strong enough to lock him down. If he'd have just kept his shenanigans to Hell, I'd have let him be. But he started screwing with Duat—the Egyptian afterlife, Varu."

"I know what Duat is," he said coldly. "I do read, Hecate."

"Of course you do." She smiled. "You see, Abaddon took issue with the fact that Duat has no hell. If your heart is not pure when weighed against the feather of Maat, then that soul is devoured and ceases to be. Thus the balance is kept. Abaddon had plans to storm Duat and steal souls. I have no idea what he wanted to do with them, but the gods and I talked and made plans.

"We captured Abaddon, slapped him with sanctions, and imprisoned him in the grimoire." Hecate turned to Varu and

Duncan. "We used vampire bloode to seal the lock. Then we hid the grimoire where no one was supposed to find it."

"Except someone found it, because it turned up in that mage's antique shop," Macy added. "And then I found it."

"Then you were *called* to find it," Mormo corrected. "You, Macy, are a Bloode Witch."

"You said that before. What does that mean?" Duncan asked.

Duncan didn't know either? Macy was relieved it hadn't meant what she'd thought, about blooding her to make a vampire meal.

Hecate looked into her eyes, maintaining a contact of power and belief. "It means Macy is a witch who gets stronger with bloode."

"*What?*" Duncan stared at Macy as if she'd grown three heads, which Hecate often did but Macy never had. He looked from her head to her toes. "She's no vampire."

"No, she's not. But she's a rare vampire ally. They used to use Bloode Witches a long time ago, special witches—likely descendants of the first vampires—bonded to rare clans within the tribes."

"Huh?" Macy had a tough time following. "I'm a witch. My mom's a witch. My dad's human." And a piece of garbage, but that was another story.

Duncan frowned. "I thought he was a mage."

"No, that's my stepdad. My bio dad is a human jerk. Drug dealer, pimp, bodyguard to criminals. You name it. He's a criminal jack-of-all-trades."

Duncan nodded thoughtfully.

"I'm not sure where it comes from, Macy." Mormo put a hand on her knee. "The power just is. And it's in you. It's why the grimoire wants you. Because you're powered through bloode, just like the lock on Abaddon's prison. With you, he can break free. And then he'll go on to break Hecate, me, anyone and everyone who stands in his way. Varu," Mormo said, turning to him. "He'll take and take and open the door to the Darkness that's coming."

"They made a pact," Hecate said. "A long time ago. I imagine Duat was supposed to be the start of the Darkness. If Abaddon gets out of the grimoire now, hell on earth is just the beginning."

"Right." Varu watched them all, Macy in particular. "So give us the grimoire and we'll keep it safe here."

"I wish I could." Frustrated, she ran a hand through her hair. "Every time Duncan has come for it, it's been in my spell room in my house. And then it vanishes. I have no idea where it goes." She paused in thought. "But I think it is inside me at some point, but not since I've been here, in this house. Since being here, I'm more me. I'm not using weird spells, have no wayward plans to trap vampires or screw with MEC."

"Too bad. Those sound like fun things to do," Duncan teased.

She glanced at him, expecting worry or caution and saw only admiration. "You're weird."

"Now that's some truth," Mormo agreed, which had Hecate laughing and Varu not frowning so hard, lightening the mood.

Duncan chuckled. "Right. Now that we all know I'm weird, how about we get back on track? We know a pack of lycans have been hexed, bespelled, ensorcelled, whatever you want to call it. MEC has them, but we know there's a malevolence in the air, and that malevolence could spread to MEC. Then we have Westhell floating about, somewhere in the city, up to no good. And someone in MEC is on his side, giving him information." He turned to Mormo. "When we breached MEC and I was being interrogated by their intelligence, I was mostly telling them stories."

"A lot like you do here." Varu lifted a brow.

"But some of what I said was true. I *did* work for EuroMEC a few decades back."

Macy blinked. "Seriously?" EuroMEC employed blood-drinkers?

"Oh, not as a vampire. They thought I was a mage."

"Nice work." Varu nodded.

"I've been keeping abreast of what goes on there, at least, up until my time with the Night Bloode. There's a leak in MEC. Westhell is always one step ahead of enforcement, and that's by design."

Macy was still trying to wrap her mind around being connected to vampires. She didn't understand what that meant, exactly. She now had to drink blood to have power? Gross. Wait. A leak in MEC? Did her father know about this?

"We need to get Westhell's MEC contact. Bait them and feed false intel to flush them out," Duncan continued. "We get to Westhell, maybe we can get our hooks into Abaddon. Macy's an obvious link, but until we understand how she can unlock the grimoire, we need to keep her away from it."

"I agree." Varu nodded. "But we don't know where it is, so how can we keep it away from her?"

"It's at her house," Hecate said. "Until she reads from it or it needs to hide. Then it pulls on her vast well of power and hides itself. In another realm, in her, in a pocket dimension. Who knows? The point is, we need to break her from the grimoire. To do that, she needs to become a true Bloode Witch."

"I'm still really confused on that." Macy rubbed her head, feeling a headache coming on.

"Me too. Do I need to feed her? Feed from her?" Duncan asked, sounding calm, as usual. Did anything faze the revenant?

"I'll look into it and let you know," Mormo said, glancing from Duncan to Macy and back again.

Varu stirred. "Perhaps I should lend my bloode. We do want the most powerful—"

"No." Duncan stared at Varu, his eyes turning red.

What the heck?

"I'm merely suggesting—"

"No. She's mine. My prey."

Well, at least he hadn't called her his pet. Macy kept her misplaced amusement to herself, because it wasn't really funny, and she shouldn't be laughing at the idea of being kept by a vampire.

"This is great, really. I love being in the middle of a vampire tug of war," she said drily, "but if you're serious about MEC, I have an idea of how you can plant the seeds to unearth your traitor."

"Oh?" Duncan asked, though he had yet to look away from Varu, snarling in silence.

Varu finally threw his hands up and growled, "Fine. She's yours for the time being. But we need to figure out this power and our tie to a witch." He sniffed. "Bad enough we have to deal with Hecate."

"Hey. You be nice," Macy snapped. "She's a goddess and demands respect."

Mormo gave her a soft smile. "That was lovely, Macy. And so true."

Varu didn't snap back at her. He looked from Macy to Duncan and gave the revenant a slow nod. "Keep an eye on her."

"Of course." Duncan paused. "Just as you keep an eye on Fara."

"Ha. I knew it." Mormo slapped his knee.

"Knew what?" Macy was really confused.

Mormo cleared his throat. "Right. Let's discuss Macy's plan to go back to MEC and dig out the traitor."

"That's a shit plan," Duncan said at the same time Varu frowned and Hecate nodded.

Knowing she'd have her work cut out for her, Macy put forth

valid arguments for going back. "I know MEC. They know me. Cho will have my back."

"Who is Cho?" Varu asked.

"A half-demon with a powerful father. I'm not sure he'll have the firepower to back her up properly." Duncan sighed, as if put out. "I'll have to go instead."

"Nope." Macy shook her head. "I work during the day, when the sun is out. I need a day partner. And that's Cho."

Mormo said, "Cho sounds fine, but I want someone more for you. And I have the perfect male in mind. He can go out in daylight or the night, and he blends well with a human or magir populace."

Duncan shared a horrified glance with Varu, and said, "No, Mormo. No way. You can't send him."

"Can and will. Macy, we'll call your friend Cho and invite him and the two agents investigating Westhell to our house. It's time we had a chat."

"The agents are my dad and uncle—Cho's dad."

"That's fine."

"That's less than smart,' Varu said. "We want to let MEC know where we are? They hate us."

"Everyone hates you," Macy said.

"Not helpful."

But true.

Duncan stood, moving to the back of her chair and looming. "I don't like it either. We should meet them on neutral territory."

"And we will." Mormo nodded. "I'll invite them into a pocket dimension."

"But they have to access that pocket dimension through our home, correct?" Duncan placed his hands on her shoulders and squeezed in reassurance.

Why his presence made her feel so safe, she didn't know. But she'd take it at this point.

"No. We'll send them to a different address where I have access." Mormo thought about it. "Augusta's Coffee."

"Where?" Macy asked.

"A magir shop nearby. Trust me. It'll be open for us."

She felt better about getting her father involved. He and Uncle Anton knew how to handle rough magir. And having a demon on hand to battle a demon made sense. "Okay. So we have them meet us there. When? It's a little late now."

"Tomorrow night," Duncan said. "Before then, we need to talk about how this Bloode Witch magic is supposed to work."

Mormo shrugged. "No time like the present."

Macy wasn't ready. "Ah, do you think we could take a short break? I need to wrap my mind around all of this."

Hecate nodded. "You three take some time. Macy, come with me. I want to show you something."

Not sure if she could handle much more weirdness, Macy paused before saying, "I'm honored. But please, if what you have to show me involves vampires, demons, or drinking blood, I might need a few minutes."

Hecate smiled. "I wasn't thinking blood, more like a cocktail or two."

Macy sighed. "Why not? It's five o'clock somewhere, right?"

More like two in the morning, but who was counting?

# CHAPTER TWENTY

Macy looked around at the basement, at what had started out as an entertainment center where Kraft and Orion battled over a video game and Onvyr added his input and was ignored. She walked through a shimmer in the air, and the video games and vampires vanished.

To be replaced with a magical speakeasy complete with creatures from multiple planes. Music and the muted noise of customers eating and drinking at a supernatural bar filled the gigantic space. The ceiling seemed to have no limit, the floors made of bamboo and stone in some places. The atmosphere felt classy, shadowy, and intimate. Like a pricy wine bar staffed by... the dead?

Gods, goddesses, minotaurs, sprites, fates, and even a few banshees mingled while clearly dead witches and a few necromancers served drinks behind the bars or went table to table taking orders while a Lady Gaga tune played.

"I'm partial to speakeasies, but I like modern music," Hecate said, now looking like a young flapper from the 1920s.

"Killer dress," a mermaid said as she walked by on two scaley legs, nude from the waist up.

"Thanks." Hecate winked. "I got it on sale." She twirled, and the fringes of her dress twirled with her. "Catherine, we need two refreshing drinks. And maybe a kick for strength."

A pale witch behind the bar nodded and moved away to fix two fancy drinks in oddly shaped glasses with paper umbrellas and lots of fruit. She slid them down the bar, where they came to a complete stop in front of Hecate and Macy.

Hecate held up her drink for a toast. "What should we drink to?"

Sitting and drinking with her goddess in a bar. If Macy was dreaming, she didn't want to wake up until she'd at least had a sip of crazy.

"To living through all this," Macy said.

"To interesting times," Hecate said. "And love."

*Not touching that with a fifty foot pole.* Especially when an image of a conceited, handsome-as-sin, annoying vampire came to mind.

Macy drank the fruity cocktail and felt revived after just one sip. "Oh wow. I needed that."

"Another winner, Catherine," Hecate called out.

The witch gave her a wide grin and a thumbs up before turning to help a ghoul.

Macy sipped and studied her surroundings, astounded by the myriad beings all around. Then she spotted one she'd seen before. "Hey, I know him."

Hecate spun to see the dark-haired giant—not such a giant anymore—walking toward them. Macy noted his clean jeans and tee-shirt, a long step away from that ripped toga in her dream. He saw her and stopped in place, his brows drawn in a severe frown.

"You." He looked as if he wanted to clomp over but walked with too smooth a gait, gliding instead. He glared down at Hecate, his eyes blazing gold. Macy felt definite "don't touch me" vibes coming from him. "If I'd known what I was getting into, I'd never—"

"Have helped and seen what's coming," Hecate said firmly. "I'm tired of this godly bullshit. And not just from you." She raised her voice. "It's coming for all of us."

The crowd ignored her.

"Assholes."

The handsome guy put his hair up in a manbun and should have looked ridiculous. But all that man-muscle, gorgeous hair, and killer cheekbones had him looking like a male model instead.

"Morpheus, meet Macy. Macy, the god of dreams."

Slack-jawed, Macy could only nod. Oh right. The god of dreams.

He looked much better than he had the other night.

"Macy Bishop-Dunwich, it's an honor." He clasped her hand and brought it to his lips for a kiss. "Oh my. That's a pretty strong signature."

"The demon?" Macy cringed.

"The vampire." Morpheus grinned. "You should have seen what they were wearing in that dream, Hecate. Yowza."

"Did you kill it? The hell-beast?" Macy had to know.

"I wish. That fucker kept me busy for two days." He sobered. "And that wasn't the real thing, only his shadow left behind to keep an eye on you." To Hecate, he said, "We need to move fast."

"I know."

"I feel the Darkness. I'm a convert. I'll help when I can." He paused. "But I also meant what I said earlier."

"About?"

"I want time with the servant."

Hecate blinked. "Bella?"

"No, you idiot. Mormo."

Macy was taken aback. One, to learn Mormo had a fan. Two, that this god had called her goddess an idiot.

But Hecate only laughed. "Good luck with that. I can barely get him to meet me for cocktails down here."

Morpheus shrugged. "I just need to talk to him. He keeps avoiding me."

"Because you make suggestive comments whenever he's around."

He laughed. "Of course I do. He's cute, and he makes a huge deal out of being embarrassed. No wonder you love having him around. He's adorable."

Hecate snickered, and Macy wondered if poor Mormo knew he was a hot topic of conversation.

"But in all seriousness" —he turned to Macy— "I scrubbed him from your dreams, little witch. You got rid of most of him when you crossed Hecate's boundary. But his shadow lingered."

"And lingers still." Hecate nodded to her back.

Morpheus took a peek under Macy's shirt. "Damn. He marked you good. Abaddon's such a dick."

Hecate snorted. "No kidding. He's a demon."

"Who doesn't take care of his nightmares. He's beyond ridiculous. I'm planning on talking to Hades about him sooner than later. I mean, if he doesn't want the responsibilities of having pets, he should free his stables. I'd take them in a heartbeat."

While Hecate talked with Morpheus, Macy sipped her drink and found, to her surprise, she'd finished it. The dead witch walked over to give her another.

"Thanks."

"You look like you needed it."

Macy sighed. "Yeah. Demons, end of the world, falling for a vampire." Oh crap. She'd admitted the bar truth out loud. "Take your pick."

The witch's eyes widened at something over Macy's shoulder. "I would, but I'd say he's already picked you." She smiled and turned away. Macy spun to see who had made the witch leave and looked into Duncan's angry eyes.

Duncan couldn't believe Macy had let that Morpheus prick kiss the back of her hand. "How's the drink?"

Macy frowned. "How did you get here?"

"I took the stairs." Duncan had visited the basement many times, often finding his way to this speakeasy filled with gods and monsters from other planes. He'd even gone so far as to visit Kur, the Sumerian afterlife ruled by a quirky goddess with a bland personality. The place had been pretty bleak, the dead not prone to lively conversation or adventure. But the goddess's messenger had been a decent chap. And he'd been more than obliging when Duncan had been in the mood for a fight.

But none of that mattered a damn when some pervy sleep god slobbered over Duncan's mate—*witch*. Not mate. No way he'd found a female to bear his young, to cleave to, when he'd just met her and didn't even know if he liked her.

Okay, that was a whopper of a lie. He liked her. *A lot.* But Duncan had always liked women. Human and otherwise. He'd have sex, enjoy himself, and leave. He rarely ever repeated an intimate encounter with the same female.

So why the hell couldn't he get Macy out of his mind? He had no idea if she preferred a cauldron over a simple witch's fire. Did she like blood sacrifices? Had she ever thought of going warlock? Well, that one he knew. No. She had definite opinions on helping people. She worked for MEC, after all.

But she had such passion, a sense of humor, and true grit. He liked that about her. Most humans with even a remote intelligence feared him and his kind. Not Macy.

*Bollocks.* He should talk to his father about her. Or his uncle. Or Varu.

No, wait. Varu?

Well, Varu did have a mate he seemed to... love. A foreign concept for a species that knew only how to covet and possess, yet Varu had announced to them all that he loved his fae.

Perhaps Hecate had cursed the clan, fating them to find mates. But why?

He saw the goddess still arguing with Morpheus and tugged Macy with him.

"What are you doing?"

Stubborn witch. "Luv, I'd like to talk to you."

"With our clothes on or off?" She flushed.

Which made him grin. "Well, if it's dealer's choice, then off. But I was hoping for a word."

She sighed, downed the drink, and followed him into a shady corner in the bar, where a troll and wood nymph sat chatting and paid them no mind.

"What word did you want, Duncan?"

He opened his mouth and closed it, now not sure what to say.

"Well?"

The dead witch Hecate seemed to favor walked by with two fruity drinks on a tray and stopped next to them.

"Oh, thank you."

Duncan took one as well, staring at it.

Macy took a big sip, so he did as well.

"Holy shit." He blinked, knockered, and not sure why the room was spinning.

"Duncan?"

"I need to sit." He stumbled to a nearby couch and dropped.

"Wow." She gaped. "You look drunk."

He grinned. "Haven't felt this off since my first drain as a lad."

"Drain?"

"We eat regular food when young. Revenants do, at least. We don't drink the blood until puberty hits."

"I had no idea."

"No, you didn't." He chuckled. "But I don't know anything about you either, and I want to."

"Why?"

He frowned. "I have no idea. You fascinate me." He stared at her hair and reached for a strand, nearly falling off the couch.

She helped him get his balance and fell on top of him. But when she tried to get up, he wouldn't let her. "Oof. Duncan, I'm too heavy."

"You're not."

"Duncan." She blushed, looking around but seeing no one nearby. Even the troll and nymph had vanished. The light dimmed, leaving them alone.

"I want to fuck."

"Duncan, hush." Macy slapped a hand over his mouth.

"But I want to talk more."

She slowly pulled her hand away.

"What do you like?" he asked, staring at her face, entranced.

"Um, well, I like chocolate. A nice wine. Tea."

"So it's food and drink, eh?"

"What?"

"Go on. What else?"

"I love my family. I love Cho."

He tensed. "He's a demon."

"He's a *half*-demon, and he's my best friend. Has been since I was a kid."

"Just a friend?"

"Like you and Orion."

"We're not friends."

"Yes, you are."

Duncan thought on that. "Maybe."

"I know vampires don't like each other much, but do you have family or friends from before?"

"Before I became Night Bloode, you mean?"

She nodded.

Just having her near felt good, connected not only by blood but by body and mind. He couldn't explain it, even to himself. Not yet.

"I don't know. I liked, and still like, to talk to my father and uncle."

"No mother?"

"No." He didn't miss what he'd never had. "Most females don't linger in clans. Females are tolerated to breed, for sex, sometimes even fun. But once they birth a vampire, they leave." He sighed. "Or are driven out. I don't remember my mother, but I do know she had stayed with us. Then one day, she went out shopping and never came back, ripped apart by a flock of harpies." He frowned. "I don't remember much, but I do know life with my kin was good. We're smart, and we love to learn."

"I do too. Love to learn."

"Yes, you would. You've a brain that keeps whirling, don't you?"

"What got me in trouble with the grimoire, probably." She sighed and petted his chest, making him want to purr. "I'm worried about this demon, Duncan."

"I'm not. All living things can die, and Abaddon is a living thing. They all fear death. But vampires don't."

"You're not afraid to die?"

"I welcome the rest. One day. And the only way to go down is with a fight."

"I like that sentiment."

He stroked her ribs, taken with her sharp breath. "I like you."

She blinked down at him. "Your pet witch, you mean?"

He should have felt badly about that but didn't. "You're still upset about that, aren't you?"

"What gave it away?" She glared at him.

He pulled her down for a kiss and ran his hands up her back, under her shirt. "Do you know what I can't get out of my mind?" he asked in between kisses.

"No, what?" She was panting.

"That dream we had. Of you taking my bloode inside you."

"You mean when I bit you?" She rubbed her fingers over the spot she'd bitten in the dream. "It felt so good. Did it hurt you?"

"No. Not at all, and that surprised me. Being fed on, as a vampire, is painful. Always. Because our bodies fight to hold onto the bloode, our magic in the red stuff flowing through our veins." He paused, looking at her and knowing he'd never seen anything more fascinating in his life. "But with you, it didn't hurt."

"In the dream."

He nodded. "In the dream." Then he lengthened a fingernail and cut into his throat, where bloode began to well. "Drink from me, Macy. Let's see what it feels like to bloode my witch."

"Not what they said," she murmured, appearing mesmerized by Duncan's bloode. "It looks gross.'"

"It is. Totally gross," he said with a smile. "Just a taste, then kiss me."

"Just a taste."

He nodded.

She neared his neck, obviously drawn to him but not sure why.

His arousal felt oversensitive, the anticipation an aphrodisiac.

Just a sip...

She took a taste.

And the rush of power knocked them both out.

# CHAPTER TWENTY-ONE

Cho didn't know what the hell Macy was playing at, but he was tired of being worried. He called her parents again, only to learn they'd found nothing new. She'd disappeared Thursday. It had been two days. That shouldn't be a big deal, but she hadn't called or texted. And she hadn't been home. He'd checked with his key, alarmed to find her spell room a shambles.

He stood there Saturday afternoon, beyond concerned, when his phone rang.

He answered right away. "Macy?"

"This is a new friend of hers. Macy needs to talk to you. Bring her father and uncle. Your father, I presume."

Cho glanced at the number, which was unknown. The deep, sure voice of the male on the phone promised a man of power. "I want to talk to her."

The man sighed. "So do I, but she's napping right now after overindulging. Witches."

Cho blinked. "Who are you?"

"Mormo the White."

Cho thought he detected a hint of humor. "Macy's okay, isn't she?"

"She's fine. Stubborn, sweet, and sassy. She's running rings around her new friends." Mormo chuckled, and Cho felt relieved. "We have a problem with MEC."

"Who's we?"

"Tell no one of this meeting. Just you, Will Dunwich, and Anton Novak. Come alone and make sure not to be followed. Augusta's Coffee tonight. Eleven p.m."

The call disconnected.

Cho had no reason to trust what Mormo said was true, but the man's description of Macy was spot on. He hurriedly called his father and told him when to meet.

"I'll call Will," his dad said. "And we're going into this with caution. But I agree. MEC is a problem. Keep this between us, Cho. You, me, and Uncle Will. The three of us will fix what's broken. Bring your A game, son.

"Will do."

"Good. Pick me and Will up early at the house. And load up for war." His dad hung up.

Cho would do whatever he could for his best friend. He didn't understand the worry about MEC, but that his father agreed made him wonder. There had been some dark stuff happening around town with some magir. Folks acting oddly aggressive, nearly outing themselves to humans. Even a dryad had gotten snippy when asked to stop attacking people, causing a media frenzy about a supposed "haunted tree" randomly knocking people out with pinecones. Dryads tended to be shy, not wanting attention. Her actions had been beyond strange.

Perhaps Macy had found something more than those vampires. He paused. *Should I tell Dad and Uncle Will about the vampires? Yes.* But then, Macy might get in trouble. And if there were vampires involved, they wouldn't call to set up a meeting. Cho would have already been sucked dry.

Their kind never played well with others.

No, he'd meet with Macy on Mormo's terms. And he'd bring a few extra spells for firepower, eager to show Macy the new tricks he'd been learning to aspire to Special Forces.

Later that night, Corson watched the half-demon drive away. "Follow him, Lil."

His human servant drove after Cho, keeping far enough away, in addition to the vehicle being under a no-notice spell, that he didn't worry the young magir might spot him. But when they pulled up near a domicile radiating power, he hastily erected a spell to cover the entire vehicle.

Lil didn't talk, still just a shell, doing his bidding. He liked her better this way, honestly. A human servant without opinions.

The obnoxious pair getting into the half-demon's vehicle would be a problem. That grand mind mage and higher demon had been tracking him for years. They still hadn't gotten tired of their pursuit. And with Corson being so close to finally serving his master, he couldn't let anything go to chance.

"Keep on them. We need to see where this is taking us. And don't worry, Lil. Pretty soon, you'll be on assignment, attached to our fair witch. Just as soon as the tease stops hiding."

They drove to Mercer Island and pulled into an affluent neighborhood. He felt a taste of crossroad energy and swore. He knew *exactly* where he was, though he'd only managed to get in and out of the basement through a dimensional gateway.

Fucking Hecate.

Well, Abaddon had said he was right where he wanted to be.

Corson would wait and watch. And when the opportunity came, he'd take it.

He'd torture and kill Hecate and all her minions, even if it took the rest of his lifetime to do it.

MACY WOKE up in Duncan's bed, and it took her a moment to recall what they'd been doing. She'd tasted him and *bam.* Everything turned white and then dark as a rush of lightning branched through her.

Vampire blood, or bloode, she supposed, had a punch to it. She'd tasted Duncan briefly when making love—*having sex, you ninny*—just yesterday. Er, last night.

She couldn't believe it had been just a short period of time. It felt like she'd known him for a lot longer.

What to make of his behavior last night, though? He'd been flirty, acting like he was into her. Had his attention been real? He'd acted drunk, so did that mean he was finally being honest with her, his inhibitions gone thanks to the booze? Or that he'd made everything up and didn't actually like her that way?

"Gosh, maybe if I'm lucky I can get Mormo to pass a note to him in a class and we'll go to the prom together," she said in a goofy voice, feeling like an idiot for acting boy crazy. *You're twenty-eight, not fourteen. Act like it!* How many times had she cautioned her younger sister not to wrap herself up in bad boys, and then Macy acted gooey over a vampire. The scourge of the magir. Death-bringers. Killers. Apex predators. And she thought Duncan might like-like her?

She slapped herself in the head and realized the bane of her existence lay next to her, his chest not moving. In a vampiric torpor. She noted the time and realized she had a few hours until sunset. Freedom from vampires, and she didn't feel too tired to move during the day.

Her sleep schedule had been all out of whack lately. But that would soon change. She had a job and life to get back to. And it totally didn't bother her to think of not being around Duncan anymore.

She studied him in sleep, seeing how incredibly handsome he was. He had a stubble on his cheeks, which fascinated her. She hadn't thought vampires could grow facial hair. For that matter, she hadn't realized they really did cast reflections. But since Duncan only let himself be seen by humans when he wanted to, she could understand the myths about his kind.

Unable to stop herself, she stroked his cheek and felt her heart flutter when he sighed and moved into the touch.

Completely vulnerable. She could stake him, set him on fire, kill him in any number of ways.

She stilled, holding onto the tiny urge to destroy him, a remnant of the damned grimoire. It had to be. That or his bloode making her a teensy bit murderous.

But as she watched him lie there, the killing thought left as if it had never been. Instead, her heart felt full. Able to watch him without being judged, she admitted to herself how much she liked him. How amazing the sex had been, and his treatment of her afterward just as delightful.

If Duncan truly cared, he'd be the perfect boyfriend. Husband? Mate? Vampires didn't marry, but they did mate, if she wasn't mistaken. But they bred babies and ditched the mom. And if Macy ever had a kid, she'd keep it. Boy or girl, vampire or witch. It wouldn't matter. She'd keep what belonged to her.

Huh. A flash of possessiveness. *That* felt a lot like Duncan.

Making herself crazy wasn't going to help, so she showered and found new clothes in his armoire, tailored to fit *her*.

A new lacy panty and bra set—who was picking this stuff out? —jeans, and a sweatshirt with UW printed on the front. After fixing her hair, she left his room.

The corridor remained quiet, still. All signs of life absent.

Macy let herself just breathe.

She'd been surrounded by close-up danger for too long if being by herself felt like heaven.

Shaking off her uneasiness, she grabbed an amazing smoothie from the magic refrigerator then went into the living room and plopped on the sectional. Demons and Darkness were soon coming to destroy the world. So she'd make time for a few episodes of *The Office,* because who didn't love idiot bosses?

She grinned, wondering if Ishaan, one of the most powerful witches at MEC, would ever realize he'd been bespelled by an S&I nerd. How far she'd come.

After watching the employees of Dunder Mifflin arguing over a stapler inside a gelatin mold and wondering how tough that might be to do herself, she put her favorite sitcom on hold and stretched, feeling normal once more.

Until a spark lit inside her. Energy popping like corn kernels, exploding then settling, revving her blood. It felt good yet strange, and she wanted to think she was leveling up, somehow, and not getting ready to spontaneously combust.

The reaction stopped as suddenly as it had begun. She should go ask Mormo about it. But she wanted more time to relax. So she put on another TV show, grabbed a peanut butter and jelly sandwich from the kitchen, and relaxed.

Before she knew it, she felt like a new woman. Outside, the sun started to set, but it hadn't gone down all the way yet.

*"Mew. Mew."*

A cat? She recalled Orion finding a kitten with matted fur.

There. She heard it again. A tiny meow echoing, though she couldn't see the little guy. She followed the sound down the hallway, past Duncan's room, to the stairwell. She paused at the top, but the kitten kept crying.

"I'm coming," she called and descended the steps, praying not to run into Hecate or her crossroads bar again.

Thinking about it now, in the light of day, made it all feel like a dream. Sure, Macy was part of the magir world though not magir herself. A witch, she'd been around magic her entire life.

At MEC she frequently worked with people who weren't human and had no problem with that.

But meeting Hecate, her patron goddess, was on another level entirely. Her mother would be beyond thrilled to know her daughter had met the goddess of witchcraft—the entire cornerstone on which their lives revolved. And to take it a step further, Macy hadn't just talked with the deity. She'd been in a legendary Between space, a liminal passage connecting more than just worlds, but life and the afterlife.

She hadn't been able to absorb it all last night, but now that she thought about it, her knees started to shake. She sat on the same sofa the vampires had used while playing their games. To her relief, the room seemed normal. Overly large, with an enormous TV, game console, and comfy furniture in a game room built to entertain large males who liked to brawl.

"Thank you, goddess." Macy sighed.

A ball of black fluff landed on her stomach and stared at her.

The kitten, black with bright green eyes, just stared. Macy felt a hint of animage in the little beast.

"My goodness. You're a familiar, aren't you?" Like humans, some animals possessed magic. Not all humans were witches, but all witches were humans. And not all animals were familiars, but all familiars were animals. Well, usually. She'd once heard rumor of a shifter acting as a witch's familiar in an emergency situation. But Macy couldn't imagine pulling magic through a human the way she'd once pulled through a toad.

Macy stroked the little furball, and it started to purr.

Taken with the cat, she kept petting it, doing her best not to magically reach out because she knew Orion had adopted the little thing. But would he treat it right? He wouldn't try to drink from it, would he?

She lifted the kitten and drew it close, staring into its eyes and seeing the question there. An invitation to enter and join. Claws bit into her hands, drawing pinpricks of blood to the surface. The kitten squirmed, but she only heard the offer To Become...

She didn't hear the danger until it was too late.

"Let him go," Orion snarled, ripping the kitten from her hands while tossing her into a wall at the same time.

She hit hard, but surprisingly, the throw hadn't hurt her. As Macy stood, she saw Orion snarling at her while cradling the kitten against his chest. Then he put the little beast aside and rushed her.

Annoyed that he'd interrupted a witch's right to commune with a possible familiar, she met his attack and rebuffed it, sending Orion into the wall she'd just dented.

He hit hard but bounced up without issue and blinked at her. "What did you just do?"

"Huh?" She opened and closed her hands, letting the tiny drops of blood grow. Nothing that some water and a tiny healing spell might not fix, but the blood would naturally draw a vampire.

"You smell like Duncan." His eyes narrowed. "And you hit like him too. Weak but effective."

Before she could ask what he meant by that, still intrigued with the power in her fists, she met his next attack by accident. She'd made a fist and punched at the air, in his direction. And it *hit him*. Before he could knock into her, her air fist smashed him into the other wall.

"Holy crap." Macy gaped at her fists. "I'm super witch."

"No, you're a Bloode Witch," Mormo said, appearing from out of nowhere behind her.

She screamed in fright and shot a bolt of fire at the interloper.

He vanished and reappeared next to her, waving a hand to smother the fiery couch.

"I'm so sorry," she apologized, embarrassed at losing control.

Orion reappeared with the kitten in hand. "You threw me against two different walls. Not bad."

She swallowed. "Sorry."

"I'm impressed." He nodded. "Not bad for a human."

"Not bad for a non-vampire," Mormo corrected. "Macy's a Bloode Witch. She's Night Bloode."

"What? No." She shook her head at the same time Orion shook his.

Neither of them wanted her attached to the clan.

"She's human. Food."

"A witch. Part of our fight against what's coming."

"She tried to take my cat," Orion growled.

"No, I was just looking at him, and he invited me to bond. Kind of."

"Back off, witch. He's mine. Aren't you, Mr. Mittens?" Orion asked the kitten before snuggling with it.

Both hers and Mormo's jaws dropped.

"Is he messing with us?" she asked Mormo while Orion stomped away to get Mr. Mittens some milk.

"I wish he was. Orion is a hothead, but I like that better than this *cat person* he's turned into," Mormo said with disdain.

She had to bite her lip not to laugh. A magician who tolerated vampires and death but not people who liked cats?

Macy cleared her throat. "Right. So, um, can you explain the power I'm holding? I can't access it, exactly. But I feel it." She focused and recalled the sigils the grimoire had burned into her brain. "I see the sigil spells the grimoire gave me. I can probably use them now, with all this power."

"Don't," Mormo ordered. "The bloode magic is strong, meant to protect your kin. It's not for the demon inside the grimoire. I'm afraid if you use it, you'll just make it that much easier for Abaddon to take hold of you once more."

She turned and lifted her shirt up in back. "Do the marks look different?"

"They've faded some. The work of Duncan's blood-bond with you."

"Blood-bond?" She dropped her shirt and turned back around.

"Some of that is the power of the revenant, the ability to seduce. He drank from you, and you drank from him. A bond is there that time will of course lessen. But... " Mormo stared at her. "There's something deeper between you."

She blushed. "We just met. I barely know the guy."

Mormo raised a brow. "The magic of bloode to blood is strong. I meant nothing of a personal attachment." Then he slowly smiled. "Do tell."

"Stop it."

He chuckled.

She opened her mouth and closed it. "You're wearing regular clothes."

"Jeans and a sweater. Yes. We're having company, and I wanted to impress them with my normal attire."

"No more Mormo the White?"

"We're doing a Hobbit night next week. You'll see."

Next week? Did Mormo actually think she'd still be around next week?

"If I can make it. I have to get back to my life, you know."

Mormo smiled, showing fangs, and his eyes turned a bright red. "This is your life now, Macy. Just you wait and see."

She didn't know what to make of that comment. But she didn't get a chance to ask for more information. The house seemed to vibrate.

He turned to her with a surprised look. "You felt that too?"

She nodded.

"Powerful guests indeed. Come." He held an arm out to her which she took, and they walked back upstairs. "Time to receive your father, friend, and uncle. Gather the others for me, would you? And bring them upstairs."

"Upstairs?"

"Where we'll use my gateway to journey to Augusta's Coffee." He snorted. "You didn't think we'd *drive* there, did you?"

"Well, yes."

"Macy, you're a Bloode Witch. Cars are pedestrian. We're going big tonight." He smiled and vanished.

Bemused, Macy grabbed a crabby Duncan and waited while he gathered Orion and Varu. But Khent, Rolf, and Kraft had been assigned another mission.

Orion walked with them up the stairs to Mormo's office, filling them in about Macy's new powers as She-Hulk.

Someone reads, she thought, amused.

"Where's the feline?" Varu asked. "Fara wants Onvyr to see it."

"To *talk* to it. Who knows what nonsense he'll put in my furry-buddy's head?" Orion snarled at Macy, which caused Duncan to snarl back.

"Watch it, vryko," Duncan warned.

"Hey, your witch tried to fuck with the little guy."

Macy sighed. "I did not. He's a familiar, Orion. It's only natural for a witch to—"

"See? *Proof.*" He glared at her, and she stepped back. "Keep your witchy hands off my cat."

"Vampires tend to be possessive," Varu commented as they continued up the stairs to Mormo's office. "I don't recommend trying to steal the feline."

Did no one listen to her? "I wasn't stealing him. I was just petting him."

Duncan pushed himself between her and Orion and warned, "You touch her and I'll break your cat in half."

"Duncan." Alarmed, because he seemed to mean it, she second-guessed her affection for someone who could harm a tiny, defenseless kitty. But then he turned to her and winked before looking back at Orion with the stone-cold face of a killer. "Do we understand each other?"

Orion stared from Duncan to Macy before deflating. "Fine. I wasn't trying to hurt her. I was just protecting Timon. That's his name now. Mr. Mittens didn't fit."

"Timon." Macy paused. "The meerkat from *The Lion King?*"

"What? Timon is a cat, like a meerkat."

Varu frowned. "That's not at all the same thing."

"Yeah, well, anyway, the witch tossed my ass around like it was nothing."

"What?" Duncan's eyes narrowed, so Macy quickly explained to him what had happened, which made him grin. "She kicked your arse, eh?"

"Barely. I wasn't trying to hurt her. Mormo keeps calling her the clan's Bloode Witch. She's dangerous." Orion pointed from his eyes to hers. "I'm watching you."

And that didn't make anything better at all.

Varu seemed to find their interaction amusing, his eyes crinkling as he said, "Now, now. Orion, let her be. It's typical for females to get nervous when their partners first meet the parents."

Duncan flipped him off. "Ignore him. He's in a mood."

Orion snickered. "A mating mood. Oh, so that's why you're so bitchy lately, Duncan. You're worried about impressing your mate's father."

Macy refused to listen to any more and rushed up the stairs, ignoring a lot of unnecessary laughter, then stopped in her tracks and turned to confront three death-bringers.

"Not one word about mates or sex or sharing blood to my father. Do you hear me?" She pointed at all of them. "Or I will boil the bloode you seem so fond of. Do I make myself clear?"

She ignored the fact her entire body seemed aglow in red.

Duncan and Orion nodded, their eyes wide, and took a step

back. Varu didn't react, though his eyes crinkled again. She had the feeling he found her amusing.

Macy headed up the stairs once more, realized she'd threatened *vampires* and gotten away with it, and figured, *Fuck it.* On a roll, she hurried to warn Mormo to behave as well.

She might only be a witch, but a girl had to pull out all the stops when bringing a boy with fangs to meet her dad.

# CHAPTER TWENTY-TWO

Duncan couldn't believe what he'd just heard and witnessed. Waking without Macy beside him, even after sleeping alone for over two hundred years, had felt odd. Not right, somehow.

But after tracking her down and learning she'd kicked Orion's ass? Granted, if Orion had really wanted to hurt her, she'd be dead now. But those not Of the Bloode didn't throw around a vryko like Orion.

Duncan had a serious case of the hots for Macy, even more than he'd had before.

And then she'd threatened not only him and Orion, but Varu as well?

*Is this what love feels like?*

He stared after her, grinning when he heard her yell at Mormo.

Orion nudged him. "Your female. She's a little scary."

"Right?" Duncan's smile widened, and Orion scowled and stomped away.

"She might prove useful to the clan," Varu said, watching

Duncan carefully. "I can feel your bloode inside her. It's a natural fit."

"Interesting." Duncan didn't want to think too hard about why he and Macy worked well together.

"We should see if she can harness Orion or Kraft's power as well. Is she limited to one vampire? Our clan?" Varu deliberately paused. "Her mate?"

Duncan wanted to brush him off, but for a revenant usually in command of all his faculties, he had a few issues that made him uncomfortable. Like having a human all over him while he slept. Or for that matter, falling asleep next to her, giving her the power to end his life while he rejuvenated. He didn't seem to see her as a threat to him, when he still considered his fellow kin to be dangerous to his well-being.

And this fixation on her, wanting more sex, more time spent watching her smile. By the Night, he sounded besotted.

"Duncan, when it comes for you, you need only accept and open to it."

"It?"

"The uncomfortable need for a female." Varu made a face. "It's still new to me, but I can tell you, that time when I thought Fara dead? I often imagined walking into the sun and letting it take me away. I never want to feel that again." He scowled, looking a lot more like the dangerous strigoi Duncan respected than some lovelorn magir. "And we will not talk about this again until the others feel the same vulnerabilities. Then we'll taunt them for their 'feelings' and weakness."

Duncan nodded, relieved. "Good. I'd rather go kill something than think about my emotions right now. I'm a revenant. We have little fucks to give."

"Exactly." Varu nodded and followed the others.

While Duncan pushed through the spatial gate Mormo had

created, keeping Macy between him and the magician, he studied her. A witch, one of Hecate's people.

Had the goddess set him up? Duncan would never have thought about taking a mate, not so soon in his lifetime. He didn't yet want progeny. Did he? He felt funny, and his witch must have noticed.

"What's your problem?" she whispered as they walked to the back of Augusta's Coffee, past a host of night-loving magir who gave them plenty of space.

"You," he growled low. "Stop picking on Orion and his kitten."

She blinked, looking adorable in her pique. His heartbeat changed, adapting to hers, beating in sync.

*I'm so fucked.*

Duncan had a mate. Now what did he do with her?

"Are you okay? You look weird." She looked him over. "And you're not dressed up to your usual standards. What's up with the casual look? Jeans and a button down shirt without a tie? Slumming, Duncan?" She teased.

Meanwhile, she looked gorgeous in jeans and a sweatshirt, her full lips and laughing eyes driving him to distraction.

A male approached too fast for Duncan's liking, and Duncan put himself between the male and Macy, growling a warning.

The big guy looked familiar. Oh, right. Cho. Her friend.

Macy tried to push past Duncan, who wasn't moving. "Orion, move him, will you?"

Orion muttered, "Get too close to a woman and lose your mind. Pathetic." He yanked Duncan back, ignoring all the swearing.

"Thank you." Macy left the safety of his arms and gave the big half-demon a hug.

And just her being that close to another not kin sent him into a rage he had a tough time containing.

"Great time for this to happen." Mormo sighed. "Macy, one moment." He smiled at Cho and the two men behind him. "Can you wait for us in the back room? We'll be right along."

The mage and the demon frowned but turned to leave, the demon dragging his son with him.

"But Dad, I—"

"Come."

Varu and Orion followed.

Mormo grabbed Duncan and Macy close.

"Watch it," Duncan warned. Magician or not, the arse was close to losing a limb. And not just for grabbing Duncan. Duncan didn't like seeing Macy yanked around either.

"What's wrong, Mormo?"

"Duncan and you have bonded, so he's bound to be overprotective for a while until the bond settles. Try not to get too close to others, okay?"

She stared at Duncan, and if he could have, he would have blushed.

He tried to act casual. "It's no big deal. Feel free to share emotion with your father."

"But not the others?"

"I don't care."

Mormo shook his head. "He cares. Steer clear of the others."

Macy blinked. "Are you *jealous?*" She started laughing. "This is awesome."

"I'm not jealous," Duncan hissed. "And I don't find it amusing."

"So you do like-like me." She clapped like a toddler.

"What is wrong with you?" Then he realized she was taking enjoyment from his discomfort. Such a vampire-like thing to do. Pleased, he smiled. "Ah, I see. You're turning vampire on us."

"Ha. Hold on. What?"

Mormo bared his teeth. "Save your mating arguments for

later. We have pressing business. Remember? The grimoire? End of the world? Doom?" He stalked away.

Before Macy could rib him about that mating comment, Duncan tugged her to follow Mormo.

She refused to move and whispered, "Did he say *mating?*"

Duncan looked deeply into her eyes. "You ignore the mating part, I'll be on my best behavior with your father. Deal?" It didn't occur to him to seduce her into doing his bidding, or threatening her to get his way.

*Damn it. Something has definitely changed between us.*

"I'll— Okay. No mating talk, and you're nice to my dad, Uncle Anton, *and* Cho."

"Fine." He held out a hand for her to shake.

"Fine." She took it.

"Fine," he said again, feeling like an idiot. But the warmth of her hand aroused him. Her scent aroused him. The sight of her eyes clouding with passion aroused him.

Duncan shook it off and nudged her ahead of him. "Focus, Macy. You can lust after me later."

"Oh, you." She fumed, as he'd thought she might, and stormed into the back room.

He followed, his arousal once more under control, and tried to keep himself together as he met her father again. This time as himself, under no spells or glamours. Vampire to mage. And he told himself to stop thinking of how tasty some mage blood might be right about now to take the edge off.

MACY HUGGED her dad and uncle, not lingering, and sat with the vampires and Mormo across from her family.

"What the hell is going on?" her dad asked, his voice icy. She could feel his magic at the ready, just waiting for an excuse to fight.

Next to him, Uncle Anton bristled, looking extremely demonly in his human form, several inches taller than he normally was, his frame noticeably huge even sitting down.

"I'm Mormo. The one who called Cho." Mormo nodded to her bestie.

Cho nodded back, his gaze concerned for Macy.

"I work with Hecate."

Anton snarled, "We know who you are. But why do you have my niece?"

"Because she's mine," Duncan said before anyone could stop him.

"Shit," Orion muttered.

"What did you say?" Her father's hands lit up, and he frowned as he stared at Duncan. "It's you. The one who came into MEC. In Brown's office," he said to Anton.

She could feel a confrontation building, growing as the vampires and demons fed off their rage. She really didn't like the deadly grin on Orion's face.

"Okay, everyone needs to settle down before the world ends."

"Wait." Mormo held up a hand. "Continue, Macy. We're sealed. Everything said here stays here."

Her father shot Duncan another angry look. "Macy, we work for MEC. The world is always ending."

Anton sniffed, and smoke came from his nose. "Truth."

"But not at the hands of a demon who marked me."

That had her father snapping his attention back to her. "*What?*"

Macy explained from the beginning, leaving only the intimate parts between her and Duncan out.

Anton stared at her in awe. "A real Bloode Witch?"

"You've heard of them?" Varu asked.

"Yes. Back when I attended court in the Underworld, a long time ago, we occasionally dealt with powerful vampire clans. And the big clans always had a Bloode Witch. No more than one, and she or he had always bonded with a vampire, cementing the loyalty of a human to those Of the Bloode."

"Macy is not a Bloode Witch," her dad said. "She's extremely powerful with spells, but she lacks the bridge to utilize her power."

"Exactly," Mormo said. "Because the bloode is the bridge. There aren't many of them born any more. But your daughter came into our lives for a reason. She's the only thing Corson Westhell wants right now. Because once he has her, he can use her to unlock the grimoire."

"And set Abaddon free," her dad said.

"Yes." Mormo sat back, sounding tired. "He's a danger to us all. Vampire, witch, mage, demon. Abaddon wants only to create chaos, to bring the worlds back to destruction and disorder. Once he's free of the grimoire—his prison—he'll use Macy to do terrible things."

"Like what?" Anton stared at the vampires, lingering on Varu. "Destroy vampires, maybe?"

"Or use us to kill the world," Varu said. "Think on that, demon. Do you really want us all working together, for a demon?"

Cho cringed. "God, no."

Orion chuckled. "Yeah, we don't want that either. So we need to kill Westhell, destroy the grimoire, and call it a day."

"You can't destroy the grimoire," Anton said. "But you can put it back where it belongs. In Hell, under lock and key. Every demon knows of this book, an abomination built to contain threats to demonkind. And if demonkind is concerned, the rest of the worlds should be as well. Even if you kill Westhell, you'll still need to destroy Abaddon."

"That's a tall order," Mormo said. "But it's a necessity. To that end, we need Corson Westhell."

Her father nodded to Duncan. "The vampire fed us some story about problems in MEC."

"It's true," Duncan said. "It's the only explanation that makes sense. Unless you and your partner are that bad at your jobs."

Anton growled. "Watch your mouth, bloodsucker."

"Or what? You'll track me down and kill me the way you've done Westhell? Bollocks."

Macy had to hand it to Duncan. He used his polished, snotty voice to full effect. Anton looked as if he wanted to burn Duncan to a crisp.

"Dad, relax," Cho warned when his father's horns appeared.

"Duncan," Macy said. "Be nice."

"Luv, I'm being honest. And if your uncle and father thought about it for a minute, they'd realize the truth. There's no way a demon, even one as powerful as Westhell, could have avoided MEC for so long unless he had someone helping him."

Her father sighed. "He's right, Anton."

"Fuck, I know."

Cho asked the question she'd been waiting for. "So what do we do to capture him? You want to use the three of us on the inside?"

"Four," Macy said, waiting for her father to object.

"No."

"Right on cue," she murmured. "Dad, listen. The grimoire is bound to me. Westhell will come after me, and then we grab him. No one at MEC except you guys knows I'm working with vampires."

"Which is still a huge problem for me," her dad growled. "I understand how you got to this point, but we need to protect you. From them." He glared at Duncan especially.

Macy put her hand on Duncan's shoulder and squeezed. A warning to stay silent. "Look, Dad. This is my fault. I used the grimoire."

"More like it used you," Mormo said.

"In any case, its magic is in me. Westhell will want to use it to free Abaddon, so we use that to finally nail him. And in the process, you guys keep an eye out and find the leak inside MEC. We don't want to keep Westhell's friend in place, do we?"

"It's not a bad plan, but you need more backup," Anton said.

"I agree." Mormo looked at Cho. "You're dependable, I'm sure, but you're in a different department than Macy. We can't be there, because, you know, the sun."

Her dad grunted.

Duncan frowned. "Technically, we can. I could—"

Macy stopped him before he got started, not comfortable with Duncan being vulnerable. "No, you can't."

Orion muttered something that had Duncan telling him to shut up. She was glad not to know what he said.

Mormo continued, "I'm sure you two can mask your presence, or do extra rounds near Macy. But too much will be suspicious. We have to draw in Westhell before he spooks and vanishes for another hundred years. Best to fix this while we have the assets to do so. We have the perfect person to put undercover with her. And to make sure he's close, Macy can be training him."

She sighed. "Great. More training."

"What are his qualifications?" Cho wanted to know, seeming eager to have her protected.

She gave him the look.

He gave it right back and mouthed, "Later."

Crap. He was going to lecture her. She just knew it.

"We have a fae warrior we'll stick with Macy. He can work a glamour that will hide his identity."

"Is he strong enough?" Anton asked.

"He nearly killed Varu a few times," Duncan said.

"Not me," Varu was quick to respond, bristling with arrogance. "He did nearly kill Rolf though."

"Too bad he didn't succeed." Orion sounded disappointed.

"We'll have her monitored," Duncan said. "And I'll be around in case I'm needed."

"I said no." Macy frowned at him.

"We'll talk about it later."

Her father watched them, a little too keenly for Macy's peace of mind. "Right. Well, it's best if she's back to normal, especially if Westhell's keeping an eye on her. She can come back to stay with me."

"Dad, I'm fine on my own."

"A good plan," Mormo said to stymie more arguments, and Macy could sense Duncan glaring at him. "Between Cho, Will, Anton, and our backup, she'll be covered."

"Yes, but I'm worried about Westhell's insider," Anton said. "I have a bad feeling the demon has someone powerful on his side."

And so the discussion returned to whom it might be, how to counter any opposition, and subtle threats about not stabbing each other in the back. Her dad and Anton didn't trust the vampires, nor should they. But Macy believed that they were all after the same thing and prayed Mormo wouldn't let the others mess with MEC.

The group broke up, Macy leaving with Cho and the others, doing her best not to look back to see how Duncan was taking her departure. She'd almost reached Cho's car when a stiff breeze blew.

In a blink, strong arms had carried her back to the hallway to the restroom in Augusta's Coffee.

"What the—"

Before she could finish, Duncan kissed her, a bold claiming that set her on fire to have him.

"Be good, luv. Be safe. I'll find you in a few."

She blinked and stood near Cho's car once more, behind her father, who looked around in puzzlement.

"Where did you go?"

"Nowhere, Dad." She accepted his hug and joined him behind Uncle Anton and Cho. "Still here." *And still confused about what that kiss meant, and why I feel so sad without my vampire.*

What was a witch to do when nothing made sense anymore?

# CHAPTER
# TWENTY-THREE

"You're shacking up with a vampire?" Cho's voice rose.
She and Cho had convinced her dad that she'd be fine staying at her own place with Cho for added protection. So after swinging by Cho's house so he could grab some things, they then drove to Macy's. Both her father and Uncle Anton had added protection to the spells guarding her house then reluctantly left them alone.

Cho stretched out on her couch with a spare pillow and blanket while she lay on the floor nearby, harkening back to their old sleepover days.

"Shh." She didn't want Duncan to overhear, should he be nearby. "Did you check to make sure it's just us, no ravens or vampires allowed?"

"Yep. We're good. Plus we have super reinforced wards around the house. It's just us." Cho wore his favorite pajamas, green flannel pants covered in cartoon pizza slices and a tee-shirt with more holes than Swiss cheese. "Tell me about the vamp."

"Which one?"

"The one that stared at you throughout the meeting and growled if I so much as sniffed your way."

She flushed. "Duncan's okay."

"He's into you."

"He's a vampire."

"I know. He'd like to eat you for sure." After an awkward pause, he flushed. "I meant... Not... I... ugh. I'm talking about your blood, not sex stuff." He grimaced, never able to see her as anything but his sister. And though she teased him about women, she felt the same, not wanting details about his love life either. She'd already forced herself to forget his *friendship* with those muses.

"Duncan and I are friends. I think."

"Friends? With a vampire?"

She sighed. "I like him, Cho. But I'm not sure what we are together. I drank his bloode." She told Cho what it was like to command that kind of power.

He stared at her. "Macy, this is *huge*. You're a *vampire's bitch*."

She choked. "Cho!"

"Kidding. But you are a clan witch. A witch connected to vampires. It actually makes an odd kind of sense."

"How so?"

"You've always seemed powerful to me, and it never made sense you couldn't cast spells, that you could only create them. Hell, you're a ton more powerful than that sniveling Debman. Yet he's a higher rank in S&I. See? You were always kickass, just needing a bloode-bridge to get there. How cool is that? You're so powerful you work with *vampires*. And not any vampires, but the new super clan in the city. Shit, girl. If that doesn't promote you, nothing will."

She tried to feel his excitement, but she felt nothing but blah at the thought of going back to her old life. No arrogant vampire to bicker with. No magic fridge from which to grab food. No kitten to steal. No goddess to drink with. What the hell had become of her life that she missed all that weirdness, and the vampire most of all?

He groaned. "Don't tell me you miss him."

"I don't." She stared at the ceiling, seeing a few cracks. "I do." She sighed. "So much has happened in just the past few days, but it feels like a lifetime has gone by. Did I tell you I drank with Hecate in a crossover bar?"

He leaned over the couch to stare down at her. "Are you shitting me?"

As she described her many adventures, she realized how much fun she'd had surrounded by predators considered the boogeymen of the magir world. For so much of her life she'd followed the rules and played it safe. But just a few short nights around vampires and her worldview had shifted.

"I liked being around them. The vampires. They're rough and scary, but also fun. It makes no sense, I know."

"Maybe it makes sense to you because you belong there. Vampires hate anyone not kin. I mean, they for sure hate each other. But sometimes they tolerate us non-vamps. Tonight, none of them looked at you as if you were beneath them. You were a part of the team."

"You think so?"

"Yeah. Heck, they protected you in there, Macy. Your boyfriend watched every move we made. His big friend watched your back. Varu, the really scary one, watched the door, and the magician kept an eye on everything. Not like your family would hurt you, but they still kept you on their side of the table."

She'd *chosen* that side of the table. "How can I like Duncan so much when I just met him?"

"I have no idea. But I do know these vampires are different. While you were cleaning up and settling in after we got back, I overhead my dad and your dad talking about the Night Bloode. A vampire clan backed by Hecate and her powerful sidekick,

Mormo, has some real juice. Plus, we heard that Varujan took out his dad. That makes him a master." Cho swallowed. "Macy, Atanase ruled all of the strigoi, the most terrifying of all the vamps. Varu killed him then left the tribe to the others. He walked away from power, which for a vampire, is unheard of. And now he's living with vampires from different tribes and clans, which should be impossible. *And* he's made peace with the upir clan. How can this be happening?"

She frowned. "They mentioned Ambrogio's Tears."

He grimaced.

"What?"

"I need to talk to Dad."

"I wouldn't worry about the Night Bloode. Not with Hecate's guidance. As much as they claim they hate gods and goddesses, they're working with her."

"For now." He settled his head back on his pillow. "I'm here for you, Macy. I don't care how powerful Duncan is, if he doesn't treat you right, I'll fry him. I've been working on my fire, and it's growing bigger."

"Nice."

"Yeah." He sounded pleased with himself. Then she heard a yawn. "Kaia came by to see me yesterday. She's worried about you too."

Macy groaned. "I'll talk to her soon." She had enough on her plate with a demon and vampires. "The thing that scares me the most about all this is making a mistake and letting Abaddon go free."

"Never happen," Cho said, his voice sleepy. "Between you, me, and the doom squad, we'll figure it out."

"Yeah, well, don't call them the doom squad within hearing, or they'll beat you up. And I'll help." Cho wasn't the best with nicknames.

"Whatever. I'm tired."

"Goodnight, Cho." She crawled up to kiss his cheek, then took herself to bed.

But not a full minute after her head hit the pillow, a hard body blanketed her. She would have screamed if a large hand hadn't settled over her mouth.

"Shh. Can't have you screaming now, can we, witch?"

DUNCAN GLARED down at his mate, not pleased that she smelled like demon. "You're mine," he reminded her. Apparently, she needed more than words to remember.

He kissed her, already naked and aroused. More than ready to fuck her into submission. But as always with his witch, the tables turned. Duncan was kissing her, stripping that awful sleepshirt from her body, when she flipped them over and kissed her way down his body.

Lost to her touch, he watched her panties go flying and dragged his hand to her thick hair, loving the way the red strands looked against his stomach. The sight of her moving lower had him ready to come, right then, right there.

"Luv, slow down— *Fuck.*" He sucked in a breath when her hot mouth engulfed him, taking his cock to the back of her throat. So sad he had little stamina when it came to Macy. Embarrassing if he hadn't scented her need as well. Hungry for her, he shifted her body so that she straddled his face while she continued to send him closer to bliss.

He sucked her clit between his lips while she bobbed up and down over him.

The sixty-nine felt like a special version of hell, because he had the taste of her in his mouth but couldn't get deep enough for satisfaction. She kept up a steady rhythm, but it wasn't enough.

For either of them.

In a burst of speed, he turned, positioned her under him, and thrust into her, the feel of her making him lightheaded.

"Duncan," she breathed. "What—? How—? Oh God. More." She moaned as he increased his speed, meeting him thrust for thrust as he continued to pump.

"Need to come, deep in you," he admitted, his voice like gravel.

"Yes, harder."

He kissed her, nicking her lip, and tasted her *bloode*—a combination of witch and vampire—and he felt the truth of their bond. A mate's first kiss.

The climax rushed over and through them both, the ecstasy leaving Duncan powerless and powerful at the same time. "Mine. My female," he roared as he continued to come. *My mate.*

Some time later, finally spent, he felt boneless as he rested inside her. He stroked her breasts and belly, having turned them on their sides to spoon her from behind. The lazy caress felt right, his female content in his arms, settling his predatory nature to rest.

"What was that?" She petted his arms holding her, the tender touch meaning more than it should.

"What?" he asked, nibbling along her shoulder. Tiny love bites without drawing blood.

She moaned. "I don't know why, but I love when you do that."

He did it again and smiled when she sighed his name.

"Why do you call me yours, Duncan? What does it mean?" A pause. "Are we mates?"

Would she be upset to know she now belonged to him? And why should it bother him if she was? "You're mine."

"But what does that mean, exactly?"

"That you're mine," he repeated, not sure why he didn't just commit them aloud as mates. He knew it as surely as he knew his own name. "This, us, I didn't plan for it. It just happened. Our situation is unique. I've never known a Bloode Witch before."

"And I've never been one before." She clutched his arms to hold her tighter. "Heck, Duncan, I've never even met a vampire before you. I'd heard you were cruel and violent and kill everything in your path."

He smiled. "You say the sweetest things."

She chuckled. "I know that's true. But... you and your kin are different."

"We are. I'm not sure if it's due to Mormo's magic, Hecate's interference, or something else, but six vampires who should have killed each other now tease and live together. It's not normal."

"Or maybe it is. The only reason you all don't get along is because you were cursed."

"For a reason, Macy. Varujan is a powerful patriarch, but he loves a fae. Vampires don't love. As odd as it might sound, my father is still considered slightly mental because he didn't kill his mate after she gave him a son, having done her duty and served her purpose. And that was two hundred years ago."

She stiffened.

"Relax. I have no intention of killing you. Unless it's with pleasure."

She eased in his arms. "Sweet talker."

He chuckled and inhaled her scent, so at peace he didn't understand how he'd lived so many years without this. Without *her*.

"Or are you just waiting to get me pregnant? Then you'll kill me?"

The idea of Macy round with his child sent a tingle of—something—through him. His heart jumped, and a spear of joy made it difficult to talk. He had to clear the emotion from his throat. "You're way too valuable to me alive. I'm intrigued by the idea of procreating." He nuzzled her neck and flexed his hips, aroused once more. "We need to keep practicing."

"Whoa." She tried to turn around, but joined and trapped in his arms, she couldn't and sighed when he slid inside her. "I'm not ready for babies, vampire. And if I did have one, I wouldn't be leaving without him or her."

"Shh. Easy, luv." He started moving, slow thrusts that made all talk of the future, of the past, fade as unimportant. He shifted a hand between her legs, letting the other massage her breasts. "Nothing will ever hurt you while I'm around."

"I..." She groaned. "I can't think when you touch me." She leaned her head forward, and he licked her neck, needing to bite. "Duncan, I like you. A lot."

The confession seemed grudging, and he loved that about her. Her honesty, her trickery, her stubbornness.

"Ah, sweet, not as much as I like you." He continued his slow pace, frustrating them both as they teetered on the brink of climax.

She dug her nails into his arm. "Stop playing around and bite me, damn it." She ground his hand down between her legs with her own and seized around his cock.

Lost to his mate, Duncan slid his fangs into her throat and moaned as he poured into her, the orgasm one huge wave of pleasure, cresting over them both.

Once again, unaware of anything but Macy, he lay vulnerable as he spent his seed, pleasure like a drug he couldn't get enough of. Thoughts of making young with his witch didn't seem so far-fetched.

"Just have to get rid of that blasted demon and protect her from what's coming."

"Did you say something?" she asked, her voice husky, her hands entwined with his over her breast and between her legs.

"Nothing, Macy. You—"

The door burst open, and Duncan, still drugged with the taste of her, thoroughly pleasured by his mate, didn't move. Something he never would have let happen with any other being in existence. To protect himself at least, or Macy, but he wanted nothing but for Cho to see her fully claimed.

Cho stood tall, his powerful build full of corded muscle, his chest bare and backed by wide, black wings, his demon form apparent in the horns and tail. He stood, his fists closed, ready to attack. Until he saw a naked Macy in bed, Duncan curled possessively behind her.

"Ack. My eyes! My eyes!" The demon covered his face with hands the size of dinner plates, the claws like knives. "I came to save you, but now I'm blind with something I can never unsee. What foul hell is this?"

Macy screeched and tried to cover them up with a blanket, but Duncan remained buried inside her, making it impossible to move. "Do something, vampire," she pleaded. "I can't let my brother see me naked."

He smiled and kissed her neck again, shifting inside her, his cock thick, ready for another go. *Nope. Not done yet.*

"Oh my God. Stop molesting her, you monster," Cho said from behind his hands. "At least wait until I'm gone."

Macy groaned. "This is beyond embarrassing."

Duncan gave an evil-henchman chuckle. "Go away. My mate and I are bonding."

Cho shouted, "Mate? I knew it. Shit, Macy. What are your parents going to think?"

"Can we please talk about this later?" Macy begged, desperate and aroused, her scent thick with lust.

Duncan gave a throaty moan, on purpose, and watched with amusement as the demon fled, slamming the door behind him, loudly complaining about being scarred for life.

An amusing demon who showed no animosity or hunger for

Duncan's mate. Cho, Duncan could work with. For a lesser being, he was a funny guy.

"That was mean." Macy managed to pull herself away from him, only to flatten him to the bed, fitting him inside her once more, and start riding him. "And embarrassing."

Angry and aroused, the perfect combination. He couldn't get enough of her.

"You're going to get me off again, and then we're going to talk about how you're going to start getting along with my best friend. And no more sex talk in front of him either." Her body flushed, glowing with a red power that lit up her eyes.

Duncan knew there would never be another for him, not after experiencing the treasure of his Bloode Witch.

"Right. No talking." He gave her what she wanted and more.

Then, instead of doing the smart thing and taking them both back to the house where it was safe, he watched her sleep. And pulled out his phone.

"Oy, what took you so bloody long?"

Another voice joined on speaker. "What the fuck, boy? You're late."

He cringed. "Apologies, Sire, Uncle Brock. There have a been a few... developments." He brushed Macy's hair from her cheek, his heart as soft as his brain. "Got a new problem with Abaddon. That Darkness I told you about is rearing its head again."

"Trouble's best to know in advance," Uncle Brock said.

Duncan swallowed. "And oh, I got myself a mate."

The silence on the other end was deafening. And then the shouting started. The cursing. The threats. And the shocking news his father already knew about his witch.

"How do you know about Macy?" Not that Duncan should be surprised. He'd learned how to gather information from his dad and uncle, after all.

Edward snorted. "Who the bloody hell do you think arranged all this? That Hecate, that's who. Well now, I'd say we're even."

Uncle Brock grunted. "You've thrown a right spanner in the works, lad. But we'll work around it."

"Her, you mean," his dad said drily. "You sure she's your mate, Duncan?"

"She's lovely," Duncan murmured. "And mine. Touch her and die."

His uncle had the audacity to laugh. "Ah, he's gone daft, Edward. Just like you were with Mona."

His father growled. "Shut it, Brock. Boy, make ready to receive us. We'll be there in a shake to talk this out."

"What?" Duncan blinked, waking from his goofy daydreams of a future with his mate.

"We're just north of you. Be seeing you soon, jack-o. And you can explain this new independence you think you have," his father ended in a growl and disconnected.

Duncan stared at his phone, not sure what to think.

As if he didn't have enough to worry about.

# CHAPTER TWENTY-FOUR

The next evening, while Macy spent time with her father, Duncan and his clan, to include Mormo and Hecate, sat around the dining table and discussed their plans to take out Abaddon. Duncan advised the group to expect visitors.

"Your father and uncle are coming for a visit?" Varu blinked. "Do I have that right?"

Duncan normally kept his feelings behind a dry expression of mockery and distaste. But Macy was changing him. And he had to wonder if it was for the better. He groaned and knocked his head against the table.

Mormo wore a stupid grin, as did Rolf, Kraft, and Orion. Khent stared at him in amazement. Only Onvyr—and who had invited him?—looked at him with genuine delight.

"My clan is close-knit. We defend each other, aren't prone to unnecessary violence." Duncan glanced at Orion and Kraft, who didn't seem to see the jibe though Khent quirked his lips. "We gather information about threats to our tribe and pass it along to our master. We know a lot about everything and everyone. Nothing happens that the Tizona clan isn't aware of."

"Including all of us and my mistress. You've been talking out of turn, Duncan," Mormo said, a slice of threat in those words.

Varu frowned. "I hate to agree with Mormo, but you are Night Bloode now."

"I don't deny I am." It had taken him a while, but Duncan felt fully immersed in his new clan. "But my ties to the Tizona aren't broken."

Mormo's face cleared of all menace. "You feel a kinship with your family. Your father and uncle."

"Duncan, I had no idea you were so soft." Khent looked disapproving.

Rolf shrugged. "There's our weak link. Who knew it would be the revenant? I thought it was the vryko."

"Funny, Rolf." Orion glared at him, the kitten crawling over his shoulders ignoring all the vampire hostility.

"Say what you want," Duncan said. "But I won't let my clan go unprotected. They need to know what we know. And half of what you lot have learned over the past eleven months has come from me and my contacts, both overseas in and this city. Yeah, think on that."

"He's got a point," Onvyr said.

Defended by a dusk elf? Not what Duncan might have hoped for.

"The animals talk to me, and they tell me things," Onvyr was saying. "Smoky wants to stay with Orion, but he also needs to work with Macy to unlock more of her power. He said his brother would make a better familiar for her, though."

"Wait. Who's Smoky?" Orion asked as the kitten jumped to the table and walked across it to investigate a bowl of fruit.

"The cat." Onvyr nodded to the little guy. "That's his real name, not *Timon*." He frowned. "You need to go back and grab his brother for Macy." He pause to listen to Smoky chirp and flicker his tail and whiskers. "Oh, okay. So Smoky said his brother is in Ahnessa's hidden room under the stairs. There are some potions in there Macy might be able to use."

Everyone stared at Onvyr, who continued dropping bombshells. "I'm glad my sister found someone to love. Varu's a good mate for her. Now we have Duncan who also has a mate. Before long, you'll all find mates, which only makes sense."

"Why does that make sense?" Rolf asked, clearly humoring the dusk elf.

"Because you need love to balance your hate, your violence. Or at least, that's what Gaia would say."

"Gaia?" Kraft blinked.

"You know, his earth goddess," Orion told him.

"Not a goddess. Gaia is life."

"Here we go." Kraft groaned. "Can we not talk about gods and goddesses for a while? Bad enough we have to live with one.'"

Hecate smirked.

Onvyr shrugged. "Truth is you're all unbalanced. To defeat the Darkness that comes, you'll have to be at your strongest. Just sayin'." He reached for a red and yellow ripe apple. "Oh, I love these." The elf opened his mouth, showing small fangs, and ripped into the fruit. "Honeycrisp, right? My favorite," he said with his mouth full.

Mormo shook his head. "Onvyr, you constantly surprise me."

"I'm not taking a mate," Khent said, his brows drawn in offense.

"Me neither." Kraft chuckled. "Though I have no doubt Orion will fall hard for a female who loathes him."

"Fuck you." Orion glared but gently settled Smoky on his shoulder. "Sorry, Smoky. We'll grab your brother soon."

The kitten rubbed its head on Orion's jaw, and even Duncan had to admit the feline was cute and growing on him.

"Mated?" Rolf laughed hysterically. "No wonder the

revenant's losing it. But then, he found an authentic Bloode Witch. I can't fault him for that. The witch will be brimming with power." He turned a serious gaze to Duncan. "That's a huge temptation for a demon of Abaddon's caliber. Wish I could stay to help. But I can't." He nodded to Khent. "Come on, bro. Varu, you too. Let's go grab a Bloode Stone."

Mormo perked up. "You actually found it?"

"Yes, in Canada. In Nunavut, of all places. A mess of upir have it, and they're not going to willingly hand it over. We'll need the strigoi."

Varu frowned. "The strigoi has a name. I'm your patriarch."

"Whatever."

And that, there, was why this clan would never be typical. Rolf couldn't care less about Varu's standing as patriarch, yet Varu didn't slit his throat for it. Duncan shook his head, amused.

Mormo of course, had to have his say. "Varu, we need that stone. We'll handle Abaddon."

"But Duncan's kin are coming. I'll..." He paused and cocked his head, then started talking to himself the way he did sometimes.

"I'd swear he was batty if I didn't know he and the Bloode Stone talked." Duncan was glad he didn't have to deal with a sentient stone. That would drive him mad.

Varu shrugged. "Fine." He fisted his hand then opened it, showing a tiny red stone. "Don't worry. This is just a piece of the stone. It needs to stay with you while I'm gone. You'll be able to keep the peace, especially with your relatives."

"Um, thanks?" Duncan hesitated for a second before putting his hand out. Varu dropped the stone shard into it, and everyone watched as the stone sank into Duncan's hand and disappeared.

"Wow. Does it hurt?" Orion asked.

"No. But it's not entirely comfortable." *Can you hear me?*

Silence met his query, and he felt silly reaching out to a gem.

Not seeing any drama, everyone turned back to the conversation at hand.

Kraft sighed. "Mormo, honestly, is it that big a deal if we let Abaddon have what he wants? A little bit of chaos never hurt anyone. And really, what can he do to us?"

"He can chain you," Hecate, who'd been quiet up to that point, said. She wore a youthful appearance, with bronze skin, dark hair and dark eyes, and an hourglass figure. The picture of health and beauty. "Abaddon will use Macy to free himself, then he'll use her bond with Duncan to work through all of you. And yes, he can do that. You're bloode-bound as kin.

"Then, with the power of the Bloode Stone under his control, he'll wipe out any resistance to his rule using the Bloode Empire to do so. And then of course, he'll feed on you until there's nothing left. You say you hate gods and goddesses because we try to rule you. What do you think the demon lord will do when you tell him no?"

Everyone considered that scenario, one that might still come to pass. Duncan refused to let any harm come to Macy or his kin and would do everything in his power to destroy the demon. Looking around, he thought the others likely felt the same.

"But what a glorious battle it would be." Kraft sounded dreamy.

Rolf chuckled.

Varu slapped Kraft in the back of the head. "Don't be stupid."

"Hey." Kraft snapped his teeth. "It was just a thought."

"Yeah? Well, go back to normal and stop having them," Orion growled.

"Fuck you."

"Fuck you back. Fighting it out with a demon for our souls? Get real, wolfie."

"What? Tell me a grand fight with a worthy opponent doesn't get you excited."

Rolf tapped his cheek. "He's got a point. We haven't fought anyone strong since the strigoi, and honestly, it was only Atanase who put up a good fight."

"True." Khent stared at Kraft, as if considering his words.

"No." Duncan stood, clenching his jaw. "You idiots are not going to give in, sacrifice *my mate* and the other tribes and clans, just so you can have a free-for-all with chaos. I'll kill you myself before I'll let you dance with Darkness."

"So now you've got a mate and you're all heroic and shit." Orion shook his head, but Duncan caught a twinkle in his eye.

Rolf winked. "Told you Kraft would get him going." He held out a hand, and the others grumbled as they put bills and charms into it. Even Varu handed over a golden coin.

Duncan gaped then snapped his jaw shut. "You're all assholes."

Everyone laughed. Khent, Rolf, and Varu teased him before readying to prepare for their battle with the upir up north.

Kraft slapped him on the back. "That's what you get for making me be nice to the Seattle Bloode."

"What?" Duncan scowled. "Look, dickhead, telling you not to kill any upir has been Mormo's rule since day one. No clan wars in the city, remember? And we were at the university to be a *distraction,* not there to cause a war."

"Still, I blame you." The nachzehrer smiled, showing sharp fangs, then gave a wolf howl of laughter as he left.

Khent, Rolf, and Varu followed. "Good luck," Varu said over his shoulder. "Don't lose or I'll gut you myself."

"Ah, now there's a pep talk worthy of a patriarch," Mormo said drily.

Hecate laughed then vanished in the blink of an eye.

Only Mormo, Onvyr, Duncan, and Orion remained.

"I'll go get Smoky's brother," Orion said. "Macy might need him." He left with the kitten.

Onvyr jumped to his feet, bouncing with enthusiasm. "I'll get ready to blend with the humans."

"Don't forget to wear your glamour," Mormo warned. "MEC isn't used to elves, and we don't want anyone knowing about you, do we?"

"No." He left the dining area and ran into his sister, who agreed to help him with his glamour.

"I still think it's a mistake sending him with us," Duncan said. "He's like a too-eager puppy. He'll get someone killed."

"So what?" Mormo shrugged. "Death-bringers no longer want death?"

Duncan glared at the white-haired magician. "Your death, sure. But not my kin or Macy."

"Well, now, it seems like you're finally a part of our clan, aren't you, Duncan of the Night Bloode?" Mormo seemed pleased with himself.

"Is that what this is all about? Making sure I remain a part of this wacky group of blood-drinkers?"

"Yes and no. The threat we face is real, and I'm extremely concerned about Macy. We need her, Duncan."

*Tell me something I don't know.* He never would have guessed he'd have... feelings... for a human. And a witch at that.

"It's imperative we locate Corson Westhell. He's the key to stopping Abaddon. If we can't get him, then we need to make sure Macy never gets near him. Because if he gets his hands on her, I'm not sure she'll be strong enough to prevent the coming apocalypse."

"You're a real downer, you know that, Mormo?" As if Duncan wasn't already not liking this plan. Not that he was worried, exactly, just not comfortable with Macy out of his sight.

"I believe in being prepared." Mormo smiled. "Now, I think it would be best if we kept an eye on our Bloode Witch until she heads into work in the morning. Don't you?"

"I'm already gone." Not like Duncan needed Mormo to tell him what to do. Until he figured out how to handle having a mate in his life, he'd—

"Don't forget to take your father and uncle with you."

Duncan frowned. "What?"

The house shuddered. Mormo smirked. "It's for you."

Duncan hurried to the front door and opened it to find his dad and uncle standing there, waiting.

His father studied him. To look at them, one would think them all brothers. Vampires aged slowly, and though his dad and uncle had more than three hundred years on him, none of them looked much older than a human male in his late twenties. And like Duncan, his family knew how to dress. Wearing tailored suits and looking like high priced executives, they grimaced at his wardrobe.

"I worried about this," Uncle Brock said. "He's dressing like a commoner and rolling in the hay with a witch. Boy's got problems."

"Good thing we're here to fix them." Edward smiled, his mirth something Duncan could have done without.

"Right. Good thing." Duncan sighed. "Well, come on, then. I need to keep watch so my new mate doesn't get mauled by a demon."

His uncle shoved past him into the house. "You two go on. I've got some catching up to do with Hecate."

As if he'd summoned her, the goddess appeared and stood with her arms out, her divine beauty breathtaking. "Brock, you old devil."

Not wanting to see his uncle flirting with Hecate, Duncan turned. "Let's go, Dad. I don't have the stomach for this."

"Eh, me either. Now tell me about your witch. And if she passes muster, I might not kill her."

"Have I mentioned how great it is that you're here?"

"No. Tell me again." His father grinned, showing long, sharp fangs. "But this time act like you mean it."

# CHAPTER TWENTY-FIVE

Macy spent her Tuesday at work the same way she spent her Monday. In training.

It was the most boring aspect of her job. Not her education, but educating others. Every time they got a new witch or mage into S&I, Ishaan would assign mentors to the newbies.

Needing Macy's skills to create top-level spells for their enforcers and SO agents, Ishaan normally let her off the hook despite the rotation all their agents had. But he seemed less than pleased with her because someone—*Dad, you're going to get it for this*—had spilled the beans about her being on a demon's hit list.

Her two trainees, one a "human" witch named Vic who seemed dazzled by everything in MEC, never stopped asking questions. Although Onvyr had been assigned to watch over her, he took his role as a new witch seriously.

Looking at him now, one would never suspect the six foot two skinny guy with short, brown hair to be a smoking hot dusk elf with height and muscle and the prettiest long hair framing a face she'd more than once gotten caught admiring. She had to admit though, that she felt safe with him always a step or two nearby.

Her other trainee, a witch new to her power, seemed afraid of her own shadow.

It didn't happen often, but adults had been known to find they suddenly had magic. Lucy, a beautiful blond close to Macy's age with a lot of potential but little ability to steer her craft, shadowed Macy's every step.

"So, wait." Lucy frowned. "I'm still confused about how you make up spells but can't use them."

"That's just me," Macy said *again*. "Lots of witches and mages in S&I both craft the spells and use them. But my spells tend to be higher-level, so it takes someone with more magic to use them."

"Or more magir together to cast one of your spells, correct?" Onvyr asked, paying attention.

"Yes, that's right."

Lucy frowned. "You're a big spellmaker but not a spellcaster. That seems like a waste."

Rude to point it out, but the woman wasn't wrong. "It's something I've gotten used to. But now—"

"What about blood magic?"

Macy paused. "What's that?"

"I've heard of people using blood with spells. Isn't that why vampires are so strong? Because the magic is tied somehow to their bloode?"

"An interesting idea," Onvyr answered. "But the magic is in fact fused to their bloode. And that's blood with an E on the end."

Macy answered Lucy's question. "Witches and mages don't work with blood spells. Sacrifice and pain fuel dark magic. While it can be powerful, we don't use it."

"Why not?" Lucy wanted to know.

"Because that kind of magic takes its toll. It corrupts, turning witches into warlocks, mages into sorceri. What we do comes from the earth, from deep inside our connection to life. Those who take from others to fuel their magic are continually drawn to darkness until they can't exist without it."

"Like demons?" she asked in a small voice.

"Yes. They're incredibly strong, especially in their own plane. They live off hurting others. It's how they're made."

Lucy looked thoughtful. "So demons are evil."

Onvyr shook his head. "No, I would postulate they do evil things. But like Macy said, magic comes from everywhere. And Gaia loves balance. Without light there's no dark. Without evil no good."

"Makes sense." Lucy nodded and studied Onvyr. "You're pretty smart."

"I am."

"So why are you so new to this?"

"I never knew I had magic until one day, it was just there. I can see it, actually, like patterns of color everywhere. And I can talk to animals."

That had Lucy more animated, as Onvyr told her true stories of his times chatting with moles, squirrels, and battle cats.

Macy needed a break. "I'm going up to talk to Ishaan for a few minutes, okay?"

They nodded, ignoring her as they talked.

*Finally.* Macy didn't mind Lucy, and she appreciated Onvyr's natural curiosity, but a witch could only take so much.

Plus, she missed Duncan. He'd sent her a text asking about her health early in the morning.

Her health. What was he, a doctor?

Nothing intimate, no phone call to make sure she was still breathing.

He'd hurt her feelings, and she hated that she'd let him. But he'd been the one calling her a mate. Was that what vampires were to each other? Fuckbuddies with the occasional text in between mattress bopping?

She sighed. *Am I silly for trying to ascribe human emotions and behaviors to a vampire?*

She had no idea how vampires dealt with relationships. Especially since all she'd heard about them said vampires didn't have them. They had sex. They made babies. And many of them then killed their baby mommas. Not a great track record. Heck, Duncan had told her about his mom dying. Although his dad seemed to have been the exception, keeping Duncan's mom around after Duncan's birth. But how long might she have stayed if harpies hadn't gotten to her?

Macy walked to Ishaan's office and stopped outside his door. He and Dr. Brown, from the Intelligence branch, seemed to be shouting at each other. She couldn't hear through his soundproof office, but they both seemed agitated.

Dr. Brown turned, saw her, and walked away from Macy's boss. She opened the door and stepped out.

"Dr. Brown." Macy nodded, conscious that the most powerful witch in Seattle had been fooled by her mate. By Duncan. With the exception of their marathon sexcapades and him calling her "mine," they hadn't discussed what being mated meant.

*And there I go thinking about him again.*

"Watch your back, Macy," Dr. Brown said in a low voice before walking away.

Ishaan watched her go, a frown on his handsome face. "Macy, a nice surprise. What's up?"

"I just wanted to know where we stand on the new vampires in the city and that lycan mob that got out of hand last week. And I need a break from training."

He grinned. "My office is your office. Tea?"

"Please." The lunch hour had come and gone, and Macy was in that hammock between lunch coma and clocking out for the day.

She sat with him at a table in the corner, overlooking the S&I

lab below. Her coworkers continued to create spells and incantations, gearing up for vampires and lycans out of control. MEC was on high alert and had been since the past Thursday night, when Duncan and his kin had infiltrated the command center.

"How are you feeling?" Ishaan asked.

Thanks to her father telling the higher ups that she'd been out sick, no one knew of her connection with the Night Bloode. "Better. I think it was a sinus infection. Dad whipped up a spell to take care of it and I was just sleepy over the weekend."

"Glad you're better." He sipped his tea, studying her. "You seem to be the picture of health. I'm only keeping you on training the next few days to make sure you're back to snuff—and of course, well away from Westhell—then I need you with the team creating some offensive bombs and spellwork. We know the Night Bloode is the new vampire clan in town, and they're unlike any others we've ever seen."

"Oh?"

He didn't tell her anything she hadn't already known, but it did surprise her to learn how much MEC knew about Duncan and the others.

"Their supposed tie to a god or goddess changes everything. If vampires start working with the gods, the power balance shifts, and we have a nightmare on our hands."

"Right." She didn't see Hecate getting greedy about power. Not with all she had to do, keeping an eye on crossover passages between realms, on witches, the dead, and certain blood rites. Personally, Macy thought the goddess could have used more than three faces.

"But that's something Special Operations is working. We continue to provide support."

She studied her boss. "Ishaan? Can I ask you a personal question?"

"Uh oh. That sounds ominous." He chuckled. "Go ahead."

"Do you ever want to do more than provide support?"

"Spoken like a true agent sniffing after field work."

Hadn't she been doing that with her off-books look into the vampires in the first place? "I love working for S&I, but sometimes I want to get out of the lab."

"I completely understand. Back when a bunch of us attended the academy together, Margery, Marquis, Asiri, and I made a pact to go as far as we could in MEC. We all had our reasons for joining, but few of us made it as far as being branch heads. I'm living my dream. It might not seem all that exciting, but what I do matters."

"No, no." She flushed. "I didn't mean that S&I isn't enough, I just wanted to know if *you'd* tried other branches before sticking here."

"I did go out on a few operations. Many of our S&I people join task forces on missions. But there's a learning curve there. You have to be able to defend yourself when out in the field, not relying on other mission-first agents who have jobs to do without looking after S&I too."

She huffed. "I know." *But I can do powerful magic now. Or I will be able to again once Duncan powers me up.* Macy retained much of the magical *oomph* she'd gotten through his bloode. But it did feel a little weaker over time. Two days since she'd tasted him. Touched him. Seen him.

Damn vampire.

"If you want to apply again for the field agent sub-designation, I'll back you on it."

She smiled. "Thanks, Ishaan."

"But I think you'd be wasted out there. Your skill with spells is remarkable, especially at your age. You're just like your mother. She chose Intelligence, to Margery's benefit. But I'm more than convinced you chose the right department to harness your skills."

Ishaan had always been a good boss. It bothered her not to confide in him about a leak in the MEC. Margery already knew. Would she have told Ishaan about it? Macy needed to talk her father.

"What do you think about your trainees?" he asked, changing the subject.

"Victor is highly curious, a nice man, and a novice witch. He doesn't feel as strong to me as Lucy does."

Ishaan nodded. "She has a great deal of potential."

"How did you find her?"

Onvyr's story was that once he'd learned he had magic, he'd first applied to a nearby magir academy specializing in hexes. Uncle Anton had easily forged some records to show Onvyr's work there as a student teacher. Lucy, she wasn't as familiar with.

Ishaan said, "She was one of the near casualties when the lycans fought the vampires last week. I think the trauma of witnessing so many magir and MEC's magical deterrents woke her magic."

"Makes sense."

"She's lucky she didn't suffer more than a few bumps and bruises." He frowned. "The lycans and vampires aren't usually so forward. I think it's that grimoire Westhell's been tracking. That or the demon himself influencing our magir."

"Grimoire?" She played stupid, since she shouldn't know about the book, especially after having fogged Ishaan's mind about it.

"Oh, that's right. You know about the demon, but we found out he's been hunting a magical grimoire for years. We tracked it to an antique shop, but the mage who owned it was killed a few months ago. Then the grimoire disappeared again. But since we've seen Westhell in various parts of the city, we think the book is still here. We don't think he's gotten his hands on it yet." Ishaan frowned and stroked his goatee. "If you hear anything about the grimoire, let me know immediately. Steer clear of that book. Witches and grimoires don't mix."

"Sure they do. They turn witches into warlocks."

"Sadly, you're right. I've seen some of our best and brightest go down that path. All I can say is, temptation can cause the best of us to do bad things."

An admission of guilt? Or a remembrance of losing someone special?

Ishaan had to take a phone call, so Macy left him to it and returned to find Onvyr and Lucy working together with an ice mage, putting together a fire-resist spell.

"Oh good. You two keep working. I'll be at my table if you need me." She waved at her area, and Onvyr nodded. He'd be able to watch her from his spot with the mage.

Lucy gave her a brief nod, her attention on the cute mage showing her how to work sigils into objects for charm spellwork, a discipline Macy hadn't explored much.

She tried to focus on her work, but she couldn't help thinking about Duncan and what he might be up to. And why he kept his distance from her when he'd been happy enough to call her "his" and "mate" when having sex.

Fuming, she did little more than think about Hecate's crew, wondering about her part in their future.

If she even had one.

# CHAPTER TWENTY-SIX

Duncan had had enough. He'd looked forward to reuniting with his family, but after three days and nights of no Macy, he was done. Wednesday evening, Duncan ditched his father, leaving him with Mormo and Orion while Uncle Brock continued to "reacquaint" himself with Hecate.

Duncan didn't even want to know what they might be getting up to.

He had been keeping watch on Macy from a distance, working with his family to learn all they could about Corson Westhell, but it was as if the demon had vanished. And that made Duncan uneasy.

He'd meant to text or call Macy several times since she'd left the house, but after that first text, something held him back. He didn't like that he'd been no more than a useful tool to scratch an itch. So he was good for sex but not conversation? She couldn't have picked up the phone to talk to *him*?

In raven form, he flew to her house and surprisingly had no trouble at all circumventing her wards. He let himself into her home, annoyed to find Cho still hanging around.

He assumed his human form and nudged the demon glued to a

television in the dark, taking satisfaction from watching Cho scream and toss a bowl of popcorn at him.

"Fuck. Don't do that," Cho growled and shot fire from his eyes.

Duncan easily dodged. "Neat trick." They both turned to watch Macy's drapes catch fire.

"Shit." Cho hurried to put the fire out.

"She upstairs?"

"You sticking around?"

"Yes."

"She's upstairs. I'm leaving."

"Good."

"Yeah, you're welcome. Tell her I'll drive us to work tomorrow." Cho locked the door behind him.

And then it was just Duncan and Macy in the house.

Duncan walked quietly up the stairs. Macy sat by the window, looking out at the moon. She wore a pair of pajama bottoms with a matching long-sleeved top, noting revealing or risqué, but he'd swear his heart beat only for her.

She turned and took a step toward him before registering his presence. He knew because she squeaked and jumped back, a hand over her racing heart. "Jesus, would you stop doing that?"

She brushed her hair from her face, and it settled in waves around her, framing such beauty she ruined him for all others. There would only ever be Macy for him. And he now had a sense of why his father had long steered clear of females since the death of Duncan's mother.

"Why are you here?"

*And* she shattered the moment. "Really? 'Why are you here?'"

She frowned. "I live here."

"Yes, my mate lives here. That's why I've come to visit. And to ask if you've gone daft, or if you think avoiding me will make me go away," he said, his words icy enough to cool that fiery temper.

"Are you kidding me?" She put her hands on her hips, pulling her shirt over her full, unbound breasts. "I've been here all week. No call? No text except to ask about my health? *My health?* Oh wait, I know. You're here because you want sex." She angrily pushed down her lounge pants and panties and held out her arms. "Well, here you go. One available pussy, Don Juan."

He blinked, staring at her, and decided to take her up on her offer. "Okay."

"What?"

He was on her before she could blink, her back against the wall while he kissed her with a need he couldn't help. She resisted for all of a moment then sucked his tongue into her mouth and refused to let go.

Goaded, he shoved down his trousers, took himself out, and wrapped her legs around his waist. Without waiting, he pushed inside her slick heat, his eyes rolling from the sheer pleasure of her fiery body.

"That what you wanted?" she panted, sounding angry and lusty at the same time.

He glared back at her. "I'm only giving you what *you* wanted. A fuck with no complications, eh, luv?" He fucked her hard, watching her while he pounded inside her.

But his witch didn't let him take. She happily gave him a rough ride, scoring his shoulders with her nails, as if his shirt weren't in the way. Nipping his lips, his tongue, then sucking on him as if blowing him. Macy fought to get closer. To make him work harder. And their almost violent coupling had him raging with lust and love.

"I'm coming," she said on a breath and cried out, dragging her nails against his neck and drawing blood.

He jerked inside her and swore, giving his mate his seed,

then moving close to press a nail into his neck, a gift of bloode he would give no other. "Drink," he ordered, caught between the agonizing pleasure of his release and utter devotion to his mate.

She lowered her lids and put her mouth over him, and he came harder as she sucked, the ecstasy almost painful. Macy moaned, drawing his essence into her, until he finally had no more seed to give.

He pulled back, his neck sealing instantly, and kissed her, tasting himself on her lips.

She gentled under him, running her fingers through his hair, and he wanted to purr like a well-fed cat. "You're a prick."

"Sure, yes." He put his nose into the crook of her neck and inhaled, taken with her scent. After drinking him, she smelled more like kin and less like witch. And the subtle difference was enchanting.

"You should have called me."

"Should have." He nibbled her neck, the love bites playful.

"Quit ignoring me, unless you only want me for my blood and body?"

"Want you always," he said gruffly. "But maybe next time *you* could call *me.* Would help a bloke to know his lady love is missing him."

She stared. "Really?"

"Fuck, Macy. For all I know, you only want me for my cock. You get off and disappear. What am I to think?"

"What... You..." She scowled and pushed him back so he had to withdraw. "Wait here."

She hustled to the bathroom and returned moments later, pulling on her clothing. "You— Do you mind putting that away?" She blushed and nodded at his stiff cock.

Once with Macy was never enough. Duncan sighed and put himself to rights.

She coughed. "You are full of crap if you want me for more than my body."

"What about your blood?" he asked, annoyed she could think so little of him. Hadn't he been a gentleman with her from the get-go?

Her expression darkened. "Of course. And my blood."

"So you think I should take off now and go fuck the next raving beauty I meet? I could do it easily. They never refuse me." At her look of hurt, he swore. "Fuck. You're a nut, you know that? I could have anyone else. Man, woman, lycan. But I only want you, though I'm not sure why." He glared at her, irritated anew when she started to soften. "Oh no. You want to blame all this emotional claptrap on me, but you're the one with the issues. I told you we mated. What the bloody hell do you think that means?"

"I don't know," she yelled, surprising him. "I'm worried about being possessed and killed by a demon. I'm scared I'll end up being the tool that kills you. And that my dad or Cho or Uncle Anton might be hurt by what's coming. Not to mention the big chaotic Darkness out to destroy mankind. Oh, and someone I work with, who might actually be a friend, could be an evil mole."

Put that way, she did have some reason to be extra stressed, not in her right mind. "Macy, I—"

"I'm not done." She poked his chest with a bony finger. "How about instead of judging me, instead of expecting me to read your mind when I have so much other bullshit to deal with, you be straight with me. All I hear is how vampires don't care, they kill their mates after breeding them, and they pretty much consider all of us non-fangers to be lesser beings. So excuse the hell out of me for not calling or texting when I'm not sure if I'm supposed to be your dinner or your girlfriend."

She was breathing hard, staring at him, and the fire in her eyes struck him mute. Such passion, such strong magic. His bloode and seed raced through her, lighting her up with a vampire's essence. The perfect blend of woman and kin, and she was all his.

"Go ahead," she said, seething. "This is the part where you kill me for disagreeing with you, right?"

He wiped all expression from his face and looked at her like the predator she accused him of being. "Right."

MACY BLINKED. Sure, she'd been overly dramatic, but she hadn't expected him to agree with her! She took a step back, then another when Duncan showed his fangs and acted like death incarnate.

She'd taken it too far. He looked livid, his eyes going from a dark brown to blood-red. A demonic death-bringer. And she was alone with him in the house. Wait. No, she wasn't. "Cho," she yelled, then screamed when Duncan pounced on her.

She managed to tear free and ran for the door, only to run into him there. No, not him, someone who looked a lot like him though.

"Is this how you entertain women these days? Chasing them around? Though the endorphins in her blood from the fear will make her taste better." Handsome, cold, and more brutish than Duncan yet looking enough like him to be his older brother, the male holding her leaned closer, his fangs looking decidedly sharp.

"Duncan," she cried and shoved the stranger back.

Amped up on Duncan's bloode, she managed to knock the male off his feet and down the stairs. But he, like Duncan, was wicked fast and rebounded, going for her neck.

Duncan stopped him with a hand on his chest, standing between the vampire and Macy. "Dad, enough."

Macy blinked. "Dad?" Good night, but Duncan's dad looked only slightly older than Duncan.

Duncan turned to her and glared. "Did you really think I was trying to kill you? Fuck, woman. You're my mate."

"What what I supposed to think, you ass? Your eyes were super red and your fangs were out."

"I was kidding."

"I'll show you 'kidding.'" She scowled.

The other vampire cleared his throat.

Duncan looked nonplussed for a moment before clearing all expression from his face. "Macy, this is my sire, Edward of the Tizona clan. Dad, my mate, Macy Bishop-Dunwich, Bloode Witch to the Night Bloode."

"And MEC agent," she added lamely. Though she had to admit, *Bloode Witch to the Night Bloode* sounded pretty badass.

The vampire looked her over. "Mate, eh? She's a right fit lass, sure enough. I feel the magic. It's strong. Yours?"

Duncan nodded. "And hers. The bloode powers her. And it's why Abaddon needs her to get free from the grimoire."

"I know. Hecate and Mormo filled us in." He studied Macy. "Used bloode to cement the lock on his prison, so he needs someone who can manipulate it to free him. A vampire would do as well for his plans."

"No. I don't think so." Duncan stood back to study her. "She's got more than just bloode, but a witch's power inside her. And Hecate is the witch who set the spell binding the demon to the book in the first place."

"Technically, she's a goddess, not a witch," Macy felt bound to clarify.

Edward smiled. "Feisty, eh? Always get a spark with a redhead."

"Dad."

"Hey." Macy paused to see Duncan looking—embarrassed? That made him seem a little human. What child didn't get mortified by their parent at some point in their life?

They stood there all staring at one another until Macy blurted, "Why don't we go downstairs and have something to drink—that doesn't involve my neck?"

"Dad," Duncan growled. "Quit staring at her throat."

"You marked her good, lad." Edward moved closer to push Macy's hair aside. "It's there, and it's not subtle."

Macy didn't move, feeling an aura of power around the older vampire. "How old are you?" she asked once he'd stepped back. Duncan shared his father's features, but Edward had longer hair and a broader frame encased by a pricey-looking suit.

She tried to hide it but couldn't contain a grin.

"What?" Edward asked.

"You and your son seem to favor fancy clothes."

"Of course. Revenants tend to be better than your average vampire. Smarter, faster, better dressed for sure."

Duncan nudged them out of the bedroom.

"We're known to finesse the ladies." He winked and offered her an arm down the stairs.

Duncan sighed, loudly, and followed them. Macy was treated to courtesy and admiration mixed with gentlemanly manners while Duncan's dad asked her all kinds of questions about her, her parents, her power, and everything and everyone connected to the grimoire and MEC.

Macy didn't realize she'd said so much until she tried to swallow and coughed, her throat dry.

Duncan handed her a glass of iced tea and glared at his father. "No more."

She followed his gaze to his dad, who sat, kicked back on her couch, one ankle over his knee.

"She wouldn't have shared if she didn't want to."

Macy realized he'd seduced the answers out of her, his power a sly trick of conquest, much less overt than his son's. "You bastard."

Edward grinned. "I do like this one."

"Duncan," she said, a little hurt. "You let your dad whammy me?"

"I tried to get you to stop talking, but you wouldn't." He frowned. "And you've got my bloode in you. We vampires remain tied to our sires throughout our lives. It's much more difficult to disobey a parent than it is a clan leader. And he's both."

"Oh." She could understand that.

"If you think he's bad, wait until you meet Uncle Brock."

"A literal lady killer." Edward chuckled, saw neither Duncan nor Macy laughing, and stopped. "Sorry. Too soon?"

"*Dad.*" Duncan growled. "Mind telling us why you're here?"

Edward nodded. "We found traces of Corson Westhell in Fremont."

Macy's heart raced. "Fremont?"

"His scent was all over a demon's house. We went through but caught nothing but brimstone and popcorn." Edward frowned down at a pile of the stuff on the floor. "Is there some human quirk with the snack food we should know about?"

Macy rushed to call Cho and got no answer.

"Macy?" Duncan watched her with concern.

"I'm not getting an answer at Cho's house."

"Dad, will you protect her while I'm gone? I'll be right back."

Edward nodded. "On my oath, your mate will come to no harm."

Duncan gave Macy a quick kiss. "I'll be right back." He left in the blink of an eye.

Too nervous to sit, she paced while Edward watched.

"So, you mated my son."

"He mated me," she corrected then wondered if it mattered. "I think it was an accident."

Edward laughed. "Duncan does nothing by accident. The little bastard plots and plans. He wanted you."

"I think he was mad because I bespelled him."

Edward leaned forward. "Oh?"

Macy told him all about it, and somehow ended up telling him how confused and worried she was to be dealing with vampires. "You guys hate each other." She paused. "So how are you, from a different clan, not trying to kill your son?"

"Ah, now. That's a family secret." He smiled at her, and though she never forgot he was a predator, she saw the warmth buried under the sophisticated ferocity. "The Tizona clan is small. We're revenants, and we do things a bit differently. Family is more important to us than it is to most of our kind. Though we've all suffered from Apollo's curse—and yes, that's what we call what they did to us, scattering our loyalties, prodding our hatred of each other—the Tizona clan has always managed to stay loyal. My one condition to allowing Hecate the use of my son, that she strengthen our bond. So that even when he left, he'd never forget his heart and home."

"His heart?"

"It beats, lass. For his father, his uncle, his new clan, and for you."

She swallowed.

"You love him, don't you?"

She wanted to laugh him off but couldn't, so she said, rather aggressively, "Maybe. But what's the point? Vampires can't love."

He barked a laugh. "Who told you that shite? Of course we love. The problem is too many vampires learned to love only themselves. We're a selfish breed. But I loved my mate before she passed, just as my stubborn brother loves the female he refuses to claim. Duncan, now, that boy has never had a problem with women. But he'd never thought to mate one, not after he saw how I pined after his mother. So if he's mated you, girl, then he surely loves you."

"He never said. And besides, we really just met." Technically they'd met months ago, but the spells she'd cast hadn't allowed for any closeness.

"Ha. My son admit to loving a woman? And a witch at that." He studied her with a smile. "My mate was a witch. A sea witch with great power. She bore me a strong son, stronger than any other revenant I know. Then she died, and I felt lost. For a vampire, that's a very big deal. We live to indulge, to war, and to defend what's ours. I lost my heart but kept my boy. And now I'm thinking of giving him over to you if you'll pledge yourself to me."

"What?"

Edward nodded. "To me and mine, we do no harm. The boy knows it. Hecate knows it. And now Mormo, that stubborn ass, knows it. It's not a case of torn loyalties, my son has. It's a rare ability to extend himself to family deeper than bloode. If you call yourself kin, then you'll feel it when the bond kicks in."

"It has to kick in?"

Edward frowned. "What has my stupid sod of a son not been tellin' you?"

Before she could answer, Duncan returned. Gone one moment, there the next.

"Cho?" she asked.

He shook his head. "He's not there. But Macy, Westhell was."

## CHAPTER TWENTY-SEVEN

Macy went into work the next day while the Night Bloode and Duncan's family worked together to find Cho. Yet it was daylight now, and she didn't think they'd be able to track anyone until the sun set. Her father and Anton had also been alerted, though, so she had faith he'd soon be found. The best thing *she* could do to help Cho would be to keep on with the plan, use herself as bait for the demon and hope he'd show himself.

Onvyr stuck close to her, asking her questions and trying to learn, keeping her occupied, for which she was grateful. Lucy hadn't arrived, apparently sick with some virus going around.

She wished she could feel better about Cho's disappearance, chalking up his absence to something less nefarious, but she believed Duncan when he said he sensed Westhell there. Still, she hadn't gone to pieces, trying to be strong for her friend, to show Duncan and his dad she could cope.

If only her vampire hadn't kissed her and held her tenderly while she sobbed herself to sleep.

She sighed.

Onvyr stepped closer and whispered, "They'll find him. I know they will."

She gripped his hand, did her best to keep her eyes dry, and nodded with a forced smile. "I know."

He looked away and frowned at a snake soaking under a heat lamp on a nearby table. "Where's Lucy? We were working on transmogrification yesterday."

Macy frowned. "Transmogrification? That's something demons like to do, transforming into the grotesque."

"I know. Lucy and Ted and I were talking about cave demons and how they sometimes mess around with trolls. Ted's a troll expert, apparently."

She nodded. "He's a good guy but a little fixated on wild fae."

Onvyr gave her a knowing look. "He didn't have much good to say about elves."

"Ah. Right."

He chuckled. "I'm going to talk to Frank if you don't mind."

"Frank?"

"The roc snake. He's fae based, did you know that?" Onvyr looked excited to reconnect with a creature from his homeworld, so she left him to it.

As she busied herself with some spells for Enforcement, she reached into her coat pocket for a pack of gum and found a stone with a note from Hecate. *Belongs to Dr. Brown. Please return.*

No time like the present. Plus, it would give her something more to do than rote spells she could craft in her sleep.

Macy sighed. She might not have what it took to become an Enforcement agent, but that didn't mean she had to be stuck with boring work forever. Maybe MEC just wasn't for her.

"Onvyr, if anyone asks, I'm heading for Intelligence to see Dr. Brown."

He frowned.

"I'll be fine. I'll stick to the main corridor and avoid shadowy stairwells."

Since the command center was busy enough, she didn't fear getting kidnapped in broad daylight.

"Call if you need me."

She knew he meant aloud, as elf hearing was off the charts, just like vampires. "Will do." She left him, greeting friends and acquaintances on her way to Dr. Brown's office in the Intelligence wing. She'd nearly reached the supreme witch's office when she felt a buzzing in her pocket.

She reached in and closed her hand around the amber colored stone. And heard Dr. Brown. Odd. She glanced around but didn't see the woman.

Macy concentrated, using Duncan's bloode to tap in to the stone.

*I don't know where it is. Why do you think I'm calling you with a fucking phone?* Dr. Brown sounded shrill.

*Relax witch. All is as it should be.*

Macy knew that deep voice.

*You never said anything about taking Novak. His father won't rest until he's found.*

*He will be. He's a part of the puzzle I'm putting together.* That familiar voice paused, and Macy's eyes widened when she realized where she'd heard it before—at the dive bar, when Corson Westhell had flirted with her.

He had Cho, and Dr. Brown knew about it. Holy crap. The supreme witch, head of Intelligence, was the leak.

Macy backtracked, looking casual, and found safety standing off to the side in the main corridor, keeping out of the way of zooming passenger trollies and fast-walking magir.

She drew out her phone, intending to text Duncan about what she'd learned when the alarm went off. At the same time, an incoming text buzzed on her phone.

She didn't recognize the number.

Then her phone rang while enforcement raced around with

guns drawn. "What's going on?" she yelled to a friend from Weapon's branch running by.

"Merfolk gone crazy at the waterfront. They've attacked a passenger vessel, and it's chaos."

"Good luck." She shook her head and answered her phone. Just another day at MEC. "Hello?"

"Macy," a voice whispered. "It's Lucy. I'm in trouble."

"Where are you?"

"I don't know. But he said he'd kill me if I didn't help. He wanted to use me as bait but I escaped." Silence.

"Lucy?"

"Hold on," she whispered, her voice wobbly. "I escaped when the demon guy drew his attention. But I don't know who to trust. He said anyone could be working with him."

"What? Who said?"

"He called himself Cho. I think he's a demon, but he's not friends with the goblins who grabbed me. I'm so confused and don't know who to trust."

"Just stay where you are. I'll come get you." Macy started running for the exit along with everyone in Special Ops, it seemed. "Are you okay?"

"I'm scared. I can't use any magic yet, and there's no way I would have escaped if Cho hadn't distracted the goblins for me. Or maybe they're orcs. I don't know." Lucy started crying.

"Can you get somewhere public? Someplace safe?"

"The cops?"

"No. Somewhere magical. Where are you?"

"I don't know. I'm underground somewhere. Hold on." After a pause, she said, "I think I'm under Trader Joe's off Roosevelt. God, I didn't even know these tunnels existed."

"Stay there."

"No way. They'll find me," she whispered.

"Fine. You need to get to a safe place. I—"

"I know one. I'll call you when I'm there. Don't tell anyone. *Please.*"

"Wait, Lucy. I can meet you."

"Promise you won't tell anyone. Not MEC, not Ishaan, not your friends. I don't trust anyone." She paused. "But I trust you."

Odd she'd mention Ishaan. What if Dr. Brown wasn't Corson Westhell's only source of information in MEC?

"Just me. Fine. Where?"

"Lincoln High School. Near the gym."

Macy checked the time. The sun was still up, so her vampire help was a no-go. She didn't want to take her dad or Anton away from looking for Cho. And she didn't trust that Westhell didn't have more informants, who might even now be spying on her in MEC.

She raced to her car and said aloud, "I'm going after Lucy. I need invisible backup. I need you, Onvyr." On the off chance Lucy was part of the demon's scheme, Macy planned to be ready. But she'd be careful, and she'd use every asset at her disposal. Including the icy bloode in her veins.

*Wake up and find me, Duncan. Or I will seriously kick your ass. No way I'm dying until you admit you love me.*

DUNCAN FROWNED AND WOKE, feeling as if in a haze. The sun hadn't yet set, but he was awake. He rubbed his heart. Something wasn't right. Was the house under attack? He listened, feeling with all his senses, but felt nothing out of the ordinary.

Still, he'd awakened for a reason. He showered and dressed in black trousers, a black sweater, and black boots, prepared for combat. Walking toward Mormo's floor, he was surprised to reach the magician without a magical runaround.

"Mormo?"

"You're awake? Interesting." Mormo stood with Hecate, and both looked worried.

"What happened?" He rubbed his heart again, feeling not himself. Stupid sun. "Any word on Cho?"

"MEC is dealing with magir attacks across the city, and they're working overtime to contain a paranormal outbreak on social media."

"And you don't think it's a coincidence that we're closing in on Westhell and this happens."

Mormo adjusted his hair into a braid down his back, his clothing casual, the magician ready for action in black as well. "No, it's no coincidence. There's more. Cho has been found by his father. Macy's father has disappeared, as has Macy."

"*What?*"

"Onvyr is trailing her. But something's wrong. Hecate can't sense the grimoire anymore. And neither can I."

"What do you mean? She could always sense it?"

"In Macy, yes," Hecate said, appearing in her maiden form. "If she's missing and I can't sense it, it's because Westhell has her. And he's going to try to free Abaddon."

"As soon as possible." Mormo and Hecate shared a look.

"What aren't you telling me?" Duncan needed to go after his mate, worry for the stubborn witch hurting him deep inside. A rage, such as he rarely felt, started to burn.

"Macy should be okay. At least for the next few hours. Corson will perform the rite either at midnight or three a.m.—the witching hour. He'll want to be precise."

"Ritual?"

Mormo gave him a sober look. "When he'll sacrifice Macy to free Abaddon. But he'll keep her shell and her power. And then he'll move on to you."

"Like hell he will." He glanced down at his phone and read the text. "Ah. Onvyr's on her tail. She asked for backup, and looks like she got it. Sorry I doubted you, elf," he muttered. "My dad and uncle?"

"In the guest wing," Mormo answered. "They and Orion will be up and ready to move in two more hours."

Hecate added, "And more good news. The crystal the demon uses to communicate with his friends in MEC. Macy has it. We can track her using that."

"Way to bury the lede, Hecate." Duncan's palms were sweating. He needed to do something, now. Waiting was killing him.

"Feed, Duncan," Mormo said. "You'll want to be at full strength."

"True. Any word on Varu and the others?" He could use the power of his patriarch to hammer down on Westhell.

"Not yet. They should be back next week if all goes right."

"And Fara? When's she coming back from Faery Land?"

Mormo snorted. "The Land of the Fae? Soon."

Duncan went to eat, then went back to his room to straighten up. Doing anything he could to distract himself. If Macy died, he — He couldn't imagine his life without her by his side. And he had no idea how she'd come to mean so much to him in such a short time. But there it was.

Edward strode into the dining area dressed in his wartime best. A long dagger strapped to his thigh and a sword at his back, he looked like a knight of old. Brock followed, dressed the same.

For war.

"You're up early," Duncan said to them.

"So are you." His father studied him. "You'll get her back, son. Even if you are a weak little Night Bloode now, you've revenant bloode in you, don't forget. We're coming along to see how far you've come."

Brock smiled, showing a lot of fang. "How fast you've come."

Duncan brightened, realizing he had the power of the

revenants' fastest vampires in the tribe. The Tizona looked after their own. And now that Duncan had claimed Macy, they'd look out for her as well. Along with Hecate, Mormo, and Orion, Duncan would bring the pain.

Corson Westhell had no idea who he'd screwed with. He'd picked the wrong witch to take, and Duncan would make sure that was the last thing he realized before he died.

# CHAPTER TWENTY-EIGHT

Macy glared at the lying witch—*bitch*—and struggled with the bonds around her wrists. She'd been knocked unconscious and woken in a large cave with high ceilings, surrounded by rock and more rock, with the ceiling open to show off a muddied moon, obscured by passing clouds.

"Oh get off it," Lucy said as she crossed her legs and smoothed down her skirt. "You wanted to play the hero. You're welcome."

"You're going to pay." Macy yanked at the chains attached to her bonds. She sat on a dirt floor close to a rock wall.

"Honey, you can't match my price. But he can." She tilted her head at Corson, who looked less human and more demon-like.

His blond hair had an ashy texture, his skin pale and his eyes a fathomless black, the whites nonexistent. He stood even taller than he'd been before, but this time he didn't bother to hide his tail or horns. To her annoyance, she found him attractive.

"I appeal to those with darkness," he said, as if reading her thoughts. "Take my lady Lilith." He nodded to Lucy. "She expects riches beyond imagining for giving you up. Your sacrifice is her gain." He crooked his fingers and waited for her to join him. "This talented young thing lied about everything. She's no witch, just a vessel for my needs. No longer of use, like Dr. Brown. She died today, sadly." He smiled. "She's been hell-sent, waiting to be claimed."

Macy tried not to cringe when he smiled at her, his teeth black and sharp. And extremely intimidating, she'd give him that. "Why don't you go back to where you came from? You don't seem to like it here."

"I hate it here," he said, still pleasant. "I was banished because of your goddess. Hecate owes me seven-hundred and fifty-two years I'll never get back. I intend to drag them out of her year by year. It'll be fun. You should watch."

"Look, I don't have the grimoire."

"Sure you do."

"When do I get my money?" Lucy asked.

"Your reward is so much more valuable than money."

Lucy eyes shone, and Macy could have told her not to trust the bastard, but she would have to find out for herself.

"Do you want it now?"

"Yes, please."

Westhell smiled and took hold of each of her arms.

"What are you doing?"

"I'm rewarding you. My master is very pleased with your assistance. He wants you to be there when he Descends."

"What?"

Westhell took hold of her arms, squeezed until her wrist bones snapped and Lucy screamed, and then pulled her in opposite directions. A human wishbone.

Macy wouldn't have believed it possible to pull a human being apart. Flesh might tear but not split. Yet she watched it, the horror splattering her and Westhell with blood. So much blood.

She retched, feeling woozy. Not sorry to see Lucy punished for her perfidy, but Lucy hadn't deserved that.

He frowned and yanked Macy to her feet, snapping the chain with his bare hands to pull her from the wall. "Aren't you a Bloode Witch? I thought I was initiating some foreplay before we really got started."

"Where's Cho?" *Don't think think about the blood and guts all over the place.*

"Who? Oh, right. You're half-demon buddy. I've been watching him. He's been most helpful, but he's a goblin problem now. With any luck, his scary daddy found him before the goblins' monthly mating ritual. Because that would be bad for him if not."

"I'm going to kill you."

"Please. I'm being polite and waiting with you for your boyfriend to show up. Which vampire is it, exactly? Duncan? Orion? Kraft? Or maybe you like a lighter flavor. Is it Hecate who really trips your switch?" He chuckled. "For your sake, I hope not. I'm going to gut that bitch and take over her station connecting the realms. You'll be dead by then, but maybe it won't be as painful as it could be. Give yourself to Abaddon and you'll only suffer a little bit, not for an eternity."

"Fuck you."

"So testy." He tsked and licked his finger clean of Lucy's blood. "You know, all this could have been avoided if Hecate had played fair. I never asked those witches to convert. They turned warlock all on their own. Only to then steal what didn't belong to them."

Macy didn't know why, but she actually felt sorry for him. "So the book was stolen, and they blamed you."

"Yes, they blamed me." He sniffed. "They took away my kingdom. Then Hecate trapped my master in the grimoire, and they tortured *me*. For years, I suffered. But that wasn't enough, because with Abaddon gone, all of Hell looked weak. They threw me out, away from my people, my home." His voice rose. "So I'm going to set it right. And you're going to help."

She swallowed the tremor working its way through. "You might as well kill me now. I don't know where it is."

He smiled and grabbed her with one large hand. With the other, he ripped her shirt away.

No matter how much she struggled, she couldn't free herself from his hold. Her bloode magic refused to come, and the spells she'd once memorized faded from memory.

A terrible pain blazed over her back, and she screamed as Westhell tore her skin off.

"See? There it is. You've had it all along."

"The tattoos," she rasped, crying and feeling sick to her stomach, the pain extreme.

"Ah, but they aren't really the grimoire. I'm just fucking with you." He snickered and tossed her skin to the ground. He said a few words she didn't understand, and the rock beneath her feet grew, becoming a small altar. Westhell read the letters of her tattoo aloud.

Furious at her treatment, and surprisingly, at Hecate for causing this mess in the first place, she screamed at the demon and watched with satisfaction when he flipped head over tail and slammed into the rock wall.

But not before a black book shimmered into existence where her skin had been. The rock like a mini altar, her pain the offering.

Westhell laughed as a loud roar echoed in the cavern, and the winds from Hell blew the scent of brimstone around.

"My master, he comes." Westhell licked his lips. "And you, my dear, will feed all my hungers. We'll start with your liver."

"The fuck you will." Duncan knocked Westhell back into the same wall Macy had shoved him into, having appeared out of nowhere

She blinked, and he was by her side. He touched her shoulder, and she felt the jolt of agony center on her back.

She must have blacked out, for when she came to, she saw the Tizona vampires attacking Westhell while Orion battled a herd of goblins—where had they come from?—and Hecate and Mormo chanted to contain a large, black void from overtaking the cavern.

"Shh. You'll be all right." Duncan continued to lick her back while pouring a powder over her that cooled the burn of pain along her spine. "The powder is some healing crap Hecate gave me. It's knitting your flesh. But you still have a lot of damage." He met her gaze, and she was shocked to see remorse in them. "I'm sorry I wasn't here sooner."

"You came. That matters." She reached for his face and froze, unable to move. Then her vision dimmed.

"A little help here," Orion yelled.

"Macy? Macy, luv, come back." Duncan stroked her face, but then she lost the feeling even in her cheeks.

Everything going black, turning numb. Except for the harsh scent of brimstone...

DUNCAN WATCHED as his mate turned into a human vessel for an insidious evil. Macy's eyes disappeared behind a film of black, and she grew weightless. He wanted to help her fight, but he had no idea how to get the evil out of her without ripping her apart. A foreign sensation, like panic, flooded him, and he tried to figure out what to do.

A glance showed his father and uncle grinning as they fought with Westhell. Probably more fun than they'd had in years. Orion had decimated the small goblin faction Westhell had planted in the tunnels. Apparently, Westhell had found this hellish cavern through a hidden passage connected to MEC.

Hecate and Mormo continued to chant, keeping the void somewhat contained.

"If he can't leave via the gate, he'll use your witch to do it." A tall man with dark hair and wearing a toga appeared next to him.

"I know you." Duncan lunged at the dickhead. "You're Morpheus. You were flirting with my mate."

"Tone it down, Romeo. Do you want her free, or do you want her to die and wander an eternity in dreamland?"

"Fuck you."

Morpheus frowned in concentration then laughed. "Your kind really is abominably annoying. I can't read you right now. Are you deliberately keeping me out? Is this a new power?"

"Fix her," Duncan ordered.

"Or else?"

"There is no or else. Fix her. Period. She dies, you die."

"You can't kill a god." Morpheus laughed, but he didn't look so sure.

Duncan leaned toward the obnoxious male. "Try me."

"Easy, little vampire. Don't get so testy." Morpheus sighed. "And Hecate calls *you* her favorite. I have no idea why." He put his hands on Macy's head and closed his eyes. "Sleep, vampire, and I can guide you to free your witch. But you have to open yourself once inside, or this won't work."

"I don't understand."

"You will."

Duncan did as the god of sleep willed, denying every instinct to preserve himself first. He needed to help his mate. To fix her, to love her forever. He couldn't help his snarls and growls of despair and rage.

Slow to anger, once enraged, Duncan wouldn't stop the killing.

He opened his eyes, not aware of having closed them, and stood on the ancient black sands of a gladiator's ring. A place where battle was welcome. And there, in the center of the victor's box, an altar upon which Macy lay.

He rushed to her side and hugged her to him. "Wake up, damn it."

"D-Duncan?"

He closed his eyes, near to crying in relief. "Macy." He pulled back and stared, his smile freezing in place. Where her eyes should have been, he saw only emptiness.

"I can't see. Where are we?"

"In your dream, Macy," Morpheus said as he appeared next to them. "Ah, Chaos's Coliseum. A fabled place where warriors and killers come to pledge service to the Lord of Doom."

"Fuck that. I'm going to crush his heart and devour it," Duncan promised.

"Then let the games begin," said the same demon Duncan had seen in a past dream.

"Morpheus, take her back."

"If I leave, you'll die."

"Do it."

"Wait. Duncan?" Macy reached for him blindly, and he settled her hand on his cheek. "Don't leave."

"Go where it's safe. I'll take care of him. I promise."

"Not without me."

"Macy, you're blind and powerless. I'd let you help if you had your magic, but that fuckhead Abaddon has taken it. Can't you feel it?"

"I can't. Duncan, Morpheus said you'll die."

"He'd die for you," Morpheus said quietly.

"But why?" she cried. "For me?"

"Tell her, revenant. Before it's too late." Morpheus took Macy in his arms and prepared to leave. She looked so small next to the god, pale and helpless. *My mate.*

Duncan could feel Abaddon's power growing. He glanced

around, seeing the real world as if a dream, a hazy state shimmering in the air. Orion continued to fight, but the goblin's champion was seriously fighting back. Westhell had given Edward and Brock more than a few broken limbs and bloodied wounds. But they continued to battle.

For his kin, for his mate, Duncan could do no less. "I love you, Macy. Stay strong."

He kissed her, and then she and Morpheus vanished. With them gone, Abaddon took form.

Everything stopped and shifted, all the players in this game now on Abaddon's board, in his realm, in Chaos's Coliseum.

Hecate and Mormo stopped chanting and looked up. And up. And up some more.

Abaddon was one giant, ugly motherfucker.

"Come, revenant. Let's see who's the stronger." The demon lord chuckled, and the walls of the coliseum trembled. "The winner shall have his prize. A soul for a soul."

"You going talk me to death or fight, you wanker?"

Mormo looked at Duncan as if he'd lost his mind.

And maybe he had. But better his mind than his mate. Because some vampires did love.

# CHAPTER TWENTY-NINE

Macy blinked her eyes open and stared at the back room of Augusta's Coffee shop. "Where's Duncan?" she asked, aware of an itching at her back. Her naked back. Pressed against a bare chest belonging to the god of dreams.

He set her down into a chair and looked at her back. "Nearly healed."

She sat topless in a coffee shop. At night? Around them, darkness filled the windows.

A woman walking by gasped and hurried away, returning with an *Augusta Coffee 4Evah* tee.

Macy hurriedly donned it. "Thanks." She turned to Morpheus. "Take me back." Morpheus had told Duncan he would die.

But Duncan *couldn't* die. She wouldn't let him. Then her eyes widened. "By Hecate, he said he loved me." She yanked Morpheus close by his toga. "He loves me."

"Congratulations. Now can you please let go?"

"I'm sorry." She smoothed the fabric gathered at his waist. "But please, Morpheus. I need to go back. I have to save him."

He cocked his head. "How? Abaddon stole your power. You

are nothing but a sacrifice your revenant doesn't want. He sent you here to live."

*But I can't live without him.*

Macy refused to give up. "No. He's mine. I'm saving him, and I don't care what we're up against."

"Oh?"

"Macy!"

She glanced up to see her father, Anton, and Cho rushing her. They exchanged hugs before Cho blurted, "It was Dr. Brown. She was in on it with Westhell."

"I know. Right now, we're fighting Westhell and Abaddon. And losing." She wiped angry tears from her face. "Duncan's going to die." She turned to her father. "He saved me, Dad."

"Oh hell. We have to help then, don't we?"

Morpheus sighed. "You can't win on your own."

"I won't have to," Macy said. "We're family, and we fight together."

"Fuck. Hold on." Morpheus whisked them back to Hell. Literally.

Abaddon must have jumped everyone into his dimension, because hell-beasts of all kinds distracted the others while he knocked Duncan around. Or tried to knock him around. Her vampire was moving so fast she could barely keep track.

"Leave the lesser demons to us," Anton said and laughed with a dark menace as he transformed into the demon form he often had to hide.

"Finally." Cho hugged Macy and did the same. She gaped, not having realized Cho could take the same dark, demonic shape as his dad. Then the fireballs started flying.

"Mage, with me," Morpheus ordered and rushed to help Mormo shut down the black void he'd been working on earlier.

Hecate was nowhere— No, she and Duncan fought together

against Abaddon, but both looked in bad shape. Duncan paused beside Macy, his gaze incredulous, then furious.

"I told you to leave," he yelled.

Abaddon's laughter hurt her ears and gave her a headache.

Duncan growled, "There's nothing but death here, Macy."

She gave him a punishing kiss. "I'd rather die here with you than live without you."

"Really?" He perked up. "Great. Then we'll be dying together for nothing, you daft witch."

"Don't you call me daft." She planted her hands on her hips and was suddenly in Duncan's arms, on the other side of the cavern, having narrowly missed being smashed into pulp by Abaddon's large fist. "He looks bigger than before."

"He is bigger than before. This is his realm. He's no shadow. It's the real deal." Duncan moved them to another spot, then another. He didn't breathe hard, didn't breathe at all. But she saw bruises and bloode, and she knew he tired.

"I can move faster than he does, but I can't outlast him."

"You can't, but *we* can." She moved closer to lick the bloode from a gash on his arm. Power lit her up.

Duncan jumped them again and again and cut his wrist. "Drink. Hurry."

Westhell caught his father and punched a hole through his side.

"Edward," his Uncle Brock growled. "That was sloppy."

"Fuck off," Edward yelled. "If you're done prancing, let's end this prick. Shite demon."

Westhell whistled, and a horde of mutant goblins appeared.

"Are you kidding me?" Orion roared. "I just killed the last one. And you brought more? You piece of shit." He hammered a blow at Westhell that connected, and the demon went flying.

The Tizona clan vampires got serious, and Westhell gurgled as they sliced into him, over and over, not letting up.

"Now," Uncle Anton said to his son, and he and Cho launched themselves at a horde of fire demons while Macy's dad worked with Orion to push through the goblins. That grew.

Macy blinked. "Aren't goblins supposed to be small?"

"Macy, focus. Your power, my speed, Hecate's magic. We can do this." Duncan looked more than tired, his energy winding down, and her drinking from him made it worse.

"Duncan..."

"Do you love me?"

"Yes."

"Then obey, woman."

"I'll give you an *obey*," she muttered, feeling happy and scared and dopey all at the same time. She looked inward, calling on her magic, on Duncan's magic, and filled it with the love she had for him. A weird combination of death magic, power, and emotion, but her love for Duncan gave her strength.

"It's working," he rasped.

Abaddon shrieked when Hecate threw lightning at him, and Morpheus kept appearing and disappearing, moving through the demon lord like a ghost. Blood and death continued to build, and Macy took her power not only from Duncan, but from the bonds he shared with his kin, with Hecate and Mormo, and with his father and uncle.

Abaddon glared at her with hate, disappearing and reappearing, so that she couldn't get a fix on him to launch the strike she knew would work.

Until he got too close.

She saw her life flash before her eyes, Abaddon's claws a hair from raking her neck and piercing her chest.

And then Duncan was there, taking the blow meant for her. It should have been impossible to deflect, yet he did, falling at her feet as the life left him, his heart no longer in his body.

She shrieked with pain and rage, needing an outlet as he bled to death in front of her eyes.

Abaddon laughed with glee, and she'd *had it.*

Using the power she'd gathered into her blood and soul, she shouted the sigil for sunder, the one Abaddon himself had taught her, and aimed a laser focus of red light at Abaddon, setting him on fire. But it wasn't a hellfire he could manipulate or control. It was the passion of a Bloode Witch, strong with death-bringer magic, a curse from gods and men alike, and powered by love.

It pierced Abaddon and burned every part of him until he was nothing more than ash and smoke.

Then Hecate, Morpheus, and Mormo gathered to bathe the smudge he left behind with celestial light and terrestrial energy.

Abaddon's bellow shook the world.

Macy had no time for anything but rushing to Duncan's body, not accepting they might come so far only to lose him in the end.

He had a hole where his heart should be, and the one thing she knew about vampires was their inability to exist without the seat of their magic.

"He's gone, Macy," Mormo said softly. "A sacrifice for you and his kin. A loss that comes from love."

Macy refused that stupid sentiment, grief tearing her apart.

She wasn't aware of anything but her pale, true-dead lover, who'd saved her time and time again.

*No. This doesn't end like this.* Macy looked to Hecate. "You control the dead. Bring him back, please."

"I cannot." Hecate's eyes watered. "His kind never pass through my domain."

His father and uncle neared. Orion stared at his kin and slumped to the ground, looking lost.

"He gave you his heart," Edward said, his voice thick though his eyes remained dry. "There is no greater honor than that."

"Bullshit," Macy spat. "He gave me his heart? Well maybe I should give him mine right on back. Stupid, pigheaded, idiotic gesture." She reached inside her chest, taking the essence of her heart and soul, her blood mixed with his bloode, and shoved it into Duncan.

A red glow covered her body and reached out to cover his. Infused with the power of the Night Bloode, she shared everything she had with the male she loved.

Time seemed to have no meaning. Forever and a second went by, and the world became red. So very quiet.

Macy had nearly given up hope until she heard him.

*"Macy?"*

"Duncan." She hugged him. *"You big jerk. You can't tell me you love me then leave me."*

*"I'm sorry, luv. But he was a pretty big demon."*

*"A pretty dead demon."*

*"Can he be killed?"*

*"I don't know. I do know he's gone. So stop playing around and come back. I need you, Duncan. I love you. You can't leave yet."*

*"Not yet, eh?" He slowly rose, dragging her with him.*

Between one breath and the next, they stood, hugging, enveloped in a red aura. Macy cried while Duncan weaved on his feet, and their allies cheered and finished with the enemy not yet dead and gone.

Until, finally, the darkness disappeared, and all that remained was a shadow over the coliseum, cast from the pale glow of victory shining from Hecate, Mormo, and Morpheus.

"Let's go home," Duncan said. "And before you ask, your place or mine, I don't care. As long as we're together."

Macy cried some more and peppered kisses over his face.

Orion watched while everyone congratulated the pair. "You're disgusting."

Duncan blinked. "What?"

Macy had to laugh. Orion looked so bothered by the two of them. He was almost cute.

"So soft. You get a mate and forget how to be tough. All this love and togetherness. Makes me want to kill more goblins and demons." He eyed their demon friends, focusing on Cho. "How about it, demon? Want a go?"

Before Cho could accept, and Macy could tell he wanted to, Uncle Anton pulled him back. "Time to go home and get clean. Your mother's coming back tonight."

"Feather-fucker," Orion muttered. "About as fierce as an angel."

Cho flipped him off, but his father refused to let him fight the vryko.

Edward slapped Orion on the back. "You, I like."

"I'll fight you," Brock offered. "But after I wash away this demon blood. That Westhell bloke stinks."

The vampires laughed and joined Mormo and Hecate, who were helping Morpheus to his feet.

Her dad came up and hugged her, including Duncan in the awkward embrace. "Welcome to the family, son."

"You do realize I'm older than you," Duncan said.

Her father smiled. "You do realize I can make you believe you're a howler monkey anytime I want. And yeah, my mojo does work on vampires."

Duncan frowned, not sure how to respond.

Macy laughed, so full of joy she didn't care about anything but living a full life. "I love you, Dad."

"Love you too, Macy. Bring him over soon. Your mom is going to want to meet him. She and Pia are back tonight. Er, later today. Hell, I'm not sure what day it is, but she'll be home soon, and she'll want to meet your boyfriend.'"

"Yes, Dad." Macy poked Duncan.

He growled, "We'd love to come."

Then the others waited by a gate Morpheus created.

"Help me, Macy," Duncan murmured. "I don't think my legs are quite right yet. I lost a lot of bloode."

"I know." She sniffed. "Let's get you home—to your home—and fix you up. Then we can decide where to go from there."

They joined the others, and Duncan said, "Right. Now about that matter of obeying. I think someone needs a dictionary, because nowhere does it say *put yourself in danger.*" He scowled. "Don't think we're not going to talk about this."

"Yes, dear."

For some reason, that made Orion laugh so hard he nearly choked.

"Your kin is weird."

"Tell me about it."

Hecate smiled, her eyes aglow as they settled on Macy. *Blessings, sister, for your heart is pure and your love is true.* "Let's go home."

# EPILOGUE

Three days later, on Halloween, Macy moved the rest of her clothing into Duncan's room. She intended to keep her house while she decided what to do about their living arrangements. But Duncan needed to live in the house to be safe from the sun, as well as safety from enemy magir, which meant everyone.

He might have saved the world from chaos, but at heart, he still wanted to drain humans dry. They'd have to work on that.

She walked into the living room to see Orion glaring at two kittens seated on the floor, staring back at him.

"Oh, kittens."

"They're little pricks," he muttered. "I don't care what Onvyr says. They're conspiring. Yeah, I'm talking to you, Smoky." The kitten chirped, looking adorable. "Dick."

Behind her, Duncan laughed.

"Orion," Macy chastised.

The big vryko had softened toward her, though he kept bugging her about fighting Cho when her friend got some time to spare. For his part, Cho wanted to rip Orion's head off. Onvyr had wanted in on the action as well after missing all the fighting. He'd run into a nest of demon-influenced gorgons on his way to help Macy and got sidetracked.

With no love lost between demon and vampire, Uncle Anton at least liked her new friends, and her father had convinced her mother not to burn the vampire nest—as she called it—to the ground. Only mention of Hecate's sponsorship had stopped Diane Bishop-Dunwich from "burning down the house."

And no, her mother didn't think it funny whenever Macy sang the Talking Heads lyrics, but Cho and her dad did.

They had a dinner to attend the next evening, and Macy couldn't wait to watch Duncan charm her family—minus the whammy. On his own, he could make people like him. Just look at what he'd done with her.

"Why are we swearing at kittens?" Duncan asked and hugged Macy from behind.

"I'll tell you why," Orion growled.

The kittens hissed at him in unison.

Macy coughed to hide a laugh.

"Smoky and I have a bond, and he likes to sleep on my pillow. Cool. But Nightmare, his brother, has a problem with me. And he's been leaving presents on my pillow that I don't appreciate."

"Mice?" Macy cringed.

"Probably birds," Duncan said. "We have no shortage of them."

"Scorpions," Orion hissed.

The one kitten hissed back, then meowed at Macy to pick him up. So she did, and Orion fumed when Duncan petted the little guy and got him purring before putting him back down again.

Mormo appeared out of nowhere and frowned. "Scorpions don't live in Seattle, do they? Are you sure that's what he caught?"

"I got stung five times. I should know."

Mormo brightened. "Oh, then you probably encountered a

wind scorpion from the Temple of Amen-Ra. They're normally the size of a small pony, but they can shrink if commanded to. No doubt he caught one of Khent's pets." Mormo shook his head. "Nightmare, he's not going to be happy if you keep stealing his creatures."

Nightmare ignored him.

"Speaking of Khent, he and the others will be returning soon. Varu called to let me know they found a Bloode Stone."

"Good, because this thing is annoying." Duncan shook his hand. "Did you know it likes to sing when its happy?"

"What are you talking about?" Macy asked him.

"You know how no one seemed to care about my dad and uncle being here? No unnecessary killing?"

"Killing is always necessary," Orion said, still glaring at Nightmare, who snarled at him. Smoky mewed, and Orion picked him up, still complaining, and walked to the couch.

"Did they get back all right?" she asked, as Edward and Brock had left yesterday through a gateway Hecate provided.

"Yes. And I had to promise we'd visit next year once we found all the Bloode Stones, so it'd be safe."

"Ambrogio's Tears, right?"

"Yep. This is what keeps the peace." He opened his hand, and a small red gem appeared. Then he explained how Bloode Stones worked.

"Oh wow." Macy stared at such a powerful tool. "That's scary."

"Yes, it is." Mormo watched her. "So, have you considered my proposal?"

"Have you?" Duncan asked, amused.

"Yes. And I'll do it."

Mormo grinned. "Congratulations to our new MEC liaison, the Night Bloode's own Bloode Witch."

"Does being the Bloode Witch come with a salary?" she teased, content with her life in a way she'd never expected to be.

Duncan kissed her on the cheek. "Free room and board and the best-looking, most dangerous mate in the clan."

"Get a room," Orion called from his spot on the couch. "Yo, Mormo, are we watching *The Hobbit* or what?"

Mormo snapped his fingers, and his black robe turned white.

Duncan sighed. "Great. Now he'll make us call him Mormo the White again. Go make some popcorn, witch." At her look, he grinned and added, "Please?"

She snickered. "You just want to drink popcorn-flavored blood later."

Orion perked up. "Is that a thing?" Smoky climbed onto his lap and sat.

"Why don't you get your own mate and find out?" Duncan suggested, stroking Nightmare, who had a thing for Macy's vampire.

"Get a mate?" Orion scoffed. "Have you been sucking off meth-heads again? No way. Females are nothing but trouble."

Macy shook her head. "Hey, Mormo, did you hear that?"

"No, what, Macy?" he asked, playing along.

"I think I just heard Cupid shooting an arrow. And bam, it just hit Orion." She wiggled her fingers to shock him from a distance, getting a handle on her bloode magic.

He jumped. "Cut it out."

They laughed, but after some popcorn and vampire snuggling, Macy swore she heard the zing of an arrow. And when Orion jumped again, she had no explanation for what she'd heard.

The kittens made funny noises, as if laughing.

The shocked look on Orion's face was priceless.

THANK you so much for reading Duncan's story! The next book revolves around stubborn Orion and the troubles he falls into—and gets out of—thanks to one sweet, sexy nymph. Don't miss ***Between Bloode and Water.***

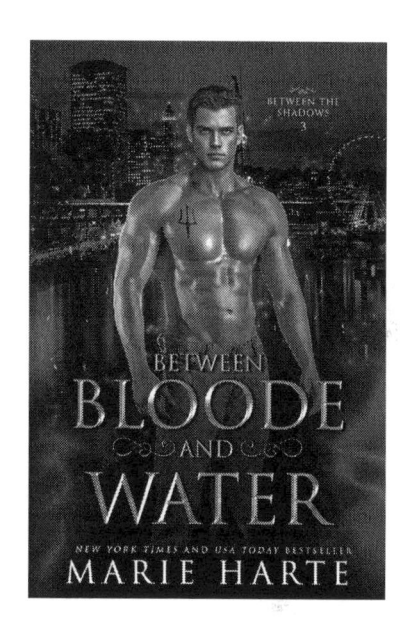

# GLOSSARY

Intelligent Beings Classification:

- **Demons**—creatures from any of the hell planes, tricksters, evil-doers, and powerful beings with a bent toward dark desires, associated with fire
- **Divinity (gods and goddesses)**—those of a divine nature and whose power is derived from creationism and worship
- **Humans**—mortal beings from the mundane world, not born with magic though some can harness its power
- **Magir**—an all-encompassing term to describe those supernatural creatures living among the human population in the mundane realm (e.g. lycans, witches, druids, mermaids, gargoyles, etc.)
- **Monsters**—animalistic creatures that aren't human or magir but do have magical properties/abilities (like fox spirits, gryphons, dragons, manticores, etc.)

## Vampire Terms:

- **Ambrogio**—the first vampire ever created, born from a curse given from the god, Apollo. Father (Primus) to the vampire species, husband to Selene, the mother of the species.
- **Blood-bond**—the psychic connection a vampire has to a blood donor
- **Bloode**—that intrinsic vampiric essence within a blood-drinker that makes him a vampire, as opposed to a demon or other dark-natured creature
- **Bloode-debt**—vampiric debt incurred by a member of one's clan, passed on through familial members until fulfilled
- **Bloode Empire**—the name for the vampire nation created in 727 BCE
- **Bloode-magic**—magic in a vampire's bloode, manipulated through the Bloode Stones or a deity with power over blood and the dead (i.e. Hecate, thus Mormo)
- **Bloode Stones**—six droplets of Ambrogio's blood or tears (split mythology on origin) congealed into power gems when they made contact with the earth. It is rumored that only a Worthy vampire can handle a Bloode Stone and instill peace within their species.
- **Bloode Witch**—a witch who uses bloode to power herself, serves his or her vampire clan and is considered kin. Very rare, more common in older times.
- **Clans**—groups of vampires within a tribe that act as family, led by a patriarch, comprised of kin (brothers/fathers/sons), anywhere in number from ten to sixty members

- **(The) Ending**—the period of time before vampires came into existence
- **Guide**—also known as bloode-guide, someone not related who mentors a young vampire through adulthood
- **Kin**—family, those vampires who do not instill an urge to kill. Another word for vampire brother, father, or son
- **Kin Wars**—legendary vampire civil war, thought to have been fought several thousand years ago, brought about by a foul curse from the gods, turning vampire against vampire and forming the ten tribes
- **Master**—vampire leader of an entire vampire tribe
- **Mate**—a vampire's bonded female partner, with whom he can sire offspring
- **Of the Bloode**—another term for vampire
- **Patriarch**—vampire leader of a vampire clan
- **Primus**—the first vampire, the father of all (Ambrogio), also refers to a pureblood vampire leader
- **Sire**—a vampire's father, also sometimes used as a term of respect for the Master of a tribe
- **Tribes**—the ten large factions of vampires, bound together according to particular traits. The tribes are as follows: Strigoi, Upir, Nachzehrer, Reaper, Draugr, Revenant, Jiangshi, Sasabonsam, Vrykolakas, and Pishachas.
- **Upir Gold**—term used to denote vampire bloode and brains, a divine delicacy
- **Vampire**—a blood-drinker and descendant of Ambrogio, always male, always naturally born. "Vampire" is also a generic term in reference to describing a blood-drinker from any of the ten tribes.

Other names for vampire are: Of the Bloode, blood-suckers, blood-drinkers, vamps, fangers, and death-bringers.
- **Worthy**—characteristic of a vampire who is the quintessential essence of the Bloode, who has the true heart of Ambrogio in his body, courageous and powerful, a leader who will do what's best for his people

## THE REALMS:

- **Celestial**—the homes of the gods, no matter what pantheon
- **Death**—also called the afterlife, the plane that harbors the dead, looked after by Hecate and several other deities, not to be confused with the hells; also sometimes referred to as the Netherworld
- **Fae**—home of the fae, to include the lands of the elves, dwarves, and faery, as well as elemental spirits
- **Hell**—the underworld planes, of which there are many, usually inhabited by demons, devils, and dark spirits, not to be confused with the Netherworld
- **Mundane**—earth, the mortal plane where humans dwell
- **Pocket**—small planes, or "pockets" of reality, created by powerful magic-users

## SPECIES:

- **Dark Elves**—Fae creatures who prefer the night, they often live in the caves and underground with dwarves in Nidavellir, which is part of the fae realm
- **Demons**—those who live in the hell plane, tricksters, evil-doers, and powerful creatures with dark desires, associated with fire
- **Druids**—humans who can do natural magic and commune with fae spirits
- **Dusk Elves**—rare (and often hunted, unwelcome among the elves) blending of light and dark elf parents, live in fae realms. Also known as mrykálfar.
- **Dwarves**—also known as dvergar, fae creatures who live in Nidavellir
- **Fae**—those who live in the fae realm, an alternate world comprised of elves, dwarves, sprites, and other creatures from a multitude of pantheons
- **Light Elves**—fae creatures who live high in the mountains in Álfheim in the fae realm
- **Lycans**—shapeshifting creatures who can assume the form of a human or large, magical direwolf
- **Mages**—magir-born, long-lived mortals who practice magic for good (also sometimes used as slang for magic users of all kinds)
- **Nymphs**—beautiful magir partial to water, generous in spirit, often sexual creatures in tune with nature
- **Necromancers**—humans who can harness death magic and command of the dead
- **Shapeshifters**—rare creatures who alternate between human and animal forms at will
- **Sorcerers**—magir-born, long-lived mortals who practice magic for evil purposes
- **Warlocks**—humans who perform magic for evil purposes, typically utilizing sacrificial magic

- **Witches**—humans who perform magic for good purposes, typically utilizing celestial or earth magic

# ALSO BY MARIE

## **PARANORMAL**

### CROSS STEP

Namesake

Kate Complete

Love the Viper

### COUGAR FALLS

Rachel's Totem

In Plain Sight

Foxy Lady

Outfoxed

A Matter of Pride

Right Wolf, Right Time

By the Tail

Prey & Prejudice

### ETHEREAL FOES

Dragons' Demon: A Dragon's Dream

Duncan's Descent: A Demon's Desire

Havoc & Hell: A Dragon's Prize

Dragon King: Not So Ordinary

### CIRCE'S RECRUITS

Roane

Zack & Ace

Derrick

Hale

DAWN ENDEAVOR

Fallon's Flame

Hayashi's Hero

Julian's Jeopardy

Gunnar's Game

Grayson's Gamble

CIRCE'S RECRUITS 2.0

Gideon

Alex

Elijah

Carter

## **SCIFI**

THE INSTINCT

A Civilized Mating

A Barbarian Bonding

A Warrior's Claiming

TALSON TEMPTATIONS

Talon's Wait

Talson's Test

Talson's Net

Talson's Match

LIFE IN THE VRAIL

Lurin's Surrender

Thief of Mardu

Engaging Gren

Seriana Found

CREATIONS

The Perfect Creation

Creation's Control

Creating Chemistry

Caging the Beast

## **CONTEMPORARY**

WICKED WARRENS

Enjoying the Show

Closing the Deal

Raising the Bar

Making the Grade

Bending the Rules

THE MCCAULEY BROTHERS

The Troublemaker Next Door

How to Handle a Heartbreaker

Ruining Mr. Perfect

What to Do with a Bad Boy

BODY SHOP BAD BOYS

Test Drive

Roadside Assistance

Zero to Sixty

Collision Course

THE DONNIGANS

A Sure Thing

Just the Thing

The Only Thing

ALL I WANT FOR HALLOWEEN

THE KISSING GAME

THE WORKS

Bodywork

Working Out

Wetwork

VETERANS MOVERS

The Whole Package

Smooth Moves

Handle with Care

Delivered with a Kiss

GOOD TO GO

A Major Attraction

A Major Seduction

A Major Distraction

A Major Connection

## BEST REVENGE

Served Cold

Served Hot

Served Sweet

## **ROMANTIC SUSPENSE**

POWERUP!

The Lost Locket

RetroCog

Whispered Words

Fortune's Favor

Flight of Fancy

Silver Tongue

Entranced

Killer Thoughts

## WESTLAKE ENTERPRISES

To Hunt a Sainte

Storming His Heart

Love in Electric Blue

## TRIGGERMAN INC.

Contract Signed

Secrets Unsealed

Satisfaction Delivered

## **AND MORE (believe it or not)!**

# ABOUT THE AUTHOR

Caffeine addict, boy referee, and romance aficionado, *New York Times* and *USA Today* bestselling author Marie Harte has over 100 books published with more constantly on the way. She's a confessed bibliophile and devotee of action movies. Whether hiking in Central Oregon, biking around town, or hanging at the local tea shop, she's constantly plotting to give everyone a happily ever after. Visit https://marieharte.com and fall in love.

And to subscribe to Marie's Newsletter, click here.

- facebook.com/marieharteauthorpage
- twitter.com/MHarte_Author
- goodreads.com/Marie_Harte
- bookbub.com/authors/marie-harte
- instagram.com/marieharteauthor

Printed in Poland
by Amazon Fulfillment
Poland Sp. z o.o., Wrocław